It Could Be You

Sue McCauley lives in Christchurch with her husband, Pat Hammond. Her first novel, *Other Halves*, won the Wattie Book of the Year Award and the New Zealand Book Award for Fiction and was made into a feature film. She has published three other novels, the most recent being *A Fancy Man* in 1996. Her short stories have appeared in anthologies and magazines. She also writes for film, television and radio.

Sue McCauley

It Could Be
You

V

VINTAGE

Random House New Zealand Ltd
(An imprint of the Random House Group)

18 Poland Road
Glenfield
Auckland 10
NEW ZEALAND

Sydney   New York   Toronto
London   Auckland   Johannesburg
and agencies throughout the world

First published 1997

Printed in New Zealand by Publishing Press Limited
ISBN 1 86941 317 2

Contents

Acknowledgements

Financial assistance from Creative New Zealand Toi Aotearoa, and from my Dad, enabled me to write these stories. My grateful thanks to both these sources.

The following stories have previously been broadcast or published:

'George' — Radio New Zealand

'The Day . . .' — *100 New Zealand Short Stories* (Tandem Press) and *Subversive Acts* (Penguin)

'Losing' — Radio New Zealand and *Metro*

'Notes for Episode Seven' — Radio New Zealand

'Trembling Annie' — Radio New Zealand and *New Women's Fiction 4* (New Women's Press)

'Arctic Circle' — *Metro*

'Said Linda' — Radio New Zealand and *Me & Marilyn Monroe* (Daphne Brasell Associates Press)

'The Remarkably Unhumble William Saroyan' — *Landfall*

'Purple Trousers' — *Subversive Acts* (Penguin)

'Boots' — *NZ Listener*

'Aunt Elly and the Rockbusters' — adapted from *Bad Music* (Hodder Moa Beckett)

'After Max' — *Metro*

An Alternative Life' — *NZ Listener, Australian Women's Weekly* and *Short Stories from New Zealand* (Highgate/Nelson Price Milburn)

'The National School of Beauty Therapy' — *New Zealand Woman's Weekly*

'Diary of the Victim' — Radio New Zealand and *Me & Marilyn Monroe*

'Distance in Kilometres' — *Erotic Writing* (Penguin)

'Do' — *Speaking With the Sun* (Bridget Williams Books)

'The Assassin Bug' — Radio New Zealand

George

H̲E̲ ̲R̲O̲D̲E̲ ̲O̲U̲T̲ of town at sundown.

In fact it was mid-morning and the sun had just reached our verandah, but my heart was tuned to sundown and a slide guitar with the credits beginning to roll. He rode off with his belongings packed into the sidecar and before he turned the corner he raised his arm in a wave but didn't look back.

I was aware that this was one of my life's major moments.

I stood out on the footpath for quite a long time half believing he would turn back. I didn't think he could do it. I'd underestimated the situation, or possibly him.

We hadn't said it was final, but neither had we said it wasn't. He's a man who likes being owned. He's nice to women and I'll be a long way away. He'll get caught up. Someone will find him.

The way I did. At the movies; *Prick Up Your Ears*. In interval, out on the freezing footpath grabbing a lungful of smoke, just the two of us.

'We're a dying breed,' he said.

'Yep,' I said. 'That damn hypothermia.'

I was thinking that I'd seen him before, then I realised it was same place same time a few days earlier. *Raising Arizona*, only that time there were a bunch of us out there gulping smoke on the footpath. So we had at least two things in common, him and me. Maybe three . . . who goes to daytime movies but those with time on their hands? Well there are also those who can't afford the night-time prices. Time and lack of cash, they go together like Laurel and Hardy, like love and heartbreak — I could write a song.

I was looking at him — puff, aaaah, puff, puff, aaaah — and plotting out a whole scenario. This, I thought, is the *inciting moment* (I once did a unit in Film Studies). So I was looking at him, only trying not to, except it's not always something you can decide for yourself.

I had a husband at home. Well, not at home much of the time. I was trying to get up the energy to leave him but instead I went to movies, always on my own because my friends still thought I had a marriage. I didn't want to admit to failure and I wasn't going to pretend. Besides I liked walking in out of the daylight to be enveloped by cinema — a ninety-minute hit of emotional massage. Who needs someone sharing your popcorn?

But why was *he* on his own? No friends? Defective personality?

Nice eyes, and he wasn't wearing a suit or a vinyl windbreaker. MOVE TO GO AND THROW AGAIN. Jeans and an indifferent sweatshirt beneath a heavy navy jacket. I like a man who looks as if his clothes are merely insulation. Smoked Kingston tobacco rolled thin. Poverty. MISS A TURN.

On the other hand my life was a poor, colourless thing. Thirty-four years old and the major emotional moments were those I spent with my cat. THROW AGAIN.

We looked at the Coming Attractions. There were three more days left of the Film Festival. I liked the look of *The Decline and Fall of the American Empire*. He said he'd booked for that already but they'd still had plenty of seats.

'So I'll see you Friday.' He flicked the tiny butt across the pavement and waited, holding the door open, while I stamped out the glow of a Pall Mall Extra Mild.

Roll on Friday, I thought insanely. The last thing I needed was an unemployed man. Money was the real reason I hadn't yet left Mark. He had a job (his own office, suits, secretary, all the trimmings), we had a house (polished rimu floors, spiral staircase, patio, one oak tree), I had a wardrobe full of clothes from When I Had a Job — an era that already felt so long ago that it had mythic, mist-shrouded qualities. We were a successful household — me, Mark and the microwave. The cat, in those days, was mainly cosmetic. Time was under our control — apportioned, prioritised, maximised. We were efficient, equal and in perfect working order. Then my employer went bankrupt.

I disintegrated. Not overnight — at first I believed there would be a job for me around this corner, then the next. Eventually I lowered my sights to unskilled. So, I discovered, had everyone else. I came to feel unemployable, believed that people could sense this — I was surrounded by a force field of unemployability.

Justin Cartwright was making a living out of people like me. I'd answered his ad: *$$$$$ EARNED CREATIVELY IN YOUR OWN HOME*. We talked on the phone. Justin ran a soft toy business. Throughout suburbia diminished people hunched over sewing machines whirring away into the night. Like busy elves, we stitched coloured felt into lumpy semblances of animals and birds. Justin delivered the felt, the patterns, the cotton and collected up the finished products. He checked the workmanship and paid two dollars fifty per creature. When I got really skilled at it, I could make one in fifty minutes.

We all specialised; Justin boasted that he matched the product with the outworker. I made parrots. Bright yellow parrots with scarlet beaks, and green feet that were sewn around a stick. Quite revolting. But I had the time, and the money paid for the movies and for the cigarettes that had somehow crept back into my pockets and my lungs, though never when in the same room as Mark, who was an advocate of wellness. A concept I had somehow lost interest in.

Having to support a wife was something Mark hadn't bargained for. His dismay was intense. One by one his life's pleasures dwindled and could not be renewed. We no longer had a selection of spirits in the liquor cabinet, or favourite restaurants. His membership at the Impact Gymnasium and the Koru Club lapsed. His Nikes grew low on tread.

He needed someone to hold responsible and there was only God, the government or me. We had belonged to the school of thought that believes in *life is what you make it*, so he blamed me. I tended to agree.

Quite early on we ran out of topics of conversation. I realised that our most satisfying dialogues had always been about what item we should buy next. This was a shock to me because I thought we had an intelligent relationship. I'd seen myself as a person of some depth; books, films and music were part of my life's schedule.

We began, in a quiet way, to avoid each other as much as possible. I moved into the spare room, preparing myself for life as a single person. I saw that it was up to me to make the break for I was the one who had caused the problem. I was poised to plunge into the great exciting sea of life, but the water looked so cold.

I'd gone in and picked up a brochure. As a single unemployed person with no dependants I'd get a welfare payment of a hundred and eight dollars and seventeen cents a week. *To live on!*

With Mark I had full board and lodging, car maintenance, and twenty or thirty dollars a week tucked reproachfully under the toaster. Survival was outweighing self-respect.

So. I was his wife, entitled to an equal share of the polished rimu, the Asian rugs, the linen drapes — but where would he live and why should he move and how long would it take? The complications built up in my head brick by brick until they became an unassailable wall.

My bus was late on the Friday (I never took my car into town because of the price of parking) and the film had started a few minutes before I got there. I sat in the dark wanting to crane my head — was he there? My mind making mountains out of mole-hills; where would we go, what would we do, and how did people *date* on a hundred and eight dollars and seventeen cents a week?

We ordered a pot of tea for two and found a table. Superannuit territory, a smell of stale biscuit crumbs (in a tin with Buckingham Palace on the lid). He poured. The stream of liquid wobbled a bit. We talked about the film but I was in another part of me, looking out, happy, liking the way he talked and laughed and moved and the mystery of all we didn't know about each other. Thinking discovery and exploration — his flesh, my fingertips. All this just from tea in the Plaza Arcade Coffee Lounge one o'clockish on a Friday afternoon.

I was in love. A new cameraman stepped behind my eyes and shot the world at crazy vivid angles. None of that dreamy soft-focus touch, I was seeing *everything*. Sharp-edged and totally surprising . . . zoom — a polyanthus in subversive shades of red . . . slow pan to — the texture of concrete, hold on a freesia, shit, it's spring! Capture it, get it on record to replay slow motion in darker days. Suddenly I had wealth in abundance, was enviable, mine was the leading role.

Is love more intense when it catches you out in the cold? With Lars I stopped eating, teetered between tender songs and self-destruction. And before that, with Angela Cannon, it was all terminal sighing and furtive verse.

In Mark's case it was more a matter of suitability — of being in the shop of life and reluctant to leave empty-handed. I believed I had matured beyond the delirium of unauthorised attraction. My point is, this was the first time it felt like a beneficent experience.

George. Pity about the name but I tried to make the best of it. George Harrison, I reminded myself, forget the others — George McElvey, who I'd once had the misfortune to work with, George Formby . . .

Blame his parents; there were seven children and he was fifth, they must have been down to basics by then. Anyway soon, in my mind, he had taken over his name and it became dear to me.

His family, or most of them, lived in Australia. They'd moved over there in dribs and drabs several years ago to what they saw as a better life. And, sure enough, that's what they'd found. But George had returned to New Zealand three months before I met him. He'd fled from a woman called Jenny who had a habit. They'd lived together for seven years. He worked as a builder, she worked in a restaurant, but they didn't earn enough to live and pay her supplier. She'd been on withdrawal programmes without success. Bit by bit, everything George owned went to the pawnbroker and never came back.

He bought tickets with his final pay plus holiday pay. He believed he would find work within a few days (I remembered the feeling). He couldn't get the dole until he'd been in the country six months — his family were all pitching in and sending him enough to survive on in the meantime.

My life, by comparison, seemed pallid but palmy.

We were seeing each other every day. We walked a lot and talked a lot and shared cigarettes. I had no expectations beyond the time when we would make love. That was inevitable and yet we delayed — not, I think, from fear of disappointment but because the anticipation was in itself so delicious. Besides, kissing was so tumultuous I thought more could mean disintegration.

George was renting a spartan room and shared amenities in a large and ugly inner-city house. The other tenants were a sad procession of the mildly insane and the seriously deformed. We would scuttle in and out self-consciously, feeling like Doctor Spock and Captain Kirk flaunting our advantages on some distressed planet. I took him once to my house — was startled to see how tasteful yet unoriginal it looked, how constricted, with its tiny bricked yard and my careful arrangement of urn-based shrubs and flowers. George said Mark was all through the house, his psyche had sprayed on every upright beam and polished corner, proclaiming territory.

So when we finally did it — naked flesh easing against naked flesh, so many nerve endings short circuiting or swoon-ing — it was in George's grim little room. Which became a magical, shimmering place tender with imperfections.

I never had any long-term expectations. I could see myself somewhere down the line blackened and depleted, a damp cardboard shell kicked beneath a hedge in late November. That wasn't a slur on George, just a lesson drawn from my recent life. It didn't put me off at all.

In fact, once we'd broken the sex barrier, things snow-balled. I couldn't go on living with Mark. I broached the subject of divorce. He was relieved, as I had suspected he might be — a financial burden removed. I pointed out that I was entitled to . . . etcetera. No problem, a pathetically eager confession; Maria from accounts would buy my half. She and Mark had been an item for some time. Her husband was buying her half of their house. Everyone, it seemed, was in on this but me. Mark had been afraid to tell me because I was such a broken reed with nothing going for me but a few stuffed birds. And I, in my miserable self-absorption, had been sure his growing dissatisfaction was all of my own doing.

'All the same,' I told him truthfully, 'I'm glad I didn't know.'

I wasn't sure I could have handled the thought of my total irrelevance. Before George, I mean.

6 George

So it all just tumbled into place. Maria bought my share at market value and Mark arranged with the finance company that my half of the mortgage should be transferable. He was bending over backwards to get me out of his hair.

George and I considered the options and decided to go country. He had friends in Carterton and houses there were cheap. We went up for three days and looked at real estate, and we looked at the plains snaked by rivers and at the dark spine of ranges and we squeezed our clasped hands and grinned as we followed estate agents up overgrown driveways.

We chose a low-slung place at the south end of town. It couldn't have been less like the place I'd left; I may have been heavily influenced by George. Tucked away among trees, but far enough back to catch the sun. A verandah, wisteria, old-style french doors, fruit trees — we couldn't believe how much you got, out here, for your money. We were staying with George's friends Jo and Malcolm. I liked them. They used to know Jenny. They told George they were glad he'd found someone nice. George passed this on to me.

We went back to Hamilton to collect my cat and what was left of our belongings. Julian didn't want me working long distance so he took me off the books. I didn't return his unused felt.

George had started collecting the dole, and now I was enrolled and waiting for my first payment. We weren't supposed to do it that way, of course, but we didn't feel married or even de facto, nothing so definite, we were just taking things as they came. Besides when I got my first payment — a hundred and twenty dollars including accommodation allowance — it was the most money I'd been in sole charge of for nearly eighteen months. I wouldn't have given that up, not even for George. And, except for Jo and Malcolm, nobody knew that we weren't just friends — a landlady and her boarder.

Malcolm worked at the local freezing works and was mates with the personnel officer. Just before Christmas a worker broke his leg in the loading bay when a bag of meal fell on him and George was called on temporarily. Then one of the old fellas had a heart attack and George applied and he got his job, permanent casual — which means 'apart from off-season'. They had waiting lists at the works a mile long, but our luck was on a run. Though, try as I did, I couldn't find work. I stayed on the dole; I'd had a taste of being supported by a man.

One Sunday we visited the bird sanctuary and I saw my first takahe, these big, clownish, clumsy birds in peacock greens with legs like plastic gumboots. It took a few trial attempts, but at home I made one — life-sized and as over-the-top as the real thing. I felt I was on to something.

Sure enough. First the local craft shop, then the Wellington tourist shops. Orders started coming in. I was making a living — only those who've been unemployed can know how good that feels. I cut myself off the dole. No more feeling underhand and furtive. We were free. We were independent.

The rest of that summer I sat on the verandah sewing, watching people walk past the gateway, waving to those I'd gotten to know. At night George would come home from work. It felt a bit clichéd and old-fashioned, but at the same time it felt pretty good. George was happy to get home to someone who wasn't pumping veins or spilling her methadone. I was happy just watching him kick off his big white gumboots and cross the verandah for a kiss.

After his first season George bought a little old motorbike so he wouldn't have to take my car to work. Then he came across a ridiculous sidecar and he bought it for me, and we had fun with it, though it always felt dangerous, being so low to the ground and unexpected.

For nearly three years that's how it was. And I still hadn't got to take it for granted; I still kept touching things to be certain they were real. I put on weight. Sometimes the thought snuck into my head *What if it goes on forever?* And I would slap it down — *Never does.*

I was so busy waiting for the enemy within I never saw what was coming straight at us.

They closed the freezing works. We saw it on the TV news — it was the off-season. Everyone laid off, just like that.

You watch a town close up like a hedgehog. All that's left are the prickles and the sense of fear. Not just our town, but all the towns around it. At first George didn't see quite how it was. He had friends, he had contacts, he had luck on his side.

The redundancy money saw him through a couple of months but even then he couldn't apply for the dole. We were a couple, we were known, and I had an income. Only it wasn't the kind of income that would support two people.

Together we visited the Social Welfare offices. We took all the paperwork from my little business. We spread this and our ordinary little lives on the woman's desk. She jabbed at her calculator.

We didn't qualify. We fell between specifications and possibly did not exist. The woman was a brick wall, we banged our heads against her.

'I don't make the rules,' she recited.

I wasn't ready to give up but George was dragging me out. 'Shove it,' he told her, 'we'll manage without.'

We couldn't, though. I could pay for the mortgage and, in a good week, basic groceries. But my orders had tailed off, even though by then I'd diversified into pukeko and paradise ducks.

George got quieter, sullen in fact. I began to think of him as a burden I had to shoulder. I felt like Mark , only a lot poorer.

Four months of this, stepping around each other, waiting, holding it together. Then one night he said, 'I'm leaving.' I felt relief. He'd go to Auckland where there still seemed to be jobs.

I could have said, no . . . please, but I said nothing. Later I went out and knelt behind the hydrangeas and cried, but I wiped my face before I went in. We'd each reclaimed our misery and gone private. I wanted to ask him to stay but there was nothing to offer.

He packed a few things. I stood watching. 'You'll write?'

He stood folding a jersey. 'I dunno.'

We didn't talk about it again. And next morning he rode out of town. I thought he would stop at the bridge and come back.

It was a lousy ending. I knew then that I'd grown to believe we were a serial — *Coronation Street* — with the world watching us growing old together. Most of that day I sat on the verandah with a watery face. I wasn't sure if I was crying because he'd gone or because it was such a shit of an ending.

Of course it may not be the ending — just intermission. He rang last night. But it was a careful call, slippery with propaganda on both sides. I didn't want to dump on him and make things harder than they were. The same with him. At least I took it to be that way — his tone was optimistic and a little remote. He's staying in a cheap boarding house and it's hard to sound intimate on a phone that sits in a public passage. I tell myself this. And I tell myself that we love each other, or seemed to, and separation will be the proof of the pudding.

But I must be realistic. George is a man who likes women. He needs to be owned.

The Day . . .

. . . THEY ARRESTED HIM I was mending our deck chair.

I'd been planning to repair it for several months. The canvas had rotted and to replace it I'd knitted an oblong of shiny blue synthetic fibre I'd bought many years before at a fire sale. It was the fibre's second incarnation. Its previous existence had been as a shirt for my husband. He only wore it twice. It looked like baby-blue chain armour and he wasn't the crusading kind. When he went he left the shirt behind and I'd kept it in case; unravelling a sleeve a year, waiting for a deck chair to come into my life.

I was attaching one end of this shiny blue creation to the bottom of the chair with a piece of old blind rail to keep it firm when his wife arrived. She was in tears. She said they'd come and taken him away without a word to her. She was upstairs and she'd looked out the window and seen her husband walking away between two policemen. They had walked in just like repo men and removed her husband.

I didn't know what to say or do so I kept on fixing the deck chair. I tried to imagine how it would feel to look out the window and see your husband walking away between two policemen, but nothing came.

It seemed to me very important that I should finish fixing the chair. I had the feeling that repairing the chair was a thread that could lead to the meaning of the universe. She sat at a table and cried while I hammered in three nails and five tacks. It took quite a long time because I am unskilled at carpentry.

When it was finished my son wanted to try out the chair. He needs to be first to do everything, which is a cross his sister has to bear. He sat down in the chair with confidence and the plastic knitting stretched until he hit the floor. We laughed at the look on his face. Her husband had been taken away and put in a cell but she laughed at this kid lying in the deck chair with his bum flat on the floor.

She wiped her face, then, and said could she use the phone to ring her friend in the city. I was feeling disappointed about the chair and all my efforts for nothing. I edged the claw of the hammer beneath the blind rail to prise it loose. And I listened to to her using the phone. *Hey,* she said first thing to her friend, *you'll never guess. After I left you last Friday I went back and bought that ridiculous dress.*

I just couldn't resist it.

Mia Culpa

AFTER ELAINE DIED — that's how he chose to think of it, to others she might be alive and working in Lambton Quay, but to Warren she was dead. The grieving process, that way, was easier. Cheryl had told him this was so. Not that she had first-hand experience of either kind of grief, except for her mother's death, and that's not at all the same; you expect to lose parents. But Warren had pictured Elaine in a coffin of pale wood, wearing the peach-coloured dress she'd bought last summer from Kimberleys. Then he had pictured himself dropping white rose petals that tumbled in slow motion past clay walls to land among the lilies which lay on the lid of the pale wood coffin. Then he drank his way through a third of a bottle of Napoleon brandy. And Cheryl was right — mourning was quite a pleasurable kind of grief compared with the other kind.

But almost ever since that day he buried Elaine, Warren had been on the lookout for someone to replace her. He didn't mean to be, he didn't want to be; he would have liked to reach out and cover the eyes of that part of him that was always peering around in hope and longing.

Wherever he went — wine bars, car park buildings, the supermarket, social gatherings — that humiliating part of him was on the alert. Many other people, he'd discovered, were watching in just the same way. Women and men, some of them even while they were sitting or walking with someone who appeared to be their partner. When Warren and Elaine were together he'd never looked around in that way. Had Elaine?

Sometimes his eyes would connect with the eyes of one of those watching women and he'd feel a small tingling jolt as if he'd laid one finger on a low-volt electric wire, even though not one of those women was what he was looking for. He didn't know what that was, exactly, but he gathered that the watchful part of him would recognise such a woman the moment he saw her.

Perhaps he just wanted another Elaine? Only one that would stay. Was that just a natural part of the grieving process, or proof that Warren was stupid?

He wanted someone his own age or a bit younger. Elaine was three years younger than him, which seemed just about right. Yet they looked so sharp, these young women, all steely and cutting edged. *Just out for themselves,* he thought, censoring Elaine from the equation so as not to think ill of the dead.

Even at work, where there was no one worth watching, Warren had caught himself glancing too often and too long at Cheryl who was, at thirty-two, only a little older than him. Cheryl wasn't the sharp-edged kind, but she was married with children. When her children grew up, would she go off and leave her Jim? You never could tell what was going on in a woman's mind.

When Elaine . . . departed, all three women in Warren's office had begun looking at him in a new and unfriendly way. That's how it felt, as if he had suddenly become the stuff of stranger danger. It made no sense. He was the same person as he'd been the week before, and the week before that. Was it his silent grief they despised? Or was it because, after seven whole years, Elaine had thrown him aside like a worn-out tracksuit? Alignment — was that what he'd seen in their evasive eyes? *She must have had a reason.*

Robert, too, had become uncomfortable in Warren's presence, juggling pity and embarrassment as if they were hot coals. As he passed the desk where Warren hunched, arms clasped across his broken heart, Robert would toss down band-aid phrases: *more fish in the sea . . . play the field . . . fancy free . . . I should be so lucky.*

'So why,' snapped Margaret, who'd overheard the last, 'do you stay with Nan?'

'You've got me there,' said Robert.

FISH SWIM ON Warren's screen when he leaves it in idle mode. There may not, he thinks, be that many left in the sea — not any more. You only have to watch them unloading crateloads from the big joint-venture fishing boats down at the wharf to wonder how many are left out there to breed. There might be more fish, already, on computer screens than in the world's oceans.

As for the other kind — the ones in public places who see him looking but pretend not to, and the others who look right back — even if they were just what he wanted, they would still be strangers.

He and Elaine had been at school together. They hadn't been friends, but at least they knew each other so that when they met again at Gareth's wedding they had a reason for talking.

'How did you and Jim meet?' Warren asks Cheryl.

'In the Barrington Mall,' said Cheryl. 'Me and my mate, Margie, used to hang out every Thursday night in the Barrington Mall. Pathetic, eh?' And she laughs.

'Arnie came to fix my washing machine,' says Margaret. Warren has heard it before. Margaret widowed with three small children; Arnie stepping through the door in his overalls. For five days she'd been doing the washing in the bath, stomping it like grapes, wringing by hand and it was winter.

'I found Ron on the Heaphy Track,' said Colleen drily. 'Should've left him there.' The others smile in sympathy.

'Pushed him over a cliff, more like, ' says Margaret. Ron is an office legend. Ten years of marriage and Colleen walked out, now can't imagine why she stuck it so long. Last year Ron was in the paper, convicted for false pretences. Not what you'd expect from a tramping man. Colleen lives alone, goes mountain climbing in her holidays with her friend Rita. Ron, she says, cured her of men.

Warren gets asthma from walking, is too old to hang around malls and never meets anyone new at this desk-bound job.

But now he remembers the man in the TV ad, the one who has been trying to get a woman for at least a year now. A perfectly presentable man, which just goes to show how hard it can be. The man in the ad had advertised. Well, he would, naturally. All the same, if *he* could, why shouldn't Warren?

At home Warren drags out Saturday's paper from the garage and reads the personal columns. He remembers how

Elaine used to spread the paper on the floor and read crouched in sphinx position. Sometimes even the small ads. The weirder ones she'd read aloud for Warren. *Athletic man seeks bi woman and partner for fun times.* They would giggle over the bizarreness of some people and Elaine's tongue would come out and lick along her bottom lip. If she stayed there reading for long enough she would sometimes leave the paper to come and sit astride him, sliding her tongue into his mouth.

Now Warren tries to remember if the two of them had laughed at the lonely ads or just the kinky ones. There are quite a lot of lonely ads — *Sincere rural gent seeks kind non-smoking woman* — but they are almost all from men. The exceptions are from a *fun-loving, roly-poly woman* and the *woman seeking sexy times.* Warren feels embarrassed on behalf of them both. A little desperately he scans the print for the word *relationship,* which has such a solid ring. *Love,* he's discovered, even *partner* cannot be trusted to mean what you might suppose. What about *soulmate?*

Looking for a soulmate. Don't be shy. Join our singles club.

SHE SOUNDED NICE, the woman who answered. 'Just don't expect miracles on your first evening.'

Warren marked the night on his kitchen calendar. This was in August. The singles club met every two weeks in members' homes. That first time, Warren was struck by two things: the number of people who said to him, 'We're all in the same boat' (sailing above all those fish?) and the way people kept their eyes to themselves, as though just having come along was all the availability they could manage.

There was no one who looked absolutely right, but there were two or three who might turn out to be if he knew them better.

In September Warren asked Karen, a solo mother, out to dinner. The slant of Karen's lips reminded him of Elaine. He watched those lips as she ate, as she talked.

Two nights later they went to a pub to hear the Warratahs. Karen joined in the line dances and Warren watched and knew for sure that she wasn't what he wanted.

He couldn't possibly tell her so.

'See you at the club on Tuesday, then,' she said, getting into her Mini.

'Yes,' said Warren. 'See you Tuesday.'

Which meant he couldn't go to the singles club anymore.

BY OCTOBER, SPRING had seeped into Warren's veins, filling him with restless impatience. The prospect of spending any more evenings alone in the flat watching television became unbearable. He thought about moving in with others — young single people who knew how to live on their own, and would have friends and friends-of-friends who came to visit. He began going out every night, driving around the streets. It was as if, without this sense of motion, he might cease to exist. Sometimes he would drive out to one of the beaches and sit for a time watching couples or the people walking their dogs. (Should he get a dog? At least for the meantime?) Other nights he would simply drive around the city, including Manchester Street, where the hookers paraded. Tried to imagine himself pulling up on the kerb alongside one, but he wasn't the type.

At least not until the night when he noticed her. *Recognised* her, in fact, as the woman that hopefully peering part of him had been looking for. Surely she couldn't be one of them? Such a pretty young woman, showing lots of leg, but otherwise properly dressed. None of that tacky thigh-boots-and-suspenders stuff. This one looked nice. And not a bit like Elaine.

All that was just an impression from the far side of the road. When Warren drove back, more slowly, on the other side, she was even lovelier than he had thought. He must stop the car, wind down the passenger window; that's how it was done.

But what if she didn't come over to talk to him? What if she did? And how much money would he need?

What if she was just a student or a barmaid, waiting for her friend?

Warren drove around the corner and parked. Sat for a moment, giving her time to meet her friend, to walk away, to climb into a stranger's car. Then he got out and walked around the corner into the chill easterly wind. She was still there. She gave him a wide-open smile.

'Nice night,' he said.

'Is it?' She shivered, but gave him another smile, just as dazzlingly friendly as the first.

It gave him the courage to ask.

'Are you, you know . . . available?'

'Very much so.' Another smile.

'Ah . . . how much . . .?'

'Depends on what you're after.'

Love, he thought. That's what I'm after. But he couldn't say that. What should he say?

'Basic,' she said, 'is sixty dollars for half an hour. Cash.'

'Right,' said Warren numbly. He realised he'd expected her to cost more, to cost so much that it was out of the question. Then he could've just gone home to bed and thought about her.

'There's a cash machine just down the road. It takes most cards.'

She pointed helpfully. The bank was a couple of hundred metres away. Westpac, Warren's bank. She saw his hesitation.

'Do you have a card?'

He nodded. A card, luckily, with overdraft facilities. 'But shouldn't we . . .?' He wasn't sure what he was trying to say.

'You go and get the money first.' Her tone of voice said, *There's a good boy.* Firm and kindly. 'Better get a bit more in case you want to do extra things.' Then, as if she was reading his mind. 'I'll still be here, it's a quiet night.'

He almost ran, glancing back a couple of times to make sure she was still waiting. While he was at the machine a car drove past him then slowed right down at her corner. He stood watching the car while the machine dealt out his banknotes, but the driver had only slowed before turning. She saw Warren looking and waved out as if he and she were old friends.

She took him, that first time, along the street and up a back stairway to a small room. In the corridor they met an older woman with aquamarine eyeshadow and prominent teeth. The two women gave each other a hug, and the older one smiled toothily at Warren and said, 'Don't worry. You're among friends here. Mia is just a lovely person.'

'That's your name? Mia?'

She nodded, wriggling fingers at her departing friend.

'I've never met anyone called Mia,' he said. 'I only know the film star, the one that was with Woody Allen.'

'Everyone says that,' she told him, unlocking a door.

Inside the room Mia took charge. She was years younger than him yet she seemed so confident, so at ease. Like the mother Warren wished he'd had: smiling, coaxing, admiring, praising. She didn't get many men as young and attractive as Warren. He was a nice person, she could tell that the moment she met him. Nice people were even rarer than young and attractive ones.

She felt so wonderful beneath his fingers, her mouth was so warm, her skin so silky, half an hour was nowhere near enough; and there were other things she was planning to show him. Luckily he'd got another eighty dollars just in case.

He walked with her back to the corner. 'Can I see you again?'

'Of course,' she said. 'I'm here Thursday, Friday, Saturday and Sunday nights.'

That hadn't been quite what he meant. There was something special between them — she'd almost said so.

It became Thursdays and Sundays. She had other regular customers, but they weren't as special as him. Only he got a ten-dollar discount, that's what she said. She wasn't used to men who treated her as nicely as he did, with so much respect.

To prove just how nice he was, Warren sometimes used the half-hour to take her to one of the nicer bars just for a drink and a talk. What with the price of the drinks on top of her fee it worked out pretty expensive, but he liked so much the attentive way she listened, leaning towards him, and her deep gurgle of a laugh. And he liked the way other men looked at them, the slightly hostile, envious glances he caught but pretended not to notice.

By mid-November she was taking him to her place instead of that bleak little room in the massage parlour. She rented an inner-city apartment (it was far too up-market to be called a *flat*) and her furniture was new and expensive, straight out of Ballantyne's or McKenzie and Willis. She liked nice things, she had impeccable taste. Warren would have hated for her to see his flat, especially now he'd sold the rimu coffee table and the video player and the settee. He didn't resent having sold them, though they'd fetched much less than he'd hoped; furniture was a small price to pay for the way he floated, blissful and buoyant, through the hours around and between Thursday and Sunday nights.

In early December Warren took out a bank loan. He said he needed to replace his car. The lie slid from his lips with surprising ease, but then it wasn't a bad kind of lie; banks wanted to lend you money and didn't really care what it was for. But a Mia-fund would have been a little hard to explain and even harder to justify, so why bother trying? Even to himself.

He had no choice, that was the bottom line; he had no choice.

At work they had seen the change in him and guessed at the cause. They probed — Margaret, Cheryl and Colleen — but he told them nothing, just sat there nursing his grin. They teased him, then, with speculation and innuendos which Warren ignored. His silence felt like a powerful thing; he sensed the women's renewed acceptance of him.

No, more than that, their *approval*.

'I shall,' he told them, 'neither confirm nor deny.'

They chorused a little squeal of delight.

The Christmas social was coming up. A Friday night. He asked Mia if she would go with him.

She bit her lovely bottom lip. 'How long would we be there?'

'Three hours? Maybe, four?'

'A pity it's on a work night,' she sighed. 'At this peak time of year. Four hours on the job and I'd take home five hundred.'

'Three hours,' said Warren, 'and I'll be paying you, of course.'

Mia smiled at him. 'Let's say two hundred and seventy —
on a special Warren Christmas discount.'

'Are you sure?' He didn't want to be costing her money.

When she nodded, he kissed her on the corner of her
mouth.

'Thank you, my love-erly Mia.'

SHE WAS WAITING outside her apartment building, dressed just
right. Classy, but in an understated way.

'How do you want me to be?' she asked him in the car.

The question surprised him.

'Just yourself,' he said. 'And I'm your boyfriend. Which is
true because that's how I think of myself.'

'You're so sweet.' She leant across and kissed him on the
cheek. 'And my name? What's my name?'

'Mia, of course.'

'What if one of my other customers is there?'

Warren felt his jaw drop. Why hadn't he thought of that?
But he knew why — he'd censored out any thoughts of what
she did for a living and who she might do it with. He'd chosen
to regard her as an astute and successful businesswoman,
which was how she seemed to see herself.

'Don't worry,' she soothed. 'It's hardly likely. This is a big
city.'

Warren felt his shoulder muscles ungripping.

'That's right. Besides, you'll just be meeting us lot from
accounts. We all stick pretty much to our own little groups at
these Christmas dos.'

THEY WERE ALL there before him, which was how he'd intended
it to be. He watched their faces as they noticed him walking
across the room with Mia's hand tucked inside his. Saw
Colleen nudge Cheryl, who leant across Jim to alert Margaret,
whose mouth fell open then composed itself and leant to
whisper in Arnie's ear, while Cheryl was pointing and grinning for Robert's benefit and Nan was looking in confusion
from one gaping or smirking face to another.

Robert's expression was the best of all. *Gobsmacked*, that
was the only word for it.

Warren sat Mia down beside the carafe of white wine and introduced her clockwise around the table.

'Mia,' they said. 'M-i-a ? Like thingee the film star?'

Jim poured her a glass of wine which she had barely brought to her lips before their more probing questions began. Warren realised with a lurch of his stomach that he hadn't really thought this thing through. Just be yourself, he'd said!

He needn't have worried; a few minutes of listening assured him of that. Mia answered all their questions so convincingly, and with such an endearing trace of diffidence, that Warren felt himself falling in love all over again with this new, shy yet down-to-earth young woman who had come to the city from Geraldine to train as a social worker.

Was some of it true? How much?

'Well!' muttered Margaret, smothering the cheese platter as she pressed her bulk across the table. 'Where on earth did you manage to find *her*?'

'Ah,' Warren pretended to flick an almost invisible something from the surface of his beer, stalling for time. 'Well, actually you should ask her — she tells it much better than me. Excuse me sweetheart,' he said to Mia, who was telling Cheryl about her three student flatmates, 'but Margaret wants to know how we met.'

He gave her a smile that felt a little desperate but which the others would surely interpret as fond and intimately significant.

'Where did we meet?' Mia looked at their now expectant faces. 'It was so corny,' she said, 'such a cliché, you wouldn't believe.' She flashed a smile at Warren then took a large mouthful of wine. Her face took on a remembering look.

'It was quite late at night,' she said, 'and my car had broken down. Well, it wasn't actually my car, it was my flatmate's, and it was a heap of junk. But this night I'd had to borrow it . . .'

Warren sat there entranced, seeing it all happening the way she described it, nodding his head, *Yes, yes, that's right* . . .

It was some time later that he noticed how quickly she emptied her glass and how often and willingly Jim, who sat on her other side, refilled it. Mia's laugh, by that time, had become rather loud and very frequent. It began on a high note and slid away, getting thinner and thinner like an anteater's tail. Warren could see from Robert's watch (he had pawned his own the month before) that he still had forty minutes of Mia's company to go. He thought they might sneak off early, back to her place — the others would understand (nudge, nudge, wink, wink). Compared with Mia, his colleagues and their partners seemed exceedingly dull and inconsequential. He wondered at himself for not having noticed this colourlessness before.

He was about to whisper to Mia that they would leave soon when she asked directions to the ladies and heaved herself out of her chair. Rather unsteadily, she set off. Should Warren go with her? No, better not to draw attention, he would just pretend he hadn't noticed.

But Colleen had. 'Is she all right?'

This wasn't directed at anyone in particular and Nan was at that moment telling Warren about the difference between the Japanese maple and the more common variety. Warren knew nothing about maples and didn't wish to, but they saved him from having to consider Mia's wavering progress across the room.

Just as Colleen got up to follow Mia, Robert rescued Warren from his horticultural wife and took him to the bar, where the senior staff and a few spendthrift juniors were buying scotch on the rocks and brandy and dry, in preference to the free wine and low-alcohol beer the company had provided.

Robert had been thinking about his future; had Warren?

Warren shook his head in instant, though perplexing, guilt. Ought he to have been thinking about Robert's future? Why?

'Well, you should,' said Robert.

At the end of next year he planned to retire and take things easy. They'd have to advertise, naturally, for his replacement, but a personal recommendation from Robert would carry much weight.

'If you get my drift,' said Robert, placing a brandy and dry ginger ale in Warren's hand.

'But . . .' Warren stared down at his glass, moved it about so the ice cubes tinkled. 'But . . . seniority? All of them are older than me, and Colleen's been there almost forever.'

'Warren, Warren, seniority . . . all that nonsense went out the window years ago. We all know that. Your colleagues are fine women but as figures of authority? What management will be looking for is a bit of get-up-and-go, plus some experience. Can't promise, of course, but you'd have every chance.'

Mia, thought Warren. It was because of her. In his whole life no one had ever before seen him as a get-up-and-goer.

'Just keep it to yourself,' said Robert, patting Warren's shoulder. 'Drink up and we'll have another. Cheers.'

'Yes,' said Warren. 'Thank you. Happy Christmas.'

HOD! Would Mia maybe consider marrying a head of department? Even if she wouldn't, at least he'd be able to pay back his bank loan and replace his settee and coffee table.

When Robert and Warren returned to the table, Mia was there, hunched forward in her chair with her head clutched in her hands. Warren had never before noticed how fragile and young her shoulders and upper arms looked. He saw this even before he became aware of the faces of those around her. The way they were looking at him.

'What is it?' said Robert.

But their eyes stayed on Warren, who was standing there almost in the middle of a very large room feeling cornered, backed up against a wall and unable to move. In a strange sort of way — precognition? — this situation felt very familiar.

Cheryl was the first to speak.

'We know!' she said. 'She told us.'

'We never,' said Margaret, 'thought you would stoop so low.'

'She's a prostitute,' Nan explained to Robert. 'It's true. He hired her for the evening. He's one of her regular customers.' She laid each word out fastidiously in a surgically gloved voice.

They all looked at Robert for his reaction, but nothing showed.

'Nineteen!' hissed Margaret. 'Our Vicki's age. Just a child.'

From Mia's hidden face came a small sound that might have been a sob.

Arnie pushed back his chair and stood up. He straightened his shoulders and pushed out his chest, his eyes on Warren. 'So what have you got to say for yourself?'

'I . . .' What was there to say? What did they want him to say?

'Mia. Mia?'

She raised her head just a fraction. Warren took a step towards her but, as he did, Margaret lunged sideways and dragged Mia protectively into her arms.

'Come on,' she ordered Arnie. 'We're taking the poor kid home to a decent bed. Some loving care — that's what she needs.'

Mia flopped like a rag doll between Margaret and Arnie as they arranged her into a transportable shape.

Jim went with them to open the doors. Warren watched until they were all out of sight.

'She got drunk awfully fast,' he said, thinking aloud.

'Who wouldn't?' Cheryl was draining the carafe of red into her glass.

'No,' said Colleen. 'It's the pills do that.'

'What pills?' Warren and Cheryl both together, but no *snap*, no linking of little fingers.

'The pills,' said Colleen, looking at no one, 'that she was taking so that she could endure all the stuff men made her do.'

'Without throwing up.' Cheryl threw out a grin that Colleen caught and tossed to Nan.

Now Robert sighed loudly and shook his head at Warren in the manner of a bull that may or may not intend to charge. Even his eyes now looked small and glinting and bull-like.

'It's an offence for the woman but not for the man,' Colleen announced. She turned to Warren. 'So you can't be arrested, you'll be pleased to know.'

'Men can do no wrong.' Halfway through a sarcastic rolling of the eyes, Cheryl remembered Robert and gave him an anxious glance. But Robert was too busy staring at Warren while pretending not to.

'I never knew Mia was taking pills.' Did that sound like some kind of pathetic plea for sympathy?

'Alison,' said Colleen. 'Her name is Alison. Mia is just a made-up name.'

Telling him, *That's how much you knew about her.* Nan giving a little smile and nodding her endorsement. Robert still glowering.

'I suppose,' Warren muttered, 'you'd all like me to resign?'

No one spoke. Snatches of conversation drifted in from the surrounding tables. Jim, rejoining them, picked up on their silence and almost tip-toed the last few steps. Warren felt a prickling at the back of his eyes. *Please don't let me cry.*

'So what do you have to say for yourself?' Nan, stepping in to save him from their cruel silence, sounded almost kindly.

Warren took a deep breath.

'It's not like that. It's not. You see, I love her.'

That silence again. Again the buzz and fragments of distant conversations.

'That's not love,' said Cheryl, and now Warren noticed that her voice was slurred. 'It's screwing. Sex and love are not the same thing, though men still haven't figured that out.'

'You don't even know her,' said Robert wearily. 'How can you love someone if you don't even know them?'

'If you don't *respect* them,' said Nan, and threw her husband an indecipherable look.

'I did resp—'

'No, you didn't,' said Colleen, 'or you wouldn't have taken advantage.'

Warren just wanted to sit down. The danger of tears was past, a small relief. *Alison*, he was thinking. *Alison!* The name didn't fit her at all. He could dislike an Alison.

'She did all right,' he said suddenly. 'I've spent a packet on her. You ought to see the way she lives. She earns more than all of us put together.'

Again they were all looking at him in that way, and now he remembered. Primary school playground; same faces, same feeling of bewildered fear.

'No wonder Elaine left you,' said Cheryl. 'No bloody wonder.'

It Could Be You

FROM THE OTHER side of the city she is transmitting to you. As you scrape the peeling paint from the windowsills, as you dead-head the roses, as you walk the dog, Anita is sending you bleats of neglect.

You are on holiday and so have no excuse. Consult your address book. Pick up the phone. That's all it will take.

Three days ago you made a list.

1. *write to M and K*
2. *B pres for Sally. W gls? Heater?*
3. *w'sills*
4. *connect answerphone*
5. *book car for o & g and t-up*
6. *Ring Jo*
7. *C for dinner Thurs? And B?*
8. *ring Anita*

Wine glasses, you settled on, for Sally. Wide enough, at the top, to get a teatowel in to remove the stain of cabernet sauvignon.

Your local garage has gone out of business. Chris recommends a Shell place in Waltham but it's so far away. Thursday suits him for dinner, but Bill can't make it that night.

Friday night's okay with Chris, though he sounded less than enthusiastic about Bill being there. Does that mean what you think it means? Best to ignore that thought. Curry or chicken?

Jo and Tony are 'sorting things out'. A highly charged phrase, that, along with 'we've had our ups and downs'. A muddle of explosive emotions crammed into one tidily wrapped expression. Your own ups and downs parade in your mind unbidden, and loneliness trickles; you would gladly have them back. But to begin all over again with someone new? Would you want that? (Chris floating involuntarily into you mind, a worrying sign.)

You connect up your brand-new answerphone according to the instructions, then phone Jo and ask her to ring you back and leave a message. 'Hi,' she says onto the tape. 'You sound like an undertaker, but at least it seems to be working okay.'

You have not yet rung Anita.

Your list now looks like this:

1. ~~write to M and K~~
2. ~~B pres for Sally. W gls? Heater?~~
3. w'sills
4. ~~connect answerphone~~
5. book car for o & g and t-up
6. ~~Ring Jo~~
7. C for dinner Thurs? ~~And B?~~
8. ring Anita
   ring Inland Rev
   sandpaper & primer
   dog reg
   pres to Sally

You have received a menacing letter from Inland Revenue demanding a hundred and ninety dollars and seventy-five cents. Which you have already paid them. You ring them and are put in a phone queue of unspecified length. You listen to Kris Kristofferson singing about a past but unregretted love and then to 'Stranger on the Shore' played, you surmise, by Acker Bilk. Halfway through a song about a clown by someone whose name you know but can't recall, you hang up.

You take the beribboned, shop-wrapped wine glasses to Sally and she opens a bottle of bubbly to christen them. Glen, her boarder, has had his cam shaft repaired by a garage called The Repair Shop. While expansively praising their workmanship, he knocks over his glass, which hits the edge of the fruit bowl. Sally says never mind, six people is a crowd, she would never have fitted them all into her kitchen.

You find a two-litre can of paint in the garage and decipher p—me– between the droolings of dried white on the label.

You prise open the lid and pierce the plasticised skin to expose several centimetres of liquid primer, which may be enough.

The Repair Shop can take your car that very day, which might be cause for concern. On the way you stop off at Mitre 10 for sandpaper. No one at The Repair Shop offers to drive you home but it's only a twenty-minute walk on a fine morning — you wish you'd brought the dog. While you are walking, you remember the name of the clown-song singer: Billy Joel.

You send off a thirty-five dollar cheque to the council on behalf of your dog whose name is Bardot (F neutered black & tan labrador X). While you are out posting it, Jo leaves a second message on your answerphone. 'It's me. Ah. Things aren't . . . hey I really need to talk to you.'

You try to ring her but her phone is always engaged. You take Bardot with you to pick up the car. They charge you at least forty dollars more than you were expecting. Is that why your local garage went out of business?

You don't get around to ringing Anita, but you haven't forgotten. How could you? She is still transmitting.

You make a new list.

1. *enamel for w'sills*
2. *ring Family Court for info (for Jo)*
3. *wine, chicken etc*
4. *hair cut*
5. *ring Inland Rev*
6. *ring Anita*

Go on.

It's such a small thing and, unlike Inland Revenue, she won't put you on hold.

Now. While you're still on holiday and have the time.

BUT THAT'S THE trouble. Come round, she'll say. Oh please come round. We can have some lunch. Do you like pickle? I've got some wonderful pickle and some lamb's tongue. I'm sure it's gone out of fashion, lamb's tongue. Nobody eats it anymore, but Colin from next door did my shopping and he got the tongue instead of luncheon. Have you met Colin? No, you won't have, they moved in during winter and it was March when you last came around. Definitely March. We went to Briscoes' autumn sale, remember? To get my electric kettle? Gina, the one with the Mongrel Mob boyfriend, she was still there then, but she's gone, and now it's Colin and Brenda. He's all right but she's a funny little thing with nothing to say, I couldn't ask *her*. I didn't need a lot but there was nothing in the cupboard, next to nothing, and I couldn't possibly go out, not even to the dairy.

Then she'll sigh and wait.

Oh dear, you'll say — your regret genuine but, alas, mainly on your own behalf — has it got worse?

You can't *imagine*, she'll sigh, how bad it has been.

Have you seen the doctor?

What else can you say? Even though you know better.

The doctor. Don't mention the doctor. I've got a new one — well you know all the nonsense I was getting from that last one. So I've got a woman, only she's not much better. I think it's these new pills she's got me on. The old ones were doing nothing, I told her that. But in retrospect — is that the word? My memory's going, it's one of the side effects; things I know perfectly well just drift out of my head. But I can tell you about it when you come round. And I've got something here for you. Funny, just before the phone went I was thinking about you. Synchronicity. Is that the word? I like to get my words right, even if I can't do much else these days.

You could pick her some daisies, the double-headers on their long stems. Her flat is on the second floor of a concrete block with tiny balconies overlooking a used car yard, the ground-floor flats with their little back gardens are too expensive. She does what she can with her balcony. Waxy geraniums and purple anemones in pots of her own invention.

Her mother was Danish. That, she has told you, is why people have always found her a little bit strange, a little bit unacceptable. It also, she believes, explains her passion for crafts.

She has made you another present. It's been waiting there for you to ring. Anita has her pride, will not ring back if her call goes unreturned. You can't say she imposes.

The gift will be something she has made with immense patience out of very little. It will not be chintzy and vaguely utilitarian in the way of those items that crowd the windows of small town craft shops. It will be quirky and ornamental, made from feathers, dried leaves, papier mâché, and artfully painted. Anita has talent.

That's how you met her. Nine years ago, when her energy level was higher, she had a stall at the weekend market. You stopped with delight and bought a covered matchbox that opened to reveal a tiny silk rose, intricately fashioned to open and close with the lid of the matchbox. Your enthusiasm pleased her. She wrote her phone number and address on the back of your cheque book and urged you to come and visit. The stall, she confided, was an experiment she would not be repeating. The day was almost over and she was still out of pocket. By the time she counted the price of a taxi to get her and her wares there and home again, plus the price of the stall . . . well, it was hopeless, really.

It wasn't fair — that's what you thought, and probably said, with indignation. This woman, still quite young and clearly talented, yet accorded no recognition, no appreciation. She deserved better.

Spurred on by murky moral outrage you went, not long after, to visit her. Nine years ago.

But that day at the market was the best it was ever going to get for Anita. That was her peak. You know that now. The doctor-defying illness that you have since become so familiar with was already encroaching, soon it would embrace — engulf — her in a world of prescription drugs and medical arrogance.

Psychosomatic, they told her — too vain (she said) to admit to diagnostic ignorance. Neurosis. Hypochondria. Words that nudge and nibble at your own reserves of sympathy and patience. But how can you know? How can anyone know? In Anita's shoes who would not become obsessive? Who would not seek out sympathy, clutch at kindness? *It could be you,* that's the thought you can't chase out of your mind.

So, sooner or later, you will ring her and go to visit. And she will welcome you in as if you are someone of immense importance. The Pope, perhaps, or the Dalai Lama — Anita is a voyager in spiritual realms. Suffering, she says, makes you aware. This would explain your own indifference to tenets and creeds; your perceptions have been blunted by an insufficiency of suffering.

You have been too lucky. Life has bestowed on you much more than a fair share of happiness, while Anita has been shortchanged. You will watch, ashamed, as she carefully arranges tomatoes and fennel and sliced cheese. It should be you preparing a meal for her, the welcome guest. In such small ways you could begin to redress the shameless inequities of fate.

She will smile as she hands you the plates and knives and forks to set on her little table, and smile some more as she pours your tea. She'll tell you about Charles from the flat below, who had sometimes invited her in for a glass of port, and knew everything you would ever want to know about antiques.

But you'll only be half listening because of the *guilt*. Why has this taken you so long? What did you imagine you were avoiding? This is a pleasant, generous woman who showers you with gifts and hospitality. If she is rather different from your other friends, is that not a good and instructive thing? How could you begrudge this person a few hours of your time!

The point about the Charles story will turn out to be that this same Charles has now warned Colin-next-door against Anita. Colin hasn't said so but she saw the two of them talking together and Colin is now avoiding her. Not that she's gone and knocked on his door; she's never done that except for the once when she'd mislaid her pills and was almost out of her mind with pain. Other times she just stayed near her own door until she heard his footsteps on the stairs. But only, that is, if there was something she really needed help with.

At about this point you will feel your guilt transforming into something twitchy and less definable. Automatically your lips will spill out a variety of innocent reasons why her neighbour might *appear* to be avoiding her. The alacrity with which she is prepared to accept any or all of these possible reasons will be disturbing.

Reassured, and therefore restored, Anita will begin to make

plans for the afternoon. She would like you to see the house she grew up in. She will describe this house with such fondness that you will be ready to agree. Where is it?, you'll ask. Rangiora, she'll say brightly as if Rangiora is just around the corner. This gives you an out. You must be home in an hour, you tell her. Your daughter is coming around, she has marriage problems.

Anita will sigh her disappointment. Never mind, she'll offer, we'll do it another day. The weekend, if you're back at work. We'll take a picnic lunch and stop by the river — that would be nice.

Anita doesn't drive. She's a sickness beneficiary and can't afford a car. If you were her you would certainly long to get out of the city now and again. Yet a picnic, a whole afternoon with Anita — the very thought fills you with claustrophobia.

While you are struggling for breath, Anita will be looking at the clock. An hour? There must be things you need from the supermarket, so would you mind very much if you both went there? It won't take an hour and she obviously can't rely on Colin.

It will have to be New World. They know her there and a friendly smile can make all the difference when you're on your own. (Yes, you'll say here, a little too quickly, driven by irritation to push yourself into the picture. It's not even true. Supermarket smiles are not a factor in your life. You are a widow, but you have family, you have friends, while Anita's life is a litany of unhappy relationships.)

Halfway along the one-way street Anita will remember that she hasn't brought her coupon book, and coupons make all the difference when you're on a benefit. Never mind, she'll say, we don't want to make you late for your daughter.

But you lied. Jo isn't coming around until after her appointment at the Family Court; you have at least three hours to spare. So at the lights you will turn back. Outside her apartment block you will wait with the motor still running, until you observe just how slowly she walks. Due to pain, or to medication? You will turn the motor off. You will fish in the dashboard where you find three loose and grubby Extra Strong mints. After minutes of indecision, then boredom, you will eat them regardless. Then you will switch on the battery and try in vain to pick up a voice, a tune, on the hopeless radio. You will be aware of your life hurtling by without you.

Eventually you will get out of the car and go upstairs where you will find her fumbling behind jars of soya flour, cornflour, gluten — her own vividly painted labels. She can't find the coupons. You will suggest she ask for a new book at the checkout counter. She'd prefer not to do that, it causes so much bother, but perhaps this once she will.

As you get back into the car you'll see the coupon book wedged on her side of the handbrake. Anita will feel sure that this is a sign; not of carelessness, but of spiritual significance.

You would like to wander around on your own and look at the shops in the mall, but Anita will insist you accompany her and the trolley through New World. She wants to discuss the brown spots on the runner beans, and whether or not they really put fresh spring water in the sardine cans. She'll point out foods that the two of you might take on your picnic.

YOU WILL NOT ring Anita. Not just yet.
Updated list.

> 1. enamel for w'sills
> 2. ring Family Court for info (for Jo)
> 3. wine, chicken etc
> 4. hair cut
> 5. ring Inland Rev
> 6. ring Anita
> J & S Wed
> return answerphone
> find Inland Rev receipt

The answerphone tape is full and you are unable to erase the messages. You try several times, following the instructions, then you disconnect the thing and look for its box, but you seem to have thrown it out. The answerphone is under guarantee.

You have finally managed to talk to someone at Inland

Revenue. They have no record of your payment. They would sooner take their computer's word than yours. The receipt you're certain they gave you is not in the drawer where you ought to have put it. Perhaps in a pocket or a handbag?

Your grandchildren, Jonno and Sarah, are staying with you so that their parents can have some time to themselves. Not time together, but time on their own — or with friends (who will have, one way or another, their own agendas).

You have roast chicken for Thursday dinner — children hardly ever like curry, and why cook twice? You feed them first and Chris is good about playing snakes and ladders and the bedtime stories. You explain about the answerphone and Chris reconnects it without once consulting the manual. Within a couple of minutes he has erased all the messages except your own. This wasn't the evening either of you had had in mind. On reflection you are grateful for this. *Possibility* is a much nicer word than *decision*.

Jonno wants to help you paint the windowsills. You say he can help restain the deck instead, though this isn't a task you had in mind for this summer. You think of it as a small deck but it is five times the size of Anita's balcony. Your deck leads off the dining room. Yes, you have a dining room. You also have a living room and a kitchen and a sunporch and two bedrooms whereas Anita has only her bedroom and a living room with a tiny alcove kitchen attached. Life has been good to you. You are a lucky person. With just a small amount of the luck you have had, Anita's life might have been very different.

But maybe her luck has already changed? Maybe this time the pills are working, her illness is in remission and she's found a friend, another beneficiary, who also has time on her hands. *His* hands? Might that not be even better? Maybe at this very moment they are picnicking beside a river. You could ring up and no one would answer. I rang, you could tell her weeks later, but you were out.

She would ask you what day, what hour, you phoned — as she has done before. Then told you exactly where she was, what she was doing (seeing the doctor/ buying eggs at the corner store) at four fifteen on that Tuesday a month before.

How lonely is that!

So, PERHAPS, YOU toss down a fair-sized glass of brandy and you dial her number. But the voice that answers is not hers.

'Good morning,' you say. 'Is Anita there?'

'Please, who is speaking?'

You give your name.

'Ah,' says the voice, which is female, foreign, less than friendly. 'Yes. So you did get my message I left on your machine?'

'What message?'

'Your name is here in her book. I thought she would want you to know.'

'I received no message,' you say carefully. 'My machine was on the blink, the tape was full and . . . What message?'

'Anita died three days ago. It was an overdose — too many tablets, a whole heap of tablets. They took her to hospital but her brain — it was too late.'

Sarah wants your attention. As she opens her mouth to speak you place your finger over her lips and scoop her up on to your lap.

'The funeral?' you whisper into the phone.

'Tomorrow. It will just be family, under the circumstances, you understand?'

'Of course,' you murmur, ashamed at the relief. You wrap your arms around your granddaughter's small body and hold her so tightly against you that she squeaks a protest.

THE INLAND REVENUE receipt for a hundred and ninety dollars and seventy-five cents was in with the packet of photos you got developed in October. It drops out on to your dining room table when your grandson Jonno is looking through the photos.

You take up your list. You cross out *find Inland Rev receipt*. Your pen (*Scripto, extra fine point permanent marker*) moves up a little and hovers above *6. ring Anita*.

~~6. ring Anita~~

Losing

HALFWAY UP THE coast road Jeff was ambushed by incapability.

The car became a malevolent beast straining to crash the frail fence and plunge to the rocks below. His hands were damp with the effort of holding the wheel in place. He couldn't glance at his wife beside him or at the mirrored reflection of their daughters singing in the back seat. He was afraid they would notice.

And yes, Alice was looking at him. He ought to pull over and let her drive. It had come to that.

He was driving too slowly? Glanced at the speedo, yes much too slow. That was all she'd noticed, ha ha. He pressed down cautiously on the pedal; the rocks were treacherous, he saw a rock sharp as a can opener slitting the roof. He saw fair fine child's hair clotted with blood.

'It's sluggish,' he shrugged for Alice. 'Seems to be missing.'

'It was okay yesterday. Perhaps it's the way you drive.' The hair-ruffling voice she'd taken to using more and more.

The girls were singing an air freshener commercial. That's why they knew it, though it had once been a song, a legitimate song that had managed perfectly well without a sponsor. He felt a welling of irritability towards his daughters for belonging to such a contemptible era.

'What's the matter?'

'Nothing. Nothing's the matter.'

'Okay,' she said. 'Okay.' Patting the air down with her palms. Calming it.

THERE WERE SHOOTS of grass growing between the rose bushes. This meant his mother, Nancy, had been off colour. She was vigilant about the garden.

She had heard the car turn in the drive and was at the door, pink-cheeked and smiling, before the girls had got their feet on gravel. 'You certainly picked a super day.'

'We certainly did.' Alice standing tip-toe to beam at his mother over the roof of the car, before gathering up the zucchini loaf, the bag of lemons, her gaping tapestry handbag. So that Jeff was left empty-handed and vulnerable, hanging back so his wife could go first, paving the way.

Alice laughing, plunking kisses, admonishing children, turning their journey into an epigrammatic adventure story . . . The ease of her transformation into Daughter-in-Law. How did she do it? Jeff felt, as always, torn between gratitude and mistrust at his wife's ability to switch on sociability like a bedside lamp.

His father had joined them, hovered above the steps in his socks. Since he retired Charles never seemed to know what to put on his feet — slippers before evening were out of the question but shoes might look like an overstatement.

'I won't come down.' He poked out a grey-socked foot by way of explanation.

'No, you stay right where you are.' Alice kept this girlish, coquettish voice just for Charles. (Why do you talk to him like that? Like *what*? Like some bloody half-witted nymphette nurse. Oh, you mean why am I nice to him? Don't you think one of us ought to be?)

Was she also *nice* to the poor sods she called 'clients'? Had she spoken like that to Jeff's former workmates when they shuffled into her official presence, no longer friends or acquaintances but *clients*? An across-the-desk voice, at once bossy and cajoling — an occupational prerequisite to be listed on her CV.

His parents seemed to find it a comfort.

Well, they were old. Old and diminished. Alice acknowledged that — why couldn't he?

Was it to do with a balance of power? With Jeff having never weighed in on that particular scale? Not even wanted to. Had only managed — Charles would say — a prolonged defiance. And now not even that. Now nothing. Now a pathetic addendum to the family. Their family and his own.

Ask him, Alice had urged. He has influence, he *still* has influence and contacts all over the place. *Ask* him.

He would offer, Jeff told her. If Charles wanted to help, he would offer. Only he'd sooner gloat.

LUNCH IS FETTUCINE and a leafy salad. Alice and his mother swapping notes. Nancy gets her recipes, and much of her conversation, from *North and South*. Jeff had told her, in the days when he still had that kind of confidence, that it was a provincial magazine tailored for rednecks. But Jeff has lost his sense of credibility, and the latest issue of *North and South* tops the pile on Nancy's bench.

The girls have a choice, and get thin slices of ham. 'I'm allowed to spoil them,' Nancy tells Alice in mock defiance.

'Don't think it's a precedent,' Alice warns her daughters.

'A *president*?' Lisa waves the ham on her fork and stares at it in disbelief. She looks smug when they laugh.

Jeff half listens to his father explaining — overexplaining — the meaning of precedent. Lisa eyes have glazed. Jeff considers the table set so casually with unchipped bone china. He fingers the scrolled edges of the silverware. He smells Nancy's fettucine and the warm bread rolls and stares, between the cork table mats, at the mottled beauty of polished walnut. All of it gives him a wistful kind of pleasure. He realises with a stab of shame how much he would like to live like this. The word *affluence* has lost its power for indignation.

He can even (for a moment) understand the urge to protect *all this* from the unpleasantness of other. And he knows for certain that the closure will not be mentioned. It's the kind of 'unnecessary' topic that Jeff would, in the past, have felt compelled to force upon them. Rubbing their noses in reality. Feeling obliged to, even though he knew it only strengthened their resistance.

Words like redundancy, unemployment, poverty had no place within these walls — except as abstract concepts demonstrating incompetence.

His mother and Alice are bouncing the chat happily back and forth. The seasoned tennis players. Sometimes they push their reluctant partners forward: wasn't it, Charles? didn't we, Jeff? And the men obediently but inexpertly lob a return, keeping their eyes safely on the women. Yet all the time Jeff wants to look at his father to see if gloating shows.

One year of university, knowing all along he would quit, a matter of self-respect, but it had taken that whole first year to get up the courage, to make it a political statement and not just rebellion. Then what? Hanging out — there was a lot of it then — six months on the Barrier, a year in the Coromandel, five years in Westport. He remembers mainly a profound sense of contentment that he tended to believe was wisdom. The recession was coming even then; it was inevitable and part of the rationale. He and his friends preparing themselves, retrieving a sense of natural order. They had prised themselves free from offices, suburbia and the national grid. Pioneers — not the dreary settler kind, sepia- toned, dragging themselves with pitiable eagerness into a technological mind trap — but pioneers of a courageous and gentle civilisation.

After the collapse.

He met Alice in Westport. She had long, softly brown hair hanging loose, three dresses, a navy blue jersey, one overcoat and no underwear. She used to bring pots to the kiln for baking. She made them by hand, coil by coil. Vases and sugar bowls, very neat, very conventional. Perhaps he should've thought on that.

When the protruberance that turned out to be Sarah began to push the dresses into a new shape, Alice started to talk about *reality* and *commitment*. They chose a country town where houses were cheap and Alice used the money her mother had left her as the deposit. Jeff built a kiln and converted the old double garage into a workshop; he worked at it happily, proud of being able to *use his hands*. He would sometimes hold them up and examine them, just for the pleasure of seeing the calluses. Or he would rub his chin surreptitiously for the sandpaper feel of his palms.

Charles couldn't even mend a window, had possibly never tried. If he'd happened to arrive home while a tradesman was still in the house he would offer a few suitably uncomplicated words on rugby and retreat to his study.

By the time Sarah was a year old Jeff was in business, making enough — just enough — to support the three of them. He felt vindicated, capable. Local people began to refer to him as *the potter*. He was glad that Alice had made them move. There were whole moments when his heart thudded with triumph — *I've done it, neither dependent nor captive.*

Their second daughter was born a year later. She was part of a national tide of inflation. Jeff sweated over how to join the flow. How much could he charge? He felt strongly that his work should be accessible to people like themselves, but his accountant and conventional wisdom assured him that he must look to the well-off. The higher the price, he was advised, the more desirable the item would seem.

Jeff settled for compromise. *Reasonable* prices, he painted in on his road sign. But fewer people were coming to look, and they were buying less. Same story with the local shops. We'll have to ride it out, he told Alice.

In the meantime he would build up stock.

But Alice had got tired of sixty-watt light bulbs and joining the worn-out sheets down the middle. She applied for a job at the local Social Welfare office, the town's only growth industry, and went off to work. Leaving Jeff at home with a toddler, a baby and wet clay drying on the wheel. Even as a junior, she was bringing home more than he had ever earned.

For almost four years he sliced up oranges, sat in the town's only playground, walked to the kindergarten and hung winter washing in front of the Kent. When (occasionally) he fired the kiln, the shelves were stacked largely with Sarah's creations — lumpy cats, horses and large, uneven marbles — though the locals, touchingly, still called him *the potter*.

His parents retired from a large city to a small one. It was closer, a two and a half-hour drive, but Jeff found reasons not to visit. When the town got its first childcare centre he enrolled Lisa (Sarah was by then at school) and got a seasonal job processing offal at the local freezing works. In the off-season he began once again to make pots, pricing them high to entice the wealthy, who nevertheless resisted. So he concentrated on improving form and texture, tried to think of it as *art* instead of *livelihood*

They began to visit his parents then, every few weekends. Jeff took initial pleasure in the discomfort caused by any mention of his freezings works job. After a couple of visits this gave way to self-censorship and silent contempt. Because of his children, he told himself, because these were the only grandparents they had.

So his work and workplace became a subject that was never mentioned in this house. All that kind of talk would centre on

Alice, and (more and more) Alice's *clients*. Charles, and sometimes Nancy, would elicit stories that demonstrated the apathy, the incompetence, or the cunning of the jobless. Alice would protest, though mildly, that this was only true of *some*, but Jeff would imagine her stories — anecdotal, anonymous and uncontested — being aired and revised over games of bridge or at the bowling club.

For Godsake, he told Alice, you're reinforcing all their half-arsed notions, they see you as an *authority*. If you must talk about your work, why not tell them about the rest? In Alice's first few week in the job she would sometimes come home and weep about those ones. But now she said, Well, that wouldn't be very amusing, would it!

Had Alice changed since she started working for the department? Or did she simply no longer bother to align herself with Jeff, not caring what he thought? Sometimes he would listen to her and feel his life was out to strangle him with déjà vu. *Jesus, I've married my parents.*

Since the freezing works was not being mentioned, neither, as he'd expected, was its closure. (I'm your son. I have lost my job and can't find another. *Brought it on yourself,* Charles would say.) The nearest thing is Nancy asking what he plans to do with his future. Jeff shrugs and is very aware that Charles is watching him, taking note. *Are you happy now?* Go on, he dares himself, say it out loud. But what would that achieve?

Standover. That's the word that has always accompanied wharfie or freezing worker in this house. Standoverman. Standovertactics. Standovermerchants. In the child Jeff's head they took form as a cross between the Beagle Boys and the local butcher — vast, sweating men in aprons clutching heavy-bladed choppers and bags of burgled money. The kind of villains who chatted to children and winked at their mothers. Even then he had sensed that he and his father were on different sides.

His father's side has won.

AFTER LUNCH THE girls hover for pool money, little parcels of towel and bathing togs sausage-rolled under their arms. Alice counts out six dollars fifty for entry fees and one packet of chippies. Alice the provider. Jeff no longer makes pots, not even in the interests of art; he can't ask Alice for the price of the glazes.

'I'll walk down with you.' Charles heaves himself from his chair. 'If you can be bothered with an old man slowing the pace.'

'Not a problem.' Lisa sounding just like her mother. Sarah is the sullen one, watchful and worrying. It goes with being the oldest, according to Alice, who was the youngest of three. Jeff's sister, who now lives in Singapore, is three years older than him. He remembers her as manipulative but outgoing.

'Go with them, dear.' These days Alice no longer bothers to cloak her orders as requests.

'Why?'

Nancy weighs in, playing mother. 'Shoo. Off with you. There'll be a pot of tea waiting when you get back.'

He thinks, they've planned this. A whole scenario, everyone in it except for me, and possibly the girls. He stacks empty plates as he stands up. A humiliating hope stirs.

All the way to the swimming pool Lisa chatters incessantly, encouraged by Charles.

Sarah falls in beside Jeff, who drags behind. She throws him a grin and whispers. 'Easy to see he doesn't have to live with it.'

Jeff gives her a look that is supposed to both empathise and discourage. He can't be sure it achieves either.

The childish screams and silver sounds of water reach them before the pool is in sight. The noises of endless childhood summers. Jeff feels a brief, sharp surge of longing not to be an adult.

The pool has upped the entrance price by fifty cents. Jeff pats his pockets in a charade of searching. When they go out together, Alice carries the money. Well, why not? He tells his daughters they have enough there anyway, they don't need food. But Charles produces a two dollar coin and pushes it into Sarah's hand. He doesn't look at Jeff. Perhaps out of kindness?

The girls run off to the dressing sheds. Lisa turns halfway and waves. Charles waves back in an exaggerated fashion. Jeff's mind has already set out on the walk home, he and his father alone and unbuffered, grating at each other like arthritic bones.

They reach the corner before Charles' silence, and the persistent hideous hope (that this journey has been stage managed by the women and his father is under orders to come up with some useful contacts — it's who you know these days), drive Jeff to say some words. About the excellence of the weather. It sounds like a grovel; he can almost feel the stones beneath his belly. Charles merely grunts.

But another block on he says amiably, 'They like their swimming, those girls of yours.'

'Yes.' Jeff hears his voice sounding wary.

Charles nods. Or perhaps just an elderly man's twitch. 'I wonder what the future will hold for them.'

'Not much, the way things are going.' Jeff warms to the chance. 'I wouldn't want to be young today.'

Charles seems to be considering this. (Looking for grounds for argument?) But then he says, 'Main trouble is they're not prepared for it — all being brought up as if it was still the fifties and sixties and there's nothing to worry about.' He looks at Jeff, who is ready to take offence. 'No, no, no, I don't just mean you and Alice — it's endemic.' He stops in the middle of the footpath. 'The same when you were young, only the other way round. Those of us my age, we knew about fear, and that's a feeling that never quite leaves you. But your generation as youngsters looked around and saw no cause for fear, you thought your parents were outmoded. So you bring your children up as you felt you should've been brought up. Except it is, again, totally inappropriate. Each generation does this, I imagine.' He smiles a little, as if this was some kind of absolution.

Jeff stands looking at him. 'But,' he says, 'which comes first? Perhaps the fear breeds the causes of fear. I mean, division, competition, winners and losers — all that stuff we were taught to believe in —'

'Rubbish.' Charles is moving again. 'You weren't taught, it's instinctive — part of our psyche.'

'Oh Christ.' Jeff takes a deep breath. 'Not mine,' he says sharply. 'Not mine.' Hearing it. Watching his chance of help blowing away like tumbleweed on a beach. Knowing, even now, that he could go after it, perhaps retrieve it. But just watching it go, and thinking, *How afraid do you have to get?*

Notes for Episode Seven

VIDEOLOGY PRODUCTIONS
FAX to Jane Meikle (03) 372 1976 from Keith Conway (09) 345 6000. Oct. 11.
PAGE ONE OF 4.

Hi Jane, Sorry about the delay — we had a major crisis. Anyway here at last are your story notes. Afraid the deadlines have to stay as is. Best of luck. Any problems/ queries give me or Colin a call.

Cheers, Keith.

CHATWIN & TE AWA — *episode seven*

Main storyline.

Hugh Middleton (boss of some multinational corporation, mover and shaker) is impressed by James' handling of the paternity charge against his son Robbie Middleton (see notes for ep 6) but James now in fact proves the woman is a total flake and the charges are dismissed. He (Hugh Middleton) is under preliminary investigation by the Fraud Squad, and doesn't feel confident that the old school firm handling his company affairs (Cawley & Associates) have what it takes to deal with this one. He approaches James. J. realises things could get messy for Chatwin & Te Awa if the Fraud Squad comes up with solid evidence. On the other hand, Middleton is too good a catch to let swim away.

James consults with Howard who is still laid up from his skiing accident (ep 5). (NB They consult by phone or fax — Lou's taking leave for three episodes, rumour is that he's booked for Hanmer.) Howard reckons leave it alone . . . timing wrong, public still nursing grudges over money they lost in the Crash etc.

James talks to his whanau, especially Aunty Whetu. He's sick of being the 'Maori culture' half of the partnership, wants to be at the cutting edge. The whanau says go for it. (Maybe check this out with Robert Heta — 09 385 6553 — but don't let him take over your story with a lot of politically correct blah.)

James goes for it. He and Middleton respect each other. M. reckons he's been set up for political ends. James, just a little deviously, uses Wendy's contacts to infiltrate the lefty scene. James and Wendy exchange words over this.

Disconcertingly, James uncovers stuff that suggests Middleton's company has been doing dodgy book-keeping.

And we need another couple of twists here. Over to you. Does he try to back out? Seeks Howard's advice? (H. is off camera remember.) Something to do with Wendy? Does she try and get back at James in some cunning way?

Then — on the eve of the Middleton's arrest — James gets evidence that the lawyer Cawley has been having a long-term steamy affair with Middleton's senior accountant. They're on the brink of shooting through to a love nest in Argentina.

Middleton's absolved. James has proved himself in the hard-nose arena. And Chatwin & Te Awa now have their first multinational client!

PAGE THREE OF 4
Storyline two.
Wendy's defending yet another small-time legal aid criminal. (So far we've had a dope grower, drunken driver, wife beater, shoplifter, flasher, drug dealer. So, anything else.) He's a hunk and Wendy becomes emotionally involved.

David susses this. They've been having a few problems as it is (see ep 6 notes). David's response is to come on to Tina (girl who plays Tina looks fabulous but can't act, so minimal dialogue). Tina is interested, if only because she's got it in for Wendy. (This feeds into an ep 8 story. You don't need to worry about the details.)

Wendy is totally convinced of her client's innocence. Her defence goes far beyond the call of duty. She gets him off. Now he no longer needs her he harshly ends the relationship. He reoffends in an in-your-face fashion.

Wendy is shattered. Seeks comfort from David, who isn't there when she needs him. (Needs up-beat resolution here.)

Storyline three.

James' niece, Marama, gets lost in the bush and the whanau mount a search. None of them have James' expertise in bushcraft, but James isn't available — too busy on Middleton's business. Some resentment from within the whanau (tribal versus individual — get some input from Robert H. on this). Keep it brief — one or two scenes at most.

Eventually James' brother, Api, takes charge and finds the little girl. A turning point for Api, who finally feels capable of filling his older brother's shoes.

NB this is the visual story. Approx. seven mins screentime. Lots of scenery, gumboots, swanndris, RTs.

Storyline four.

Comic studio story for Tim Wickens the legal clerk.

A smelly old bag lady turns up at the office and claims to be his real mother. Maybe some business with Tina and the bag lady (Tina as mute as possible, remember) . . . anyway some kind of twist . . . then the bag lady reveals herself as Kay playing a joke because she's sick of Tim's preoccupation (see eps 5 & 6) with his unknown origins.

That's it. Over to you.

Best wishes, Keith.

Videology Productions.

Fax to Jane Meikle (03) 372 1976 from Keith. Oct 13.
Hi Jane,

Brought up your concerns at today's storyline conference. None of us can see any problem with Tim and the bag lady. Guess we all have a quirky sense of humour. Just have a bash at it.

Cheers, Keith.

Videology Productions.

Fax to Jane Meikle (03) 372 1976 from Keith. Oct 27.
CHATWIN & TE AWA *Notes for Jane on scene breakdown —
episode seven.*

Oh dear. There are some nice twists, Jane, and you've done a good job interlocking the stories — but I'm afraid what you've given us is just NOT *Chatwin & Te Awa*. Perhaps you should reread eps 1 to 5 (1st draft of 6 should reach you next week) to refresh . . .

In a nutshell, *Chatwin & Te Awa* is an up-beat, up-market series about vibrant, ambitious people. At its core is the natural rivalry between two hard-nosed partner s making their way in a complex world.

What you've given us is a muddy scenario with no real winners or losers. Instead of story twists, instead of yin and yang, you've given us complexity and moral dilemmas. Not the stuff of drama.

Also (and this may be where the real problem lies) you've given Wendy far too much space. Hers is NOT the main story-line.

Let's look at how you can pull her story back —

1) Less of the David/Wendy stuff. This is a relationship that was never going to work — one of W.'s idealist fantasies. David was bound to want out sooner or later. So, sure, she's upset when she sees it crumbling, but it's not so much a life-shattering blow as a learning curve.

2) Pull back on the argument with James. It's not a conflict of ideology, just a disagreement over his methods. At heart Wendy and James like and respect each other.

3) You'll have to rethink Jason. Bank robbery is fine but Wendy needs to come up with something better than 'impassioned argument about the passive victims of alcohol abuse'. Viewers don't want *issues*, Jane. Issues are boring — they just muddy the waters and leave a lot of loose ends. Besides, Wendy's a party animal, not a moralistic wowser. Another point — by 'emotionally involved with the client' we meant sex rearing its head, not boring old touchy-feely platonic stuff.

Suggest . . . Wendy gets the hots for Jason, convincing herself he's innocent, gets him off on some fine legal point concerning identification. Once free he snubs her, she turns to David, finds he's two-timing her. Then Jason abducts her, uses her as a hostage on his next job. She grabs his gun, makes a citizen's arrest, redeeming herself. (Solves the up-beat ending problem which you haven't really addressed.)

Think you'll agree that's a more convincing scenario.

PAGE THREE OF 3

Other things to keep in mind.

a) Middleton's multinational is NOT in the liquor trade. We realise this was your way of tying the main story in with Wendy's story, but afraid it's just not appropriate. Besides, with your revised Wendy storyline, it will no longer have any relevance.

b) Small but important point — Middleton's company accountant, the one that's about to shoot through to Argentina, will be FEMALE, thank you. This is a family show. Dishonesty is one thing, bent is quite another.

c) The bush search story is fine, but don't get too specific about the scenery. Funds are stretched so looks like they'll have to shoot it out the back of Albany.

d) And story four works a treat. No worries. Tracey who plays Kay is going to be over the moon at a chance to do some real acting as the pseudo bag lady!

That's it. This really needs a second draft of the scene breakdown but time doesn't allow. So straight into first draft and any problems/queries, get back to me. I'll be out of the office most of this week so make it a fax.

Cheers, Keith.

Videology Productions, Fax to Jane Meikle (03) 372 1976 from Keith. Oct. 30.

PAGE ONE OF 2

Dear Jane,

Sorry about delay, didn't get your fax until last night. Contents surprised me a bit — not quite sure where you're coming from on this.

For instance, how can you claim the main story is boring? There's suspense, intrigue, personal conflict (James'), deception, inter-personal conflict and success. Hell, it's about power and money — how can it be boring?

As for predictable, I damned well hope so — this is TV not some obscure filmfest number.

'What's at stake,' you ask, 'for James?' I thought that was more than obvious — the future profit of Chatwin & Te Awa is at stake; James' career direction is at stake; his relationship with Howard; his relationship with his whanau.

In a nutshell, his personal mana is at stake. (But perhaps, being male mana, it doesn't count? Is that the real issue here, I wonder?)

Re your other point — Wendy coming across as some kind of emotional flake. Frankly, I just can't see the problem. This is the nineties and, as we said, this Jason is a hunk. Why shouldn't she fancy him and fancy David at the same time? Or is it to be one rule for men and one for women?

Besides, *Chatwin & Te Awa* always has at least two sex scenes, and we've done Wendy with David and James with just about every female in the cast.

We accept that you still don't think the comic story works — but 'bad taste and embarrassing'??? Have you never heard of black humour? Believe me, this'll work. Tracey's a good little comic actor who's been waiting for a break.

Hope the above has cleared some log-jams.

One last point — Robert Heta suggests that it should be a Pakeha who gets lost in the bush. Don't want to be implying that the whanau kids aren't properly supervised.

Cheers, Keith.

Videology Productions, Fax to Jane Meikle (03) 372 1976 from Keith Nov. 4.
PAGE ONE OF 2.
    Notes on CHATWIN & TE AWA — *episode seven, first draft*
Jane,

It's getting there but I'm afraid you've still got a lot of work to do. Your commercial breaks are about as gripping as ripple-sliced beetroot. I'm still working on detailed suggestions. You should receive them tomorrow or the day after. In the meantime . . .

Your revised storyline is a big improvement. However, we don't feel you've really got a handle on the characters.

James, for instance — James is not motivated by greed or personal vanity. He *is* an attractive man — he doesn't have to work at it. He's intelligent and sophisticated. But the James Te Awa you've given us is shallow and occasionally almost ludicrous. The problem, I think, is not with the dialogue but with the overall tone and the juxtaposition of scenes. E.g. it's fine for James to say, 'Achievement is a flag that we must raise as a people in order to salute it', but we don't need the cut from James' apartment to Aunty Whetu's pet goat while he says it. I'm not sure if you're trying for irony or what. If you are, it's not appropriate and could even be construed as racist. Please do keep in mind that James is the hero.

Hugh Middleton also needs to be treated seriously. He's a captain of industry, not a fixated neurotic — the two things are not in any way compatible. I imagine you were trying for humour, but comic touches should be confined to the comic storyline where they belong.

You've picked up on Wendy quite nicely, but her attitudes need to be a bit more flexible. For instance, her soft-heartedness is an instinct, not some kind of philosophy as you seem to imply in scenes 12 and 17. (In fact by ep 14 Wendy will have got her act together so well that Howard is inclined to favour her over James. That's assuming Lou's 'holiday' does the trick and Howard is still with us.)

We'll buy Wendy's argument with David in scene 6 and the getting-even motive but let's have it begin in bed. Orgasm then argument.

In the hostage scene Wendy now needs to shoot bank-robber Jason with his own gun. (Believes she's genuinely threatened or just panics.) The repercussions will feed nicely into eps 8 and 9, and we need an act of violence here to muscle-up a somewhat flabby episode. You'll still have to come up with a nice moment to end on. Maybe Jason apologises to her before he dies?

No worries with the bag-lady stuff. Truly, I laughed out loud.

Any problems . . . my fax awaits. Keith.

Videology Productions, Fax to Jane Meikle (03) 372 1976 from Colin Davenport (09) 345 6000 Nov. 16.
<small>PAGE ONE OF 1</small>
Dear Jane Meikle,

A legal document concerning termination of contract should reach you in the next day or two. We're all rather dismayed with your attitude. Keith is a most capable script editor and has bent over backwards to accommodate your views. What you choose to call 'a suitable degree of imbecility' we see as professionalism. Series writing — as we felt sure you would be aware — is a very specialised and demanding skill, and you do have a contractual obligation to us.

If you can't stand the heat it does make sense to leave the kitchen, but leaving halfway through the job causes enormous problems for a large number of people.

The really disappointing thing, Jane, is that this now means we have no women writers left on the series. You lot keep demanding an equal share of the cake, and with *Chatwin & Te Awa* we have gone all out to get that female input. Then what happens? You all pull out. When it comes down to it you just can't take the pressure.

Yours regretfully, Colin.

Videology Productions, Fax to Tracey Jubelips
Trace darl, I've been held up. Bloody Jane thingee has chucked in the towel on ep 7. God save me from these prima donnas. They all come in with some kind of agenda — just can't accept that TV is drama is *entertainment*.

Don't worry, sweetie, your big scene will be preserved.

Should be free by 8.30. Order for me — something oozing oysters.

XXXXXXX Keith

Trembling Annie

THE SPOON RISES in jerks and spasms until it's level with the teeth. The mouth waits, trembling and open. The top dentures judder against colourless gums. The spoon accelerates drunkenly towards the cavern. Too soon it tilts; the dentures snap shut, but all they have caught is a lick of thin parsley sauce. A lump of steamed fish slides down the spoon and comes to rest on brown-speckled fingers, incessantly shaking. At one corner of the twisted mouth a snuffle of white sauce emerges.

I am seventeen, a country girl, uncomfortable in my stiff pink uniform and ugly shoes. I watch the white sauce trickle down Annie Stewart's face as I place Mrs Hastings' tray between her yellow knitting and her *Woman's Weekly*. The doll-faced girl with the broken leg demands a glass of water. Old Mrs Dale wants her pillows puffed up. I do as they ask, though my job right now is trays and teas. When I look at Miss Stewart again, the spoon is once more on its erratic upward journey.

If I'm fast enough there will be a few spare minutes when all the trays are out, the special menus served, the regular meals yet to be trundled into the ward. But this is the first job I've ever had and twice I've been ordered not to feed her. *She has to do it herself.* I said but. *No buts.* They didn't tell me why.

I smile and smile and slap down the trays. I try to memorise the new names. I want to be friendly and efficient. I want to be liked.

The spoon has returned to plate level, it drums wildly against the thick china. Mrs Keogh clamps her ears, 'Oh God, she's off again. I can't stand it. I've said I can't stand it. I even told the doctor on his last rounds. He said, "I'll have a word, Mrs Keogh."'

You can hear the trolley on its way. Usually you can. I ease the spoon out of the speckled fingers. She looks at me. She has no more expression than a road drill but I choose to believe it's in gratitude that her eyes turn up to mine. I scoop up fish and sauce and pour it carefully into the open mouth. The mouth jerks shut; white overflow trickles from either side. My own stomach ripples with repugnance. I look again at the eyes and they seem to be pleading. I catch my lip between my teeth because I cry too easily.

I pour in another spoonful and another. I imagine those cavernous cheeks fleshing out, the trembling beginning to calm, her grey flesh taking on life tones. I am awed by this woman's appearance. She is the most decayed human being I have ever seen outside of photos. Her hair has no style — it is thin and grey, straight and oily. It peters out unevenly just below the shoulders. Her face clings to the bones of her skull. The skin is blotched with patches of dark pigmentation and feels as thin and dry as parchment. The teeth protrude between wide but shrunken lips.

A dead face. But the eyes still live. They are deep-set and dark. They turn again towards me and I smile a smile of desperate warmth. The eyes shy away and the spoon I should be watching chatters against the dentures.

'Nurse, what *do* you think you're doing?'

I don't look at Nurse Bailey, who has come in so quietly in her regulation soft soles. I try to wedge the spoon back beneath Annie's thumb.

'How many times,' she sighs, 'do you have to be told? Annie is to feed herself.'

'I'm sorry,' I whisper down at those grey lips, though I'm not sure if she can hear or comprehend. I've only been here a week and I'm just a nurse-aide, not privy to the reports and briefings of the proper staff. To ask questions about patients is seen as impertinence.

I gallop sedately to meet the food trolley. Everything here is done on the double; the place is chronically understaffed and besides it seems to give satisfaction if we are seen to be ceaseless. There is a walk that is almost a run; I haven't as yet quite mastered it.

Nurse Bailey is not-quite a-staff nurse. She has apple cheeks and marrow legs. I flash past her without a glance. Below her white belt the starched cotton spreads vast and smug. Her ugliness gives me little consolation.

I deliver cottage pie and limp silverbeet. My shoes go

squeak slap on the linoleum, proclaiming inexperience. Nurse Bailey looks and leaves. Her cucumber fingers don't transfer even one dinner to a waiting bed.

IN THE SLUICE room I clatter and sweat in a race against two o'clock. The bedpans scald my fingers. I think about indignity and having to get used to it; them and me. Ward Sister comes in. She's preoccupied with the test tubes she's holding. I try to stack the pans silently but they slip and shriek. She looks at me. I adjust my cap, just in case. I take a deep breath. 'Sister, that Miss Stewart . . .'

She looks at her watch. 'Yes?'

I nudge my words into a trot. 'Can she understand? I mean, what you say to her?'

'Of course.' Just automatically. She's given it no thought at all. 'Get the trays in before you take those out.'

'I thought this way they'd have more time to finish their teas.' I say it without thinking. It's a habit the staff are helping me to get rid of. I tend to have what they call *a nerve*. Sister is halfway out the door. She pauses and looks over her shoulder. She sighs. 'Would you like to be looking at a bedpan while you eat your lunch?'

I want to say, quite truthfully, that I would prefer that to having my cup cleared away before I'd finished with it, but I can see that she doesn't require an answer. I trot back to the ward and begin to collect up the trays, ready or not.

On Miss Stewart's plate lumps of cold fish sulk in congealed sauce. I take the napkin and wipe her witch's chin. I coax her long, bony fingers through the handle of the cup. The ward clock says sixteen minutes to visiting.

Miss Stewart concentrates. I feel her concentration and I surround it with my own. The cup rises, trembling. Lukewarm tea splashes on to her hand and the cuff of her plaid dressing gown; some falls onto the bleached green bedspread. I reach to steady the cup against her lips. She slurps and dribbles. I take the cup and dab the napkin at the assorted trickles, then I put the cup once more against her juddering lips. Before she begins to drink, one corner of Miss Stewart's mouth rises up in what might possibly be a smile.

Nurse Bailey is watching. I feel her eyes skewer my back. I collect up the tray, the cup, the napkin, as if that's all I was doing anyway. I risk a glance and she's staring at me. I stare back. I feel emboldened. *Miss Stewart smiled at me.*

Nothing said until we're both of us shunting the trolley out the double doors. There hasn't been time. It's twelve minutes to and the pans aren't even out.

'You a bit thick?' she asks. (No one in this place ever requires answers.) 'She just tries it on, nurse. I've seen her feed herself. She'll expect it from all of us. You're not really doing her a favour.'

'Perhaps,' I say, 'Some days the shaking's worse than others.'

'You the expert?' But she sounds almost friendly now and I am foolish enough to think that's that. Until we begin to take around the bedpans and Nurse Bailey is so quick off the mark to take her first pan halfway down the room to Annie Stewart. And she zings the curtains around that bed so purposefully that I realise I haven't been absolved. Also I get the feeling that there's more to this than I fully understand.

I trot around dealing out the pans to those who can manage for themselves. Saying, sorry, yes I know they're cold, I did try but . . . I can hear Nurse Bailey in behind the curtains. The whole ward can hear her. 'C'mon now, Trembling Annie. Hoist your bum up here, will you? Aw, get a move on. We haven't got all day.' And after a time Nurse Bailey strides out between the curtains looking like she's just won a prize at the rodeo.

Then Ward Sister calls for Bailey to help her in one of the isolation rooms, just as I'm sliding the last pan under Mrs Tackle's thunder-clouds of billowing yellow flesh. Mrs Tackle's yelp when the cold strikes sounds so muffled it's almost mystical.

'You finished?' I ask Miss Stewart. The green shade of the curtains does nothing for her. She lies against the pillows like a dislocated effigy, her chin pressed down against her collar. She seems to nod, but then she nods incessantly and it's hard to know if this nod is significantly larger.

I burrow to retrieve the pan but it appears to be firmly lodged. I push aside dressing gown, then nightgown. In the curtained gloom her thighs are ghoulish. I edge my upper arm beneath her back; her spine threatens with bunched knuckles. I heave. For a bag of bones she is extraordinarily heavy. A dead weight, as they say. But I am able to extract the pan — gently, carefully, for fear of spillage. Though I can see already that it was barely worth all this bother.

I put the pan on the floor and pull Miss Stewart into what I hope is a comfortable position. Her eyes look up but tell me nothing. I smile at her. I try to think of something meaningful to say.

'Visiting now.' It really is the best I can do. Does she get visitors, ever? There are no flowers beside her bed. Not one.

I TAKE WARD Sister her afternoon tea. I feel official and conspicuous going down the corridor among all the visitors, dodging through them with tea slopping into the saucer and four biscuits on a separate plate.

I think I could like Ward Sister if we lived in the outside world. She pours the spilt tea back into her saucer. She thanks me and says, 'Sit down a moment. Take the weight off your feet.'

So I sit down and wonder if we are about to chat. Through her partly open door I watch the visitors. They look lost and solemn. And I ask, without thinking, 'Does Miss Stewart get any visitors?'

Sister frowns and looks at me more closely. She thinks I am obsessive. 'I believe she has a nephew who comes once in a while.' She sips her tea.

I know I'm pushing my luck but I seem to be obligated by that flicker of lip I took to be a smile. I say, 'She finds it hard to manage her meals. I don't think she gets enough to eat.'

Ward Sister is shocked, I can see that. My relief is so great I feel myself smiling. But Sister's mouth has tightened and I see that she was shocked not by my revelation but by my temerity.

'Nurse,' she says icily, 'we have twenty-nine patients in this ward and care for each one as well as we are able. In nursing it is not advisable to become attached to patients and have favourites.' Ward Sister smiles a lean crystal smile. 'How long, nurse, have you been with us?'

I choose to suppose it's another rhetorical question. I whisk myself out of her office and take refuge in the sluice room.

I AM A veteran nurse-aide of three weeks' experience. I have learned to mitre corners and tighten bedspreads glacial smooth. I am nonchalant about flesh in all its variety. I have cleaned a dead woman's fingernails. I have chipped dirt from between an old man's toes. I call Miss Stewart 'Annie', though not within her hearing.

Nurse Bailey has, temporarily, been rostered on nightshift. Her replacement is Nurse Strongman. She is a third-year, the same as Bailey, but they seem to have little else in common. On her first day she said, 'I hate all this "Nurse" business. My name's Eve, what's yours?'

Eve's been on this ward often. Questions don't bother her at all, so I ask.

'How long's she been in here?'

'Ages. Eighteen months or so. Seems to me really she should be in geriatrics.'

'Is she old, then?'

'About fifty, if you call that old.'

'Isn't she gonna get better?'

'What d'you think?'

'Maybe if she was fed and things. I try when I get the time but I bet the afternoon lot don't.'

'Neither they should. It's on her charts. Doctor's instructions. She's got no spirit, that's her trouble. Won't try to help herself.'

'Maybe she tries but she can't.'

'Doctors say she can if she wants to.'

'How do they know?'

''Cause they're clever buggers, that's why.'

'Maybe they're wrong.'

'Maybe, maybe, maybe . . . Must you go on about her? Personally Annie Fanny gives me the willies.'

BUT ME, I am in love with Annie Stewart. Or at least with my own devotion. I long for the time when I shall coax from her a facial movement that is, indisputably, a smile. On the days when there are a few spare minutes between bed-baths and lunch Nurse Strongman and I slide Annie from her bed and help her balance on those spindleshanks. We clamp her trembling arms around our shoulders and march her the length of the ward and back again. It's hard to tell if she contributes to the jaunt or simply dangles between us.

SHE TALKS TO me!
After a time of intense facial preparation she will stutter out, *'Tha nky nn rse.'* But more often it's complaints. *Mm yb ackhurts. Ca ntrea ch lllo cker.* She seems to have put on a little weight. I steal flowers from those who have plenty and arrange them in a jar on her locker. And on a Friday I wash that lank grey hair and tie it back with a ribbon that came with Jill Nicholson's roses. It is a gesture; it is not a transformation. The yellow scalp shows through in streaks.

Ward Sister stops at Annie's bed and says, 'Well, we are looking nice today!'

SATURDAY, AND WE strip down old Mrs Graham's bed and disinfect away the stigma of death. The lunch trays have yet to be collected in. We work well together, Eve Strongman and I. Coordination and the habit of speed. We work to the staccato rhythm of spoon-on-plate from across the room. It's not a sound you get used to, it's a stuck-needle sound that has the nerves of the whole ward on edge.

Eve grins to herself as we pull on the cover. In a strong sweet voice she sings: 'She plays her drum for me pa-ra-pa-pum-pum.'

And I get the giggles. Disloyally, uncontrollably, I shake and snuffle and clutch my belly as other giggles from all around the ward feed and refurbish my own. Even when the joke has long died and the shaking spoon has become silent, great puffs of laughter are billowing in my stomach.

The sound has stopped. I register this slowly. The sound has stopped, unaided. I unscrew my damp eyes and, even from across the ward, I can see that the spoon is still in her hand in the plate. Not moving. Her eyes are looking at me. I turn away; there are trays to collect.

NURSE BAILEY HAS returned from a triumphant two-week run on nightshift. She rolls her eyes at the blue ribbon that hangs, a little shamefacedly, from Annie's tethered hair. 'Oh my,' she says in a voice meant for me.

EVE HAS BEEN moved to the children's ward. I sometimes see her at lunchtime. Today we have hot beetroot. I think this may be the only place in the world that serves its beetroot hot. I complain to Eve about Nurse Bailey. Eve says she just takes a bit of getting used to. 'Most people like her. She's a good nurse. She was always top in her exams.' I feel rebuked.

When I get back to the ward I see Nurse Bailey has Annie standing beside the bed, her long, bony feet shoved into tartan slippers. For Annie's sake I join them. 'I'll give you a hand.'

'It doesn't take two.' Nurse Bailey cups her hands beneath Annie's armpits and pulls her forward. 'Mrs Nicholson wants a pan.'

When I come back from the sluice room, feeling humane because the pan is still warm, I see Nurse Bailey and Annie in the middle of the floor. They appear to be dancing. I pretend not to notice. I pull the screens around Mrs Nicholson and slide the pan beneath her admirable bottom, and I hear Nurse Bailey's big voice saying, 'Come on Annie, you can do better than that. Try, woman. Try.'

When I come out, through the screens, to the wider world, Nurse Bailey is looking straight at me. She turns her attention back to Annie. 'Show us what you can do, Trembling Annie,' she commands, and in a quick and surprisingly graceful movement she releases Annie and steps aside.

For a few seconds Annie stands there alone. Then she leans forward and makes a shuffling step as if she is actually about to walk. Then she collapses. Nurse Bailey steps forward in time to catch that grey, cavernous head just before it connects with the iron railing of Mrs Hastings' bed. She wraps her arms around the long, emaciated body and hoists it up as if it's a rag doll. And she looks at me with an icy smile that I interpret as a threat. A kind of blackmail.

I TAP TWICE with my knuckles on the door of Matron's office. I think of boarding school and the disgrace of *ratting*. Matron opens the door and goes to sit behind her desk, while I stand. The only other time I've been in this office I sat in the small chair by the wall and my mother sat in the chair with the padded back. Matron and my mother talked about me while I tried to look eager. And Matron employed me.

I try to explain to Matron about Annie Stewart. About meals removed barely nibbled at, wash bowls retrieved with water untouched by soap or flannel. I can't mention the fall without naming names so I leave that out. 'I just think,' I say, limply, 'that too much is expected of her. She does try, I know she does. But sometimes she can't.'

Matron smiles and leans back in her chair. 'How long have you been with us, Nurse-aide Poole?'

'Nearly six weeks, Matron.'

She nods. 'And already you are more knowledgeable than our nurses and even our doctors.'

I say nothing. I stand there and hate her.

'Compassion,' she smiles, 'is all very fine in its place, but one must learn not to become emotionally involved with one's patients. Also to take a pride in one's appearance. What is that all over your uniform, Nurse-aide Poole?'

I look down at my chest. 'Beetroot stains,' I mumble, defeated.

I BRING TO work, hidden beneath my cardigan, a jar of orange juice, freshly squeezed. Annie drinks only a few sips. I leave the rest in a glass on her locker.

'What's this?' demands Nurse Bailey.

'Sister said,' I lie.

As I am straightening the bedspread for visiting, Annie reaches out her hand and places it carefully on top of mine. I feel weak with love. Weak and obligated.

Annie gets a visitor; the first visitor she has had when I have been on duty, unless you count the clergymen and voluntary ladies. I am searching in Miss Little's bed for the false teeth she has somehow managed to mislay and I see a timid-looking man sitting at Annie's bedside, looking unhappily out the window. A paper bag of fruit lies on the bed beside her trembling hands. I am both jealous and hopeful.

I waylay him in the corridor. 'Excuse me, but I saw you with Miss Stewart. Are you . . .?'

He shrinks back from me as if I am infectious. 'Her nephew.' His eyes avoid mine.

I gabble brightly. 'I'm glad she's got someone to visit her. How do you find her?'

He says, to the skirting boards, 'Fine.' Then his eyes slide up towards the ceiling. 'Much the same, I suppose,' he amends.

'I don't think she's happy here.' The silly understatement sliding off my tongue.

He is apologetic. 'I suppose she is a bit of a complainer. They have mentioned . . .'

'Oh no, I didn't mean . . . You see, she has reason to complain. I think you should take any complaints she has made very seriously. I think you should do something about them, talk to someone.'

He laughs. A nervous, irritable sound. 'I don't know why you're saying this or what your motive is. My aunt is very comfortable here. You can see they keep her clean and tidy. I really don't know what you're talking about. We don't want any trouble, either of us.'

'IT'S YOUR DECISION. I hope you won't regret it.' Matron holds out her hand but I am pretending not to see it. 'Between you and me, 'she says, 'I don't think you were cut out to be a nurse.'

'No,' I say, though today my uniform is unblemished.

TEN MINUTES, ONLY ten, to go, and Annie Fanny's talons grip my hand. *Lll astnnnn ight, she hisses, cc oold. More blll . . .* She draws back her lips in a canine grimace. She is ugly with age and decay.

'I'll tell them,' I say. I hear the impatience in my voice. Her fingers are brittle and cold. Revulsion seeps up my arm and I have to pull my hand from hers. In nine minutes and thirty-five seconds I'll walk out of this place for ever.

Arctic Circle

THE NIGHT BEFORE she flew north she saw Billy Connolly gambolling in Arctic snow with nothing on but his boots.

The camera was far enough away for decency to be preserved. A white Scottish body with pubic fuzz and what appeared to be gumboots. She'd walked into the room after packing her bag and there he was. A few moments later, clothed, he talked to the camera about the experience of being alone. If you felt loved, he said, you were never lonely.

LOOKING DOWN AT a landscape of white clouds, Rita thinks of snow and Billy Connolly. She, too, feels loved. *Is* loved. The realisation surprises her, and for a moment her confidence wavers. Is it not presumptuous to attribute to others an emotion she has no absolute proof of? Is testimony sufficient evidence? Or is the need to make declarations in itself a reason for doubt?

Love you, Ross will sometimes say, out of a silence. They might be driving, or pulling weeds, or dividing up the evening paper. Rita takes it to be not so much an assurance, as an incantation to ward off forces bent on destroying comfortable old affections.

And her boys, having cringed all through puberty at their television peers, now admit to loving no one, least of all their mother. But they do love her.

The dog loves her too. This isn't just the anxious adoration of dependency, but a deep and mutual affection. The dog also loves Ross, but not as much. Testosterone, Ross insists, though the dog is thoroughly neutered.

And — Rita adding up her bounty — her friends love her. Of course they do. As she loves them. Especially the ones that go way back.

The young, thinks Rita, have no old friends. It feels like a profound and startling observation.

So that was it! she thinks, fifty-seven and flying north, amazed that something so obvious should occur to her only now, too late to be of use or comfort. (Yet flying does that, she's noticed. At least with a window seat. At a certain altitude the bird's-eye view of land and sea promote an overview of life. It is not possible to gaze down at an uninhabited coastline and think about a suitable colour for architraves, or the contents of the freezer.)

Rita has not always felt loved. Not feeling loved is there inside her like a movie she remembers incompletely. Fingers — her own — threading the rope over the rafters in the garage and knotting it just the way she'd learnt for her school ties. (But it wasn't loneliness she sought an end to, it was the screaming pain of failure. The person who surely knew her best did not love her; Rita had failed at being lovable.)

There was also — to be perfectly truthful — the childish thought that, finding her there, dangling like an old hooked fish, would serve him right.

The rope like a lover's hands around her throat. But before she kicked away the chrome-legged stool she thought, what if it wasn't him who came into the garage first?

'Why didn't you see a doctor?' asked Maggie years later in a voice that quavered with incredulity. When *her* first husband left her, Maggie saw a doctor and was tranquillised for three and a half years, or until she met Barney. Whichever came first — and Maggie couldn't remember.

If, back then, Maggie had been an old friend, Rita would have called her and Maggie would have told Rita to see a doctor. If Rita had had an old friend who loved her she would not have felt so unlovable. If Rita had had a mother and father who . . .

An airline tray hovers above the empty seat next to Rita. The steward peers down over it.

'Sorry,' Rita says, in case he's been standing there for ages. She unlatches the fold-down table and accepts the plastic tray. It contains a club sandwich on half a leaf of crinkly lettuce, cheddar and crackers, a peanut brownie, mineral water and an after-dinner mint. Rita is pleased with all of it. Thirty thousand feet above National Park (she's guessing both the altitude and what part of the country lies beneath the cloud) she is about to eat a private picnic lunch that someone else has prepared for her. How could she be anything less than delighted ?

HER MOTHER'S HAIR is now as white and wispy as thistledown. The scalp shows through, pink and vulnerable as a new baby's. The three of them sit in the sunporch, catching the pale autumn rays. The tray was carried from the kitchen by Rita who is gripped by an unfamiliar instinct to *be in charge*. On the tray was a teapot, a small jug of milk, the tea strainer, the sugar bowl, three cups and saucers and five banana muffins Belinda had taken from the freezer and warmed in the microwave. The sunporch is at the other end of the house from the kitchen. Joe and Belinda have lived in this house for fifty years. It's a big house for an old couple but they're determined to stay here, and Rita can't imagine them living anywhere else. If she wasn't here they wouldn't bother with elaborate rituals like afternoon tea in the sunporch. This is a kind of celebration.

After two noisy slurps of his tea Joe has fallen asleep with his chin on his chest. Belinda rescues the cup and puts it back on the tray without a break in her description of Phil's Canadian scholarship. Phil is one of the grandchildren — Tom's son. Tom is Rita's half-brother.

Joe, in his sleep, gives little snorts and grunts. The skin on his temple is shining parchment, tracing his skull. He was a small, wiry man from Idaho who never quite matched Belinda's height, and now he was shrinking faster than she was. Seeing them as she entered the airport, Rita's first — shocked — thought was that her stepfather looked like a dressed-up chimpanzee.

She'd expected to be met by her half-sister Jill, because Stratford was almost an hour's drive from the airport. But there were just the two of them. Belinda turned eighty-nine last spring and Joe is a year older. *Remarkable for their age!* There is a special kind of voice, Rita has noticed, that people use for commenting on human feats like learning to walk, becoming potty trained, staying alive . . .

'He does that now,' says Belinda, of Joe. 'Nods off anywhere. He's even done it standing up. We think it's the pills.'

'Then I'm glad you did the driving,' Rita tells her. Joe still has his licence.

When they realised it was Rita behind the grey hair their faces had *lit up* — that really was the only way to describe it. She should come more often. But it's not as though they are alone. Jill and her daughter, Shelley, live barely two blocks away. (Jill, they explained in that initial burst of exchanged news, is in Auckland for a retraining seminar, and won't be back until Friday. In any case, Joe pointed out, they wouldn't have let Jill drive to the airport — she takes the corners at sixty k's.)

'Your father's wrist has mended well,' says Belinda now, on a slow medical train of thought. 'You knew about the fall?'

Rita feels her body snap to attention. On guard, she makes a non-committal sound that she perfected years ago for these occasions.

'I popped in to see him,' Belinda says.

Rita's mouth opens. She's aware of holding her breath and thinks, in a dissociated fashion, *She has taken my breath away!*

'Last week . . . no, the week before,' Belinda is saying. 'I took him some lemons, they were falling off the tree. And rhubarb. He was very fond of rhubarb as I remember. But he took one look and said he'd gone off rhubarb years ago. I'll bet he hasn't at all. But I brought it home again. I said, "Fine, we'll eat it ourselves." Hmph.'

When she grins Belinda's teeth look too white, too perfect, for her aged face.

'But we had a nice chat,' she adds.

Rita claps the arms of her wicker chair and stares at her mother. Possible reactions spin in her head — relief, anger, suspicion, joy. It's like watching a roulette wheel slowing down — *what will it be?* She has an urge to laugh but she chokes it back.

'You ought to take the car and pop over tomorrow,' Belinda advises, as if this is about Rita's niece, Shelley, or perhaps some old family friend.

Rita finds a voice. 'Yes,' she says. 'Yes. I'll do that.'

'He might like to come back for dinner,' says Belinda. 'Do you think?'

Rita's jaw hangs open.

'Ask him anyway,' Belinda says. 'You can give me a ring. There's a leg of lamb in the freezer. We'll take it out tonight.'

'I'll ask him. Yes,' whispers Rita.

It's six years since her father was widowed and moved back to Stratford. 'It makes no sense. The old fool just wants to upset us,' Belinda had written.

When Rita asked Charlie why he'd come back, he said, 'I liked it here. I like the mountain.'

It was no kind of answer. Belinda was probably right. Rita had been angry. 'It makes things hard for me. You must realise that.'

He'd shrugged. 'It needn't. That's up to you.'

Trying to make her choose!

He'd bought a small brick house on the outskirts of town. Twice Rita had visited him there. The first time she stayed with Belinda and Joe and walked until she found the place. She didn't say where she was going or where she had been and nobody asked. The second time she drove up, spent the whole day with her father and drove back again. Belinda and Joe didn't even know she was in town. She kept to the back streets and drove in her sunglasses on an overcast day. The deception felt ugly. But it wasn't her fault. Ross said she had to remember that, and he was right, of course — it *wasn't* her fault. It just felt like it was.

Even talking about it to Ross — that ought to have been a release, yet it felt, every time, like betrayal. And Rita knew all about betrayal. By spending time with Belinda and Joe she betrayed Charlie, and in spending time with Charlie she betrayed Belinda and Joe. 'Crap,' said Ross. But Rita has read it in their eyes. *Et tu, Rita!*

She takes another banana muffin, consoling herself.

'You wouldn't remember that time at the railway station,' says Belinda, probing. Rita, beyond surprise now, registers only that this is the first time her mother has acknowledged this event.

'Oh yes, I remember it,' Rita says. The Man on the Mantelpiece, though barely recognisable and no longer in the crisp, brave uniform, had his arm against her chest. Blocking the way in case Rita was of a mind to jump down those high steps, though the train was already hissing and clanking. Her mother and Joe were down on the platform. Belinda's embarrassing belly was poking out from her coat like a balloon in a doorway, and her cheeks were wet and shining under the station lights. They were, all three of them, shouting. Hate hung in the air, harsh when Rita breathed in. Something was moving; it seemed to be the platform but it wasn't. Rita was wearing brand new shiny T-bar shoes.

'I should've leapt on to that train and grabbed you back,' Belinda says. 'I should've. He was in no fit condition . . .'

Rita shakes her head, meaning she doesn't want to talk about it. Not now. It's lain there too long to be so suddenly exhumed. Yet, over and over, she'd imagined just that scene — Belinda or Joe bounding up those high metal steps to save her.

Of course she understands, now, why they didn't. Guilt; moral right was on Charlie's side. So Belinda and Joe just stood on the platform growing smaller as the train pulled away. Rita remembers this part the most clearly of all; she remembers a pain that wasn't an actual tummy ache kind of pain, and she remembers thinking, *This is how it feels when your heart is torn apart.*

It was almost three years before she saw them again.

For the first year and a bit Rita and Charlie lived with Charlie's mother in Taupo. The house was dark with heavy net curtains and it smelt of dead fish and caustic soda. Charlie stared at Rita a lot, but never had much to say. Grandma Rawlings talked almost all the time, as if she was obliged to make enough noise for all of them. At night Charlie would sit on Rita's bed and read to her from books he'd had when he was a boy. They were much too young for Rita but she didn't tell him this. Finally, when he'd turned out the light and she'd heard him return to what Grandma Rawlings called the 'front room', Rita would think of her mother and Joe and cry herself to sleep.

When Charlie wasn't around Grandma Rawlings talked about *that hussy, Belinda, and her sneaky little Yank.* Rita didn't defend them. This shamed her, but she'd learnt the importance of staying on her grandmother's 'good side'. Grandma Rawlings' bad side was a frightening thing. Besides, a part of Rita understood that this was her grandmother's way of sticking up for

Charlie. *Her father* — she was beginning to think of him that way, turning Joe into the interloper who stood between her and her parents. With a little help from Grandma Rawlings, Rita was able to overlook her stepfather's steadfast and kindly affection.

By piecing together her grandmother's insults Rita came to an understanding of her parents' situation. Charlie, who had managed a bicycle shop, had married Belinda, a maker of hats, in nineteen thirty-nine. Their first child, a son, died within the first few weeks of life. Then came Rita. She was six months old when Charlie enlisted.

Back then, in Grandma Rawlings' house, Rita had liked that part of the story. Her father — this man who sat in the sun throwing pebbles at the fence, or cleaning their shoes, all the shoes he could find, over and over — was a brave and adventurous man.

When she got older, it was Belinda Rita thought about. Left at home holding the baby — how did that feel? What did she think had compelled him to go? Adventure? Honour? The chance to escape from her and the child?

Whatever she guessed to be the reason, Belinda would never know for sure. Nor would Rita. Charlie talked to no one about the war. Not even his new wife. Audrey had told Rita that much.

'He just shuts down,' she'd said, in a hurt voice. 'I guess I have to respect that.'

Why had it felt like an accusation?

Deserted (and possibly resentful), Belinda and her baby moved into a boarding house. Belinda made hats in her room. Rita wants to remember those hats but can't. She doesn't even remember back to before Joe, or the two years between his early visits and when he came back with metal plates in his shoulder. By then Charlie had disappeared — *missing in action* (the phrase sounded like a code for something unimaginably sinister).

In nineteen forty-six Charlie turned up on Belinda's doorstep, but he was too late.

If he couldn't have his wife back the least he deserved was his daughter. But Belinda wasn't prepared to part with Rita, so Charlie snatched the girl away.

He needed her, that was the truth of it. This father who had claimed Rita was a shambling, childlike man who had nothing and no one except his bossy mother. Rita cried herself to sleep at night, but did not hold this against her father. He wasn't to blame. No one was to blame.

She ought to be saying that, now, to Belinda, whose lips are pressed together too tightly. Belinda had been about to shoulder the blame and ask forgiveness when Rita cut her off. Rita should get up, put her arms around her mother and tell her that it doesn't matter, that everything's okay.

Except it isn't okay. Suddenly Rita is angry, she wants to shout at Belinda, 'For Chrissake, that was half a century ago. Half a bloody century. How could you leave it so long with me in the middle being torn apart?'

But instead she says, in a hasty, wrapping-things-up voice. 'Yes, I'll ask Dad and if he wants to come we'll get back early so I can give you a hand.'

Belinda raises her eyebrows. 'Good gracious, Reet, I'm still capable of cooking a dinner!'

IN CHARLIE'S NEAT little unit Rita feels caged. He sold the house last year and moved into this retirement home. It reminds Rita of a holiday camp, the TV kind — *Hi De Hi*. She suggests they go for a drive.

'If you want to,' he says. 'But not on my behalf. Nothing around here to see that I haven't seen already.' He grunts. 'If I could see, that is!'

Last year he'd failed the eye test for a licence and it rankles. He sold the car and the brick house and came to this place, which is, unreasonably, five kilometres from the town. Rita suspects his reluctance to go driving is simply cussedness: since he's not allowed to drive, he'll refuse to be driven.

He's making them coffee. Instant. She stands in the doorway of the tiny kitchen watching him. For the first time in years his hands are not traced with embedded black grease.

When they discharged him from hospital Charlie changed from fixing bicycles to fixing cars. It was his livelihood and his hobby; get his head beneath a bonnet and Charlie would turn into a whistler, a teller of jokes, a cheerful gossip. Rita suddenly remembers when Charlie's hands were very clean and never still, the constant abstracted stroking, tossing, tapping. Except when she'd trap his fingers in hers.

His clean hands are not a good sign.

'Your mother called round,' he says, pouring the water with his left hand because the other wrist is still weak. His tone is casual but he's watching Rita for her reaction.

'She said.' Rita's voice is non-committal. She braces herself, a learned response, for some snide remark about Belinda.

'She's looking well,' he says. 'Always was a good-looking woman.'

He passes Rita a mug of coffee. Her fingers fumble, limp with incredulity and release.

'She said would you like to come for dinner.'

She watches him trying to hide his pleasure.

'I'll think about it,' he tells her.

The really dreadful time was after Charlie went away to the hospital and Rita was left with only Grandma Rawlings. By then she had started school but it took up only a small part of the day, and gave her grandmother time to think up new reasons to be unpleasant. One night she boasted to Rita about having intercepted and burnt all the letters that Belinda had sent her.

Rita wrote, then, to Belinda and Joe. She wasn't sure of the address but Stratford was a small town. Her teacher gave Rita a stamp and promised to post it. But Belinda has long since confirmed that the letter never reached them. Rita, when there was no response, decided her grandmother had lied about the letters — she was capable of such devious cruelty — and that Belinda had already forgotten her daughter.

Audrey was one of the nurses at the hospital — a war widow with two school-aged children. She and Charlie were married the day he was discharged.

On a Saturday morning in the school holidays Rita went on a train to Wellington, and Charlie and Audrey and Raymond and Alison were there to meet her.

She remembers a lake with water lilies the size of dinner plates. The boy Raymond rowed through them, smashing the flowers beneath the oars. She remember a public dining room with white serviettes and the feel of her own warm, inexplicable pee stinging its way down her leg and onto the carpet.

By Wednesday she was back in Taupo with Grandma Rawlings.

It was Audrey who eventually got in touch with Belinda and Joe. ('She wanted Charlie, but not his child,' snorted Belinda. 'She knew that if we got you back we'd *never* let him steal you a second time.' But Rita thought then, and still thinks, 'Who cares about *why?* At least I finally got saved!')

From time to time Charlie wrote to her and Rita would write back. Then, when she'd left school and Taranaki, Rita would sometimes visit her father and stepmother. Raymond and Alison had left home by this time, and, if Audrey resented Rita, at least she had the courtesy not to show it.

Rita never doubted that, despite how it seemed, she mattered more to Charlie than his stepchildren ever had. And it wasn't the mountain that had drawn him back to his old home town.

AT DINNER JOE falls asleep, but Belinda is in good form. The lamb is delicious. Rita stopped off to buy garlic on the way back and tossed whole bulbs of it into the roasting pan. Her father and her mother each try a clove — Charlie wears a look of exaggerated suspicion. Belinda makes appreciative noises; Charlie chuckles and adjusts his teeth.

Rita feels like a young thing, quivery and unblemished in the manner of freshly poured concrete. Now and again she hears her voice rising in teenage excitement. She insists on doing the dishes on her own. Then Belinda wakes Joe up to tell him Charlie is leaving, though Charlie has said not to. Joe and Charlie shake hands and Belinda says Charlie must come again. 'It's taken too damn long,' she says, and Charlie says Belinda's probably right.

Rita drives Charlie home and gives him a hug. He says, 'I had a good time, girl.'

Belinda has waited up. She says, 'I'm glad I lived this long.'

'So am I,' says Rita emphatically.

Before she goes to bed Rita rings home. Ross tells her even the cat is missing her.

In her old bedroom, refurbished beyond recognition, Rita lies wide awake. She thinks about life cycles, about beginnings and endings and unbroken lines. She thinks of the beauty of circles and of Billy Connolly leaping from his tent and running naked in the snow.

Said Linda

I COULD HEAR her filing her nails. On the television Elliott was telling Ethan about death to the accompaniment of this muted *chch chch chch chch.*

She was using an emery board. I can remember, years and years back, being told by a new flatmate that it was better to use an emery board than a nail file. At the time the only emery boards I knew of were those spinning discs that shearers sharpened their cutting blades on. I imagined women queueing to grind off the tips of their fingers. I gawped at the new flatmate. *Watch her*, I warned myself.

By then Ethan had got Elliot on to God — I'd missed death completely. And she was only on to the little finger of her left hand; holding the other fingers splayed and rigid, though I only glanced. I was full of a murky kind of anger. This used to be *my* special programme. The once-a-week when I sat up late, alone, to wince or weep or laugh at people I could almost believe in. But now Linda had started 'keeping me company', and I couldn't find an acceptable way of saying *It's mine, see. Mine, Mine. Mine. And you're not allowed to sit in my armchair and watch my programme and breathe my air. So there. Nah nah nah.*

She didn't even like the programme. She watched the screen like a teacher marking exam papers, and made sure she had something else to do at the same time so the hour wouldn't be wasted. She didn't get fond of any of the characters, not even Melissa. She just didn't find them interesting, she said. But I think it was the *ambivalence* that put her off. Linda liked things to be definite: this or that, good or bad, right or wrong.

Then, a few weeks into her Women's Studies course, Linda got interested in the subliminal message. She'd explain it to me while the programme was still going and while she oiled her legs, or shaped her nails or waited for the rinse to infiltrate her hair. The subliminal message was always straightforward and it always had to do with belittling women. Clearly the makers of the programme were hostile and regressive. Her voice would take on a faint note of accusation. By liking the programme I was colluding.

So there we are, the two of us, in front of this piece of sexist propaganda, and during the commercials I am furtively glaring at Linda as she unzips her little leather tool kit and slides the emery board into its special place. Then she takes out a minute stainless steel spade.

Of course I know what it is, but I'm fascinated. I haven't seriously studied one of these things since 1951. That was when I was in Standard Five, and me and Jocelyn Holland and Anne Blythe and Neville Pickworth used to spend our lunch hours in a huddle comparing our half-moons and vitamin deficiency spots. *Cuticle* was a very significant word for a while there. But after a week or two we got bored with fingers and moved on to other parts.

Linda grinds back her cuticles in an experienced way, and, finally, I look down at my own nails. They have a rough-hewn, soil-caked, artisan look. I promise myself they will be scrubbed before bed.

MARSHALL IS STILL reading *Professional Secrets: the golfer's handbook*. He takes a glance up at my face. 'Below par tonight?' he offers, holding his thumb between the pages.

I heave myself in beside him. 'I can't imagine why she watches. She doesn't like it, she doesn't laugh in the right places or anything.'

'Never mind. It's not forever.' He crosses his fingers and holds them up towards the ceiling as if some Significant Other might be watching and prepared to intervene.

'She doesn't watch *your* programmes,' I bitch. He rolls his eyes, a martyr to my irrationality. Grudgingly, I laugh.

'It really irritates me how she talks,' he says. 'That little-girl voice.'

Knee-jerk, I defend her. 'People can't help their voices.'

'Course they can. Besides, that wasn't the voice she was born with. That's a made-up voice if ever I heard one.'

'What? Like Donald Duck?'

He puts the book, face-down, spreadeagled on his bedside table and slaps a hand over my right tit. He reads the look on my face and sighs.

'Okay — so just turn over for me.'

LINDA WAS PRECEDED by a letter from Kath, who had met her at the Unemployed Rights Centre.

She's had a really rotten time. I mean first she was laid off, then her husband lost his job, and like they sacked him so he got stood down for the dole and all that shit. So he goes and tops himself in their bathroom with this old strop razor can you imagine. Blood from arse to breakfast only lucky it wasn't her that found him but a neighbour wanting to borrow their lawnmower and saw the blood spurting out under the door. Well more likely just seeping I guess. Anyway — not surprising — she's decided to start somewhere new and put herself through university (like he left her some funds that's not a problem). Only she won't know a soul down there so I've given her your number.

Linda rang us as soon as she got off the plane. She hadn't looked for a flat; she thought we might have some ideas.

We had two spare bedrooms. 'In the meantime,' we said. 'While you get yourself organised.' We drove out to the airport to collect her. She wasn't what I'd expected, which was someone kind of bewildered and fragile. She looked tanned and capable and slightly irritated. She was in her early thirties, and her appearance didn't match her voice at all.

So she settled in and treated us in a cheerful daughterly fashion, which gave us a glow of nostalgia. She had enrolled for Business Administration because it seemed the qualification most likely to provide work. And for the Women's Studies course because our daughter had recommended it. Kath has a degree for which she studied various liberal and disputatious subjects. She's been unemployed ever since she graduated. Linda, assured us, perhaps a little too hastily, that she and Kath didn't know each other well. Kath giving our number out to confessional strangers?

In the first three weeks Linda went to look at a few shared flats but they didn't appeal. She decided she'd prefer a hostel and put her name on waiting lists. Marshall and I reassured each other; it wasn't as if she'd be staying forever.

She didn't need us. The husband was only ever mentioned in passing and always in the possessive case: Frank's funeral, Frank's parents, Frank's Citroën. Not a word about Frank himself. Of course I could have asked, but you don't like to under the circumstances. And after a time I got to thinking — why suppose the death of a spouse necessarily causes anguish?

She didn't need us, but she seemed to like us. And why not? We set a modest sum for board (because Kath sent her, because it was so temporary) and made no demands. She wasn't the kind of person I would ever seek out as a friend, but I liked her well enough. I gathered she liked me too, though I knew we didn't have nearly as much in common as her Women's Studies led her to believe.

She was the most ardent kind of convert, having been, at fifteen, Miss South Beach, and at eighteen a Miss Taranaki finalist. After leaving school she worked as a junior secretary, sniggered at women's libbers and spent her lunch hours drooling at engagement rings in Michael Hill's. But after Frank's defunction and the humiliations of unemployment she was ripe for reappraisal. Suddenly she and I were fellow victims, compatriots, sisters. She would follow me round the house identifying oppression, explaining strategy. Except I still just felt like the woman whose home she was living in. I'm a person who likes being alone.

She would say: 'You have to love your body.'

'I'd have thought you did. You give it a lot of attention.'

'*You. Your* body.'

'*This poor old thing!*'

'See! We're conditioned to think we should look like *Playboy* bunnies. Even at your age.'

'I wouldn't say I spent a *lot* of time wanting to look like a *Playboy* bunny. Or even thinking about my body. Apart from prickles, rheumatism occasionally.'

'That's a kind of denial. Give it no attention and maybe no one will notice it. You should give it attention.'

'I don't have time.'

'Oh, Fay! Come *on*. I've always looked after my body, but the point is, the point *is* — *who* was I trying to please?'

I'd know she was going to tell me.

'Frank . . . My boss . . . Men. I was trying to please men. But now it's to please *me*.'

'Right,' I'd say obsequiously.

She'd pat me on the bum. 'Be proud of it,' she'd say as she walked out the door.

Proud? It's just an everyday middle-aged arse, a bit on the large side, white. Did I really seem so desperate for self-esteem that I should invest emotion in a piece of flesh I'd never even glimpsed first-hand? I'd rush after her, shouting up the passage. 'I'm proud of the way I do my job. I'm proud of the way we've fixed up the house, I'm proud of my garden and sometimes I'm proud of my children. I don't need to be proud of my bottom.'

She'd pause in her bedroom door. 'Fay, why are you so upset?'

'Because,' I'd say.

Then one day I knew exactly why, and I told her.

'Because you're part of that new breed of people who believe that presentation is all that counts. You think people have no judgement. You think the things that matter, like beauty and truth, can be packaged. You think if we shout lies loud enough and long enough it'll make them true. People like you scare me shitless.'

There was quite a long silence. Linda began to shake her head sadly. 'I keep telling you,' she said, kindly, patiently 'that you've really got a very nice body.'

So I STAND looking over my shoulder at the mirror, my jeans around my knees.

'You got a rash or something?' asks Marshall, gripping his number seven iron exactly as it shows in the diagram in *Professional Secrets*.

'I'm just looking at it. It's mine. I'm allowed to look at it.'

'Shall I show you mine?'

GIVEN A BIT of attention, my body got demanding. It wanted

all the things it saw Linda's body getting. I bought it Oil of Ulan, and a pair of scissor tweezers, but I kept forgetting to use them.

'You always find time to look after your garden,' said Linda pointedly. She'd bought an exercycle. There's something ominous about a world where people have so little practical use for their limbs that they invent machines that simulate basic human activity. She was pedalling the thing on the lawn.

'I like gardening.'

'It's a beautiful garden.'

'Yes.' I was pleased. 'I think so too.'

'You give it so much loving attention, that's why it's beautiful.' She threw me a look of profound significance.

'Linda,' I said, 'I was never cut out to be a rose bush.'

'What about Marshall?'

'Does he want to be one?'

She grimaced. 'I mean . . . he might be . . . appreciative if you . . . invested a bit of time on yourself.'

'I thought men didn't come into this?'

She shrugged. 'No harm in improving your sex life.'

It took me a while to work out how to deal with that. 'Maybe I don't want to improve it,' I said.

In silence we both exhumed my sentence and saw it was riddled with ambiguity.

'WELL?' I DEMAND of Marshall. 'What do you reckon?'

'I'm not sure. *You* like it?'

'I should. It cost me eighty-five dollars.'

'Bloody hell. Well, come here then. Let's see how it looks on a pillow.'

Silence while the wife behaves in an obedient fashion. Then, 'Sweetheart?'

'Mmm?'

'Do you think I'm fat?'

'Cuddly.'

'I've started feeling fat.'

'I don't mind. I'm used to it.'

'*Too* fat.'

'Depends on what you want to be.'

'I want to be about Linda's size. She's got a really nice body.'

'S'pose she has. Yeah. Come to think of it. Great legs.'

'SEE. SEE.' I boast. 'They hang on me. And they were always too tight. Do I look different?'

'Hungry,' he says. 'You look hungry. Doesn't she, Linda?'

'I think she looks great.'

'You should lose a few pounds yourself. He's getting a paunch — isn't he, Linda?'

'Well . . . But it's a very nice paunch.' She smiles fondly.

'Isn't it!' A pathetic smirk. 'I'm growing increasingly fond of it. In fact I can't do enough for it. Pudding, beer, chocolate cake — whatever it fancies I make sure that it gets it.'

'Would you believe,' says Linda, 'that I make wonderful chocolate cakes. Shall I make Marshall a chocolate cake? We promise not to eat it in front of Fay.'

'YOU KNOW THAT funny way Linda talks?'

'What funny way?'

'Kind of little-girlish, you said you hated it.'

'Bullshit. I never said that.'

THEY FELT I should get to stay on at the house, because of the garden and all the work I'd put into it. Our oldest son has lent me the money to buy Marshall out of his half. Marshall was shamefaced about taking the money but, as Linda said, it was best to keep everything cut and dried.

'I'm sorry, Fay.' She clutched my hand. 'But I guess you just left it all too late. By the time you started taking a pride in yourself the marriage was already dead.'

After they went I sat in the garden eating chocolate and wondering whether next year I should have delphiniums rather than cornflowers next to the white climbing rose.

The Remarkably Unhumble
William Saroyan

THREE WEEKS AGO I met your youngest daughter. I was visiting an institution — never mind why — and a staff member drew me aside. 'I want to talk to you,' she said. 'It's personal.' She led me to her office and closed the door behind us. I was decidedly apprehensive — being taken into an office brings back my schooldays.

She said your name. There's a sports commentator, these days, with the same name but this caused no confusion. 'He's my father,' she said. Perhaps she said, *was* my father. Such details, I realise now, can be important. As an observer I've always made do with impressions but as from now I'm making a real effort at accuracy. Seeking out the small but telling detail that tethers a story to the everyday world.

On my desk (I note) is a work diary with metal binding. It's three years out of date but I keep it for the photographs. It's opened on a calendar page that is ringed with coffee stains. I have scrawled myself reminders (*ring Rosemary . . . library books due . . . Helen lunch . . .*) beneath the small dewdrops of literary history that lend significance to each day. On June 23 Jean Anouilh was born in Bordeaux.

June 28 is a lesser day, marking only the birth of suspense novelist and screenwriter Eric Ambler.

On another page (I have got sidetracked — a hazard of accurate observation) William Saroyan is described as 'remarkably unhumble'.

I thought you'd like that!

It's not a diary, I find by turning to the cover, but an 'engagement calendar'. Even my most patent observations are not to be trusted.

I won the calendar at a dinner. We were all given cards inscribed with cryptic clues concerning authors or their books. Then we had to find the person with the book title clue that matched our author clue, or vice versa. The woman who had the other half of my clue was a publisher's representative with a voice that could be heard above all those other voices shouting out the deciphered names of writers and what they had written.

The only other time I'd won a prize was in the fourth form. It was the Miss Hathaway Prize for Original Verse, for which the winner received a book. Within a certain price range Miss Hathaway's beneficiaries were allowed to choose which book they would receive. I wanted *To Hell And Back* because it had a photo of Audie Murphy on the cover, playing himself in the film version of his action-packed autobiography. I had a minor crush on Audie Murphy. He won more medals than any other American soldier in World War Two but still had to stand on boxes for the important cinematic moments.

No one, these days, has even heard of Audie Murphy. Not that I've researched the matter. *Have you heard the name Audie Murphy . . . (a) frequently (b) occasionally (c) never (d) not for years and years?*

D. Which isn't to say I feel impoverished by that absence. But you do begin to know you're old when the bric-à-brac of your life turns into insignificant history. I see Audie Murphy as a paving stone in an almost endless road. If I wandered back far enough there he would be.

You're there too, possibly within jumping distance of Audie. Except you were harder to walk away from. For years I sent you intermittent memos. Sick jokes, updates on the state of the nation, cartoons, quotes — a one-way psychic transmission.

It's too bad you missed out on the fax machine. There's an invention you would have enjoyed. Lately I've been half-expecting mine to deliver a page of your dopey cartoon drawings with small comments scrawled around the edges. It would scarcely be more of a surprise than that initial meeting with your daughter.

I knew, of course, that you had daughters. But in life you so carefully compartmentalised your relationships, social and private, that it was a shock to find them merging all these years later.

Your daughter wanted to know about you. Wanted me to add flesh to her own memories, which were a child's memories of your leaving and your very occasional visits. She's a mother — you're on the way to being a great-grandfather — and as people get older they feel a serious need to fill in the empty spaces of the past.

We arranged to have lunch. She would bring her sister. I began at once to fumble around for memories that were precise and accurate. I wanted to give them you — or at least your social side — finite and framed. The Father at Bay. But most of what I came up with was subjective, imprecise and hopelessly communal.

For we were a pack. We were what you had when you didn't have a marriage, at least not one that worked. We hung out at the Duke of Edinburgh, the St George, De Bretts, the Prince of Wales . . . The batty gentility of those names reflected in the cavernous lobbies where guests occasionally scurried past those other doors, bulging and sandblasted, that were always reverberating. Always threatening to burst open and spew out the public bar inferno.

We drank upstairs in 'house' or lounge bars that were as wearily decorous as the lobbies beneath them. Lena and I wore desperately mature make-up to ward off the barmen's suspicions.

They're gone now, all those stately bars. Swept away or altered beyond recognition. These days, as far as I can gather, people hang out in gymnasiums or shopping malls. And they seem to stay within their peer groups; common age, not common interest, is what binds them.

I felt, then, I was part of an indulgent and fascinating family. I had dreamt you all up during a wistful childhood, and in my nineteenth year you materialised.

For a long time after I left Wellington I wanted to be back there, clacking up stairways in aberrant stilettos, stubbing Pall Mall Plain into monogrammed ashtrays, listening to you or to Pen.

You were the entertainers among us, and the most serious

drinkers. Your styles were poles apart. Pen was a performer. She was coyly eccentric, wilfully outrageous, parading Left Bank fantasies down Willis Street, witch's stockings on her fabulous legs.

You preferred a private audience. I remember now that you had a slight speech impediment when you got excited. A kind of stammer where your words tripped over each other and took a moment to disentangle. It seemed entirely appropriate, for no visible part of you was graced with co-ordination. You moved — drunk or sober — in a shambling but detached fashion, as if the activities of your limbs were beyond your sphere of responsibility.

Your memory was astonishing, maybe a zillion bytes. (Sorry, a nineties joke about something I barely comprehend and couldn't begin to explain.) It seemed that everything you had ever read had lodged in your brain in a tidy fashion, readily accessed. I had just a tussock of knowledge in a vast desert of ignorance, a woeful fact that I was constantly afraid my employers would discover. You were my ready reference — a combination of *Roget's Thesaurus*, the *Guinness Book of World Records*, *Pears Encyclopedia*, *International Who's Who*, *Burke's Peerage*, *Landfall*, *Straight Furrow*, *Pix*, *Truth* and *Harper's Bazaar*.

You loved the trivial facts. The absurdity of them. I imagine you saw your own life as absurd, which somehow both absolved and paralysed you. I may be reinventing you, but that's a risk you took in dying. No matter how involuntary death might be, the living find it hard to forgive. You let it happen, that's how it feels. Regardless of the feelings of others *you let it happen*. I learned about it from Lena several days later. You were still keeping your friends outside the barrier marked *private*.

When I needed to I was unable to describe your face. Because it was always putting on an act? Dolorous is the word I thought of but kept to myself. Meaning a kind of self-mocking mournfulness. It was, at least, an expression you favoured. 'A clown's face', I could have said: pale, unlined and mobile. A face dedicated to the entertainment of others.

Looking through my engagement calendar to consider faces I see Saul Bellow and a similarity. Except he is laughing in a large American way and you were a giggler and therefore essentially British.

Before meeting your daughter, the last time I had thought of you was when watching *The Tony Hancock Story*. It wasn't just the drinking. You shared a comic style, laughter like a flying fox slung across valleys of cosmic terror.

Perhaps the horror was largely mine. There came a point when your drinking frightened me. I felt like an observer watching the *Titanic* carousing through dark seas. I couldn't understand how someone with so much information could have such little regard for cause and effect.

In its three hundred and twenty-five literary snippets and fifty-two portraits my engagement calendar has no reference to any New Zealand writer. Not even Katherine Mansfield.

It was you who said to read this book called *Owls Do Cry*. And Maurice Duggan. You had great respect for fiction.

We, all of us, worked in the fringe fields of writing and nurtured secret dreams of short stories we would some day see in print. A hope too raw and bruising to be publicly exposed, even in a Wellington bar with rain hitting the windows, the smell of smoke and overcoats and that sense of being *almost* at the centre of somebody's novel.

Everything seemed so encapsulated back then, so accessible. We would sit in our circle fermenting with possibility. At six o'clock, closing time, we would gather up supplies and go home. Lumbering up the steps to my place, or Lena's or Pen's. We three were the inner-city dwellers. The inner city — walking distance — was all I understood of Wellington. Only Con had a car and where we lived he was unable to park it. I had no concept of the suburbs and lives that were lived there. If I'd known about suburbia I'd never have left the inner city.

As it was, I imagined there were people like you and Pen and Lena and Selwyn and Con all over the country. It didn't occur to me that, even if this had been so, being part of a couple made me ineligible to be one of a gang. Missing you all made me resentful. I wished I'd been the kind of girl who stayed on at home with my parents and went out on dates and looked at engagement rings. That way I'd have known no better.

You came from the other direction. The marriage and

suburbs were first and we came later. You might at least have warned me what I was in for.

In fact you still lived in the suburbs. With, at that time, your mother and father, though your daughters tell me there was also a flat. I had no image of your home. You volunteered no such information and I didn't ask. Wherever it was that you lived, you spent a lot of time elsewhere.

Your *daughters*, I said inadvertently. This time I didn't cry. I told them you were the kindest man I have ever known. And it's true. I recall a heap of kindnesses, to me and to others. Not just an offhand kindness, but acts of extreme thoughtfulness and generosity. You were the *friend in need* that I puzzled over in primary school — that confusing verbal shorthand. You qualified both ways: you could be relied on, and you were in need. I knew that, but I was only a friend and a friend's responsibilities are limited to the parameters set. Only lovers should expect unlimited access.

That's what I believed. Chose to believe.

That, I imagine, is why dead lovers can be left behind but dead friends hang about, reproachfully enigmatic.

I can't tell your daughters who you were, but I know what you liked. Who you would like now? Spalding Gray. Now there's someone I've wanted to post to you regardless of delivery conundrums. It would be like reading a mirror. An American, but he writes, talks . . . and it's your voice with a New England accent. He even looks like you, when I think about it. Not in features perhaps, but in essence. Delete Saul Bellow — he's too confident, too substantial.

Spalding Gray hasn't made it into the engagement calendar. I suspect he's a little too fresh.

Sylvia Plath was born on Dylan Thomas's birthday. A luminous but dangerous date.

My birthday is occupied by Robert Louis Stevenson's death. Suddenly, due to 'apoplexy'.

Audie Murphy died, regardless of medals, in a private plane crash in 1971.

You died on your older daughter's birthday. She was twenty-one years old. Neither she nor her sister got to go to your funeral.

Purple Trousers

THIS MORNING HE came to visit and we talked of small matters and drank tea. I kept thinking about how I was wearing ugly old purple trousers, which isn't a normal way for me to think. I was worrying about the trousers, which were tight on the thighs and low in the crotch, and worrying about the fact that I was suddenly aware of these defects, and at the same time carrying on this everyday conversation.

Worse — I was watching the conversation very carefully in case he should leave a couple of words invitingly ajar so that I would feel entitled to reach a warm hand through. And I was folding up the used conversation and hiding it on my lap so that later I could run over it with a hot iron, looking for invisible messages.

I had been hoping he would visit, but once he was sitting there drinking my tea my life became so complicated I wished he had stayed home. I'm not a child; I've been through the same kind of thing before but somehow it always surprises me and I never seem to get better at it or more decisive. I'm afraid of misinterpreting, jumping to conclusions, generally making a fool of myself. Once you get to worrying about your trousers, you're in no position to make an objective judgement about the other person's feelings.

I used to have a friend who insisted that once you got to feeling this way you could be sure it was mutual. I was happy to believe him until I realised he thought it applied to him and me.

So this morning there was this reckless voice in the back of my mind impatient for a decision one way or another, making me talk faster and louder to drown it out. Sometimes I'm so severe with my emotions that I wonder why they don't find a more sympathetic home with someone who's bold and demonstrative.

We talked about the economic package and the price of toll calls and a bit about the weather. He told me a couple of stories from his childhood and I told one from mine. We touched on the loyalty of dogs. Then he left and I went back to my normal routine, which now seemed exceedingly pointless.

So here I am. Nothing's happened but everything's changed. The inconvenience is enormous. My feet are ugly. I have a nervous laugh. I am uncertain and unsatisfactory. I write songs lyrics in my head and don't bother with dinner.

And I remember now that this is much the way it was the other times. I can't understand why I hoped he would visit me.

I treat myself gently, as I would any accident victim. I take a hot bath and bandage myself with used conversation. The invisible ink shows up in cipher. I don't understand it. I don't even try to decode it. I prefer not to know what it says.

Boots

GAIL WOKE UP to the smell of butts soaking in beer. She didn't open her eyes. Shit, another day.

She could feel a streak of sun across her back and the small dull pain in her belly, almost friendly in its familiarity. She moved a little to make sure Lenny was still there large beside her. 'Jesus,' said Lenny, 'do you mind? I was just sneaking back into a dream.'

Gail opened a little bit of eye and saw the saucer full of bloated filtertips. She reached out a hand to push the mess across the mat, away from her offended nose. Behind her Lenny thumped and heaved and sighed.

'It's gone, why didja go and wake me? It was about Garth and all.' Lenny's voice was leering. Gail closed the little bit of eye and pretended the day had not begun. Why was it Lenny even got the best dreams?

'Don't you wanta know? Eh? 'Bout what was going on?' Lenny's arm whacking across Gail's shoulder. 'Eh?'

No.

'Eh?' Another whack from Lenny.

'Leave me alone, I'm still asleep.'

'Any smokes around? C'mon, wake up, I'm gonna tell you 'bout . . . Hey where's ya boots?'

Gail's eyes both opened wide. Her mouth too. An oh of dismay sliding all the way down and settling heavy in her painful stomach. She moved around the room, pulling aside cushions and upending chairs. Lenny looking on limp with sympathy. Gail's rage spluttering.

'They was down between us. I put them there. Bet it was that turd Marty, I bet. He was wanting to try them on last night. Shit, shit, shit. I find that arsehole I'm gonna kill him.'

'Yeah,' soothed Lenny, 'that's right. You do that. Someone ought to.'

They were a kind of purple grey, with laces. Solid, you'd think, but real leather soft as skin so you could pull it up or fold it back, whichever. And soles cushioned like running shoes so the pavements turned to trampolines. In those boots Gail had flickered loose-limbed across plate-glass windows from Penrose to Princes Wharf. It was three weeks two days since Lenny had shifted the footware, so expertly, from the window display in Soles Bootique to Gail's transported feet. Her boots were the best thing Gail had ever owned. Seemed like that.

Lenny got up and threw the squab back on the sofa.

'I'd swallow nails for a decent bed. We get our own place we won't let these thieving bastards come round.'

She went through to the bedroom, Gail following. One of the three beds was empty.

'Hey, where's that Marty? Where's that cunt gone, eh?' Lenny's voice so naturally loud they would hear her at the corner dairy. 'Wait till we get our hands on that thieving little maggoty creepo.'

'Fuck up, Lenny,' said Joe's blanket, 'we're all asleep.'

Garth in the next bed opened an eye. 'Him and Ginger went out somewhere. Hours ago.'

Gail, watching Garth, thought resentfully of Lenny's unspecified dream.

'Yeah, well we know what one of them was wearing on his filthy little pinkies. This place is a scungy, thieving hole.'

'Piss off, then.' Joe's voice, muffled. 'We didn't ask yous to live here.'

Garth gave Lenny a smile regarding Joe. Lenny roared down at Joe's blanket. 'Live? You wouldn't know how to live if you took it at nightschool.'

She reached down and collected a sweatshirt from the floor. A green shirt with DOG across the front, most often worn by Marty. Lenny handed the sweatshirt to Gail as she escorted her out the door. Gail rolled the shirt up and tucked it under her arm. It smelt of sweat and beer, and she hated green.

THEY SAT ON the post office steps, moving with the sun. Lenny buried herself in the back pages of a discarded *Herald*. Gail watched the footwear parading past her like small animals, all in pairs. Gail's feet were bare. The nails of her big toes still had a bit of scarlet varnish at the edge.

'Two br, handy to shops, no pets, non-smokers.'

'You smoke.'

'Who's to know?'

'How much?'

'Doesn't say. Just a phone number.'

'Look under flatmates wanted. Ya know we can't afford a place on our own.'

'I'm not sharing,' said Lenny. 'Not me. Bugger that. Y' wanta share, y' go ahead. Not me. I got this place in my head. Third floor with a view and an inbuilt stereo.'

'Anyway, they want bonds and that.'

'Yeah. So?'

Gail pictured a home. Lumpy brown sofa weeping kapok, and a grease-caked stove. She could smell already any flat they could possibly afford. Lenny looked up from the paper to watch an office junior walk by, clutching the morning mail. She made an eager, predatory sound in her throat and swept her eyes from his smooth cheeks to the zip of his fly and back again. The young man's face reddened and he walked faster. Lenny glanced at Gail, who grinned faintly. A bit of a giggle.

But only a bit of.

Gail considered the ache in her belly. Cancer. Hunger. Ulcer. Period. Eeny meeny miney mo.

Lenny took the paper off to a phone box and Gail edged along the step to keep the sun on her feet. A woman walked past, pushing a shopping basket on wheels.

Gail said, out loud, 'My life is out of control.' The sound of herself saying it amazed her. The woman looked around for someone else to answer, but no one did.

Lenny came back dancing.

'I said we'd come and look.'

'Where?'

'Mount Eden.'

'How much?'

'We'll manage. Have no fear, Lenny's here.'

'They'll want a bond.'

Lenny sat down beside her. 'Furnished,' she said. 'TV and all.'

They sat while the day moved past.

'There's my old man,' said Lenny.

Gail looked along the street.

'I mean we could ask him.'

'I thought . . .' said Gail and left it at that.

'He's reformed. Got this new love who's dragging him back on the rails. And I know where they live.'

IT WAS ONE of a row of houses that all looked the same. Lenny had forgotten the number, but the woman at the window knew Lenny. You could see it on her face.

'Your father's at work,' she said round the edge of the door.

'Yeah?' said Lenny. 'Where's that then?'

'He won't want you coming round.'

'You gonna invite us in or what?'

The woman looked at Lenny then stepped back. 'Would you like to come in for a minute?'

'Thank you,' said Lenny. 'That's very kind.'

They all stood in the kitchen around the ironing board draped with Lenny's father's white shirt.

'So where's he working?'

The woman thought about lying, Gail could tell. 'The gas company.'

'That's nice.' Lenny almost sounded sincere. 'You're certainly doing him a lot of good.'

'Did you want to see him about something in particular or is this just a social call?'

'Bit of both really.' Lenny sat down at the kitchen table uninvited. 'This is Gail, by the way.'

'Hello Gail.' Her mouth propped up stiffly genteel, like a little finger.

'Y'see, us two've got this really good flat jacked up but we gotta have a bond and since we both just started at new jobs and don't get paid till next week I thought he might loan us, just till pay day.'

'I see. And whereabouts are you working?' She was looking at Gail.

'Nightshift,' said Gail, surprising herself. 'Takeaway place.'

'Both of you?'

'Just her. I do cleaning at the hospital. Mornings and nights.'

'Well,' the woman said with a smile of sorts, 'I don't think you need bother Graeme. If I rang your employers for you and explained the situation I'm sure they'd advance you part of your pay.'

'Oh no, really,' said Lenny, smiling back at the woman, 'we don't want to put you to all that trouble. I'm sure we can work something out. Perhaps you'd just tell him his daughter called by?'

Lenny stood up, unhurried, to leave. At the door she said, 'And you might like to remind him he has a wife and kids in Pokeno.'

'You lot aren't a family,' said the woman from her ironing board, 'you're a pack of leeches.'

'Drop dead,' said Lenny conversationally.

On the long walk back to the city Lenny talked about the woman with respect. 'I'll ring your employers! Fu...uuck, what a sly bitch.'

Gail remembered. 'I left Marty's shirt in her kitchen.'

The blue car ambled right beside the kerb.

'Girls, can I give you a lift?'

He was looking at Lenny of course. Dark glasses and a brown suit. Old. Somebody's father. They kept walking. The car nudged along beside them.

'Give your friend a break. Her feet are hurting.'

Abruptly Lenny turned. She bent down at the passenger window. 'What's it worth, creep?'

He shrugged, speechless.

'I need,' she said, 'two hundred and fifty dollars.'

'Hop in,' he told her, 'and we'll discuss it.'

Lenny turned to Gail. Her finger stabbed towards the rear of the car. 'Remember the number. Wait here. If I'm not back in a hour . . . do something.'

'What?'

'I dunno, do I? Tell someone . . . Sonny or . . . Ring the cops. I dunno.'

Gail watched the blue car leave with Lenny in the back seat. She walked up the road until she could see the clock on the Hellaby building. She walked back again and waited.

When Gail returned from her third look at the clock Lenny was there with a pocket full of notes.

'How much?'

'Two hundred.'

'Yeah? What was it like?'

'Pathetic. I'm never gonna get old. Never, never, never.'

'Y' still got the address of that place?'

'In my pocket.'

Lenny put her arm around Gail's neck. 'I bet you's worried, eh?' She tightened her arm until Gail stopped breathing. 'Y' wouldn't say to anyone how we got the money?'

Gail shook her head and was released.

'I need a drink,' said Lenny. 'I need a drink most urgently.'

THE BACK BAR half full of familiar faces. Sonny sitting with his new girl but looking all the time at Lenny. Gail took her rum and coke to a corner table where young Albie slouched alone. Lennie stayed at the bar being looked at.

'Y' okay, Albie?'

He seemed not to know her. He stared for a few unfocused seconds then his head toppled on to his arms and stayed there, mumbling now and again to the wet formica.

When Lenny brought Gail another rum she took Albie's head and turned his face to hers. 'What y' taken, kid?'

'Lenny,' he said, like an old old man remembering a past love.

'Jesus.' Lenny let go of his head and it slid sideways. 'You're okay,' she said. 'Gail's gonna look after you.' She took Gail's hand and placed it on Albie's. His fingers curled tight around Gail's palm.

Gail could feel the the rum warming and soothing the ache in her belly. She thought of her and Lenny watching the TV in their own flat and wondered if it was worth learning to knit.

Marty came in with Ginger and Amy. Wearing white sneakers.

'Cunt,' said Lenny, sharp and loud. 'Where's them boots?'

The barman told her, language.

'What boots?' Marty smiling, wanting to keep it alive.

'We'll get you,' promised Lenny. 'Don't act dumber than you already are.'

'Up your arse,' said Marty grinning.

Lenny thumped down her glass. 'It's started to pong in here all of a sudden, anybody noticed? Heap of shit just settled in somewhere.'

She hustled Gail and Albie from their table. The whole room watching. Sonny moving towards Lenny as she strode past. On purpose she sidestepped and bumped into him. 'Ooops,' she said and walked on.

On the street the wind was sharp. Albie sagged and stumbled between them. Lenny was just drunk enough to need another drink, new faces, events. She walked them down the street, across and round the corner to an unfamiliar pub. It was her money. Away in an alcove where the child Albie would be unnoticed. She brought him lemonade with a straw and a slice of lemon. The lemon frightened him. He flicked it on to the table then crushed it dead beneath the ashtray.

Two men, strangers, joined them at the table. One was blond and beefy, the other small, dark and thin. The big one kept bringing up subjects for conversation but none of them caught on. He was like a man lost in the dark, flashing his torch in one direction, then the other, but never finding the track home. The little man smiled at Gail. She smiled back. Albie lunged for the lemon wedge on the big man's glass and spilt Gail's rum. The little man insisted he buy her another. Lenny told them Albie was her kid brother and he'd drunk ten Black Russians for a dare.

The men had a party to go to. They said, 'We've got room in the car for three more.'

'Sure,' said Lenny. 'Why not.'

IT WASN'T MUCH of a party. A few women sat around in the living room wearing desperate lipstick and drinking gin. The men clustered in the kitchen and the passage, some still in overcoats. The outside doors were permanently open and people came and looked and left, as if it was a show home they wouldn't dream of buying.

They propped Albie in a corner and Lenny helped herself to rum at the kitchen bench.

'Go easy,' said Gail.

'I want your opinion I'll ask for it.'

The skinny dark man sat on a wicker chair in the kitchen and pulled Gail down on to his lap. He began kissing her. He tasted like warm yoghurt.

'Our bones clash,' she whispered, running her finger along his shoulder blade. She felt quite fond of him. The man ran his hands around her hips and across her belly.

'I need a pee,' she realised, struggling off his lap. 'D'you know where it is?'

'The passage and to the right. Don't be long, treasure.'

She kissed his nose. 'I won't.'

First on the right was a bedroom guarded by an angry man who redirected her. Lenny caught up with Gail at the loo door.

'Let's go, eh? Slack here. Albie's waiting outside.'

'We gonna walk?'

'We'll get a taxi down the road. No phone here.'

Gail sighed. 'How much you got left?'

'Enough.'

'For a taxi?'

'That's right.'

Gail took hold of Lenny's arm and looked up into her face. 'We're not ever gonna get a place, are we?'

'Don't be like that.'

'Maybe those fellas'd drive us home.'

'I'd rather crawl on my hands and knees than go with that creep.'

'I gotta pee first.'

Gail would like to have stayed a bit longer, to have said goodbye to the small dark man, but Lenny might go without her. Outside the front door Lenny was leaning into a car, shouting.

'Course you got room. There's only three of us. You can drop us at Newton Road.'

The men in the front seat objected but Lenny was already pushing Albie, then Gail, into the back. There was someone in there already but he was in the far corner and out to it, his head flopped forward against the driver's seat. It was a big car, six-cylinder, and the four of them fitted in the back near enough. The driver was snarling that he was in a hurry. He was the same man who'd been at the bedroom door, and still angry. The car slewed around the corners, old milkshake cartons leaped from the back windowsill and Gail tried to keep her mind off throwing up. Something fell against her foot and she groped a hand down to explore. It was a boot of some kind. Empty. She raised it until the streetlight lent it some shape and colour. A boot of soft leather with laces and a turn-down top. Purplish, greyish. She turned it over and looked at the sole. Newer than hers. In the dark she tried it on her foot. Her size. Almost exactly.

Her hand groped along the floor past Albie's frayed sneakers. Crumpled foil, cold potato chip, then leather as soft as an armpit. But occupied. Inside this boot there was certainly a foot. Gail looked thoughtfully past Albie at the stranger's bowed head then across to Lenny, but Lenny's eyes were closed.

The driver pulled over at the Newton Road turn-off.

LENNY WOKE GAIL up, yelling. Howling her name so that Gail stumbled up from her bed on the floor and followed the voice to the bedroom. She stood at the door blinking and bringing herself up to date. Lenny and Garth together in Garth's bed, Albie in Marty's bed, sleeping like a baby. Joe and the radio in Joe's bed.

'Hey, what street was that slack party last night? Taylor Street, right?'

'I dunno.'

Lenny told Garth, 'See it was — Taylor.' She told Gail, 'Guess what — cops came round looking for Marty and Ginger so they've shot through. Don't y'see? Means you and me can stay, least for a while.'

Lenny put her face against Garth's and smiled. Garth held his arms around Lenny and squeezed. Gail stood in the doorway looking.

'What *about* Taylor Street?' she wanted to know.

Lenny propped herself up. 'Jesus, yeah. You're not gonna believe this. Was on the radio just before. Dead guy found by the golf course — just across from Western Springs. And they reckon he was strangled at some party in Taylor Street. Then dumped. They're looking for this dude driving a brown Falcon.'

'Nineteen sixty-eight,' said Garth.

'It was a Falcon, eh? Wannit?'

'Could'a been. Was sort of brown too.'

'Y's sitting next to a corpse!' Garth was fascinated.

'Not me. Albie was, I guess.' Gail remembered. 'He had boots just like mine. The right size and all. Only one was still on and I's scared of waking him.'

Garth and Lenny started laughing. Rolling about in each other's arms shaking and gasping. Gail stood there watching them.

'What's the matter?' Lenny asked in a calm spot. 'You don't think that's funny?'

'Yeah,' said Gail. 'I guess it's funny. Yeah. It's funny all right. I'd laugh only I've got this kind of pain in my belly. Think it might be cancer.'

They started laughing again. Haw haw haw, heaving and groaning as if she was Eddie Murphy. Live. In Person.

Aunt Elly and the Rockbusters

WESTSHORE BEACH, NAPIER. FOR almost two weeks in the January of my fourteenth summer my sister and I stayed with our Aunt Elly and Uncle Roy in a beachside cabin. For secret reasons that were widely conjectured, Aunt Elly and Uncle Roy had no children of their own. She managed to imply that being childless was the cost of marrying Uncle Roy. But our mother had a different economic perspective. Aunty Elly set too high a price on herself to be burdened with kids, our mother said. (Not once, but whenever the subject of Aunt Elly arose.)

Aunt Elly didn't want just any old kids. She wanted a daughter. She wanted the two of them to wear matching mother/daughter outfits and discuss hairstyles and cuban heels. My sister said those were stupid reasons for wanting a child.

So what were good reasons ? The kind our parents had, said Jan, as if she'd been there when they decided. Assuming they did decide. I asked my mother, in the wash-house, Why did you have us? God only knows, she said.

Besides, if Aunt Elly *really* wanted a daughter, said Jan, she could adopt one. I'd thought of that myself, hopefully, on and off over the years. It wasn't that we saw a lot of Aunty Elly and Uncle Roy — they'd lived in London for much of my growing up — but the times she had visited were embossed in my memory. I didn't especially like Aunt Elly but I was enthralled by her trappings. Her earrings bedazzled me; I was transported by her shoes. Just to look at her calves in their fine tan stockings, one slung so elegantly against the other . . . the perfection of her ankles and the charming bridge of her arches in reinforced nylon . . . I was in love with Aunt Elly's clad feet.

THEY WERE RENTING a cabin three doors from ours. Four young men and not an adult in sight. In the afternoons they would travel self-importantly along the dusty road to an old hall where every Friday a movie played. War or cowboys, we'd read the posters. They'd rehearse there for a couple of hours.

In the mornings we'd see them at the dairy buying milk and marmalade — them in jackets and jeans as if they inhabited a different climate, and us with shorts on over our togs because Jan didn't think it proper that people not on the beach should get to see the crease where our legs turned into bottom. Being neighbours and fellow holidaymakers we'd all say hi or at least smile, and I'd be careful to hide my yellow rubber bathing cap beneath my towel.

Jan had a white one. Aunt Elly believed in bathing caps — salt water ruined your hair; she had bought them for us. They felt like a dead person's flesh, and if you held one over your nose it smelt of chloroform.

On the fourth day and the sixth time we'd said hi one of the musicians said, You girls want to hear us play?

I was still savouring the miracle of this invitation when Jan said, no thanks. Who do they think we are? she sniffed as I sulked behind her over the sandhills.

After one swim I manufactured a casual glance between my thighs and a groan. I've got my whatsits. I'll have to go and get something. You won't be able to go swimming, Jan said. She might have been sorry for me but she made it sound like an accusation. I shrugged. I'll have to find something else to do.

THEY STOPPED PLAYING when they saw me inside the hall. They were a Roy Orbison kind of band — basic rhythm and a singer who slid in and out of falsetto. The first musicians I'd ever seen close up. They left Aunt Elly's whole earring collection (thirty-one pairs of studs and twenty-seven drop) for dead.

They were Johnny and the Rockbusters, and on the night of Saturday week they would be playing at the Soundshell. They asked me about Jan. And about Aunt Elly, who'd caught their eye. I told them which part of the beach Jan and I had selected as ours and what times we were usually there. And I'd hardly got back down the beach, saying it must've been a false alarm, must've sat on something, when they all came trooping down to lie on the sand almost next to us and sunbathe in their jeans and denim jackets.

It was all unbelievably fortuitous and quite unlike life as I had come to accept it. So when I realised that the one who seemed to like me was the *singer*, that added leap of extraordinariness seemed totally appropriate.

He was nineteen and five foot eight. He had a pink, fleshy face and sandy hair. His pale freckles were interspersed with a few unfortunate pimples the colour of banana ice cream. But I had heard him sing. I had seen his lips hover and dip, pollinating the microphone. Already an incredulous voice in my head was recording the details of this momentous relationship.

Aunt Elly approved of boyfriends in that they were a reason for dressing up. But we didn't tell her about the Rockbusters and we tried to look sympathetic when she went on about that dreadful caterwauling down at the hall. Besides, Jan didn't seem to see the Rockbusters as boyfriend material, even when they were coming down to our part of the beach every day. Not even when a couple of them peeled off their jeans to let the sun lick at their thighs. She looked at them in the way she'd look at a sandhopper that had strayed on to the open pages of her book.

They were impressed by Jan's indifference and her ability to tackle all those words jammed together in such an unappealing fashion. It would inspire them to awed recollections of brainy people they had met. An uncle who knew poems off by heart, a neighbour's cousin who was a Quiz Kid, a boy in Standard Five who knew the capital cities of every country in the world. I wanted to make it known that I, too, read books. I wanted *Jan* to make it known. She didn't. Brainy people can be very insensitive.

As a romance there wasn't a lot happening between me and Johnny outside of my head. Down on the beach we didn't have conversations. Johnny and the Rockbusters had a line of patter they kept among themselves as if they were rehearsing a comedy routine and Jan and I were the audience. Well, only me really, because Jan seldom looked up from her book and sometimes even blocked her ears. But I thought they were wildly funny and original. And I was envious, wanting it to be me lying around with three friends, so used to being together we could pick words out of each other's mouths and blow them up and bat them about endlessly.

On the Friday the drummer joined Jan and me in the sea. He was wearing his jeans and a yellow shirt. Even so he could swim better than either of us. He said, looking at me, Johnny wants to know if you girls are going to the movies tonight? Depends what's on, said Jan. I looked at her. It's that cowboy movie — we saw the poster. I hated her for that power of being older. I wouldn't be allowed to go on my own. We might, she said.

AUNT ELLY'S WISHED-FOR daughter was the kind who was invited to pyjama parties and had Saturday night dates with tow-headed boys in navy blazers who were allowed to borrow their fathers' cars. She and Aunt Elly would spend all Saturday afternoon getting ready for Saturday night. Setting her hair, shaving her legs and under-arms, waiting for the nail polish to dry, choosing the earrings to go with the necklace and the necklace to go with the belt and the belt to go with the shoes. The more I thought about Aunt Elly's daughter, the more I didn't care for her.

Aunt Elly blamed our mother. And she blamed our mother's mother, who was Aunt Elly's mother-in-law. Brought up like savages, she hissed at Uncle Roy, who pretended not to take it personally. I believed she was mainly referring to Jan: I still took an interest in her earrings and she didn't yet know I'd let the skinny one make shanghais out of my bathing cap.

I don't suppose, Aunt Elly had sighed on our second night, either of you get the opportunity to meet any boys. We live with one, said Jan unnecessarily. For in a sense Aunt Elly was right. There were the local boys we'd known since primary school and who we now ignored on the tedious bus journey to and from the girls' and boys' high schools in town. There were farm labourers and itinerant shearers, and occasionally an unattached male townie on holiday would be brought along to the swimming hole, or the Tuesday ping pong. But no tow-headed, blue-jacketed youths to invite us on dates or call our mother Mrs Tunnicliffe or buy us sodas. Aunt Elly understood deprivation.

So we were allowed to fill our days as we pleased while Aunt Elly dragged Uncle Roy around the Napier shops, or they lay on the deck chairs that came with the cabin and read magazines. We won't come with you, Aunt Elly would say to us with unflagging optimism, we'd only cramp your style.

But at tea time the world, according to Aunt Elly, under-went a sinister change. After tea it was dangerous for us to even walk down to the beach unaccompanied by an adult. On account of larrikins and bad elements. Your mother would never forgive me, Aunt Elly would say, if *something* happened.

The time we spent with Johnny and the Rockbusters — always before tea — felt to me like an achievement. I was sure, I was *almost* sure, that Aunt Elly would be happily surprised if she walked down the beach and saw us all stretched out on the sand. Jan with her fingers in her ears and a large B for brain embossed on her back in sand glued by a fingersmear of ice cream. The skinny one making a flute kind of noise by blowing down into the mouth of an empty beer bottle. The drummer asleep and the quiet one drawing a ballpoint dinosaur on his own forearm. Johnny dribbling sand softly on to the arch of my upturned foot and smiling whenever I looked over my shoulder and and let our eyes meet.

But . . . when we got back to the cabin and Aunty Elly asked if we had a good day and how was the water, we never told her we'd *met some boys*. To be fair to Jan, she may not have noticed that Johnny and I were almost going around together. I thought about telling Aunt Elly. I wanted her to know that she could stop worrying, at least about me. But what if she wanted to meet him? Whenever I imagined Aunt Elly and Johnny in social congress I felt an oily undertow in my stomach.

Jan asked if we could go to the movies. It must have seemed, even to her, a better prospect than another evening playing Scrabble or Chinese checkers with Uncle Roy. Both Aunt Elly and Uncle Roy looked positively relieved. He gave us extra money for ice creams. They could buy a yacht with that, Aunt Elly said, snatching some of it back.

THE MOVIES WERE an amateur affair with the projector on a table and the audience on old wooden forms. The place was packed long before the projectionist had even opened the box containing the reels. Everyone slow-clapped to hurry him along. The drummer clapped in the off-beat. When the lights were turned off and the numbers on screen counted down to ten, about a hundred hands flew into the projected light and shadow-waved back at their owners.

Johnny was sitting on one side of me and Jan the other. He'd bought us both ice creams. Once the movie had started he found my hand and held it. His hand felt cool and wet like a squashed tomato until I reminded myself that this was the hand of a rock singer.

The Rockbusters were involved in the movie right from the start. They participated in screen conversations, augmented sound effects and suggested alternative courses of action. During the second reel they moved into the space that passed for an aisle, tethered their horses and conducted their part of the shootout crouched behind the water-pump heads and saloon door shoulders of giggling, gawping kids. The skinny one caught a bullet from the double-crossing sheriff and dragged himself through a plantation of jandalled feet, writhing and gasping until the drummer tore a strip from the bottom of his own shirt and made a tourniquet to staunch the blood flow.

Eventually Johnny let go my hand and got up to join them. The Rockbusters pointed to him and smiled and waved their fists high. Johnny nodded in acknowledgement and made a small movement from the waist, not quite a bow. Then up, straight and fast, with a gun spinning in each hand, and while the watching kids were still smiling he wasted the Rockbusters: one, two, three.

FOR A COUPLE of seconds the audience was stunned. The movie ran on unattended. Then a mass of kids heaved towards Johnny, drawing their guns. Trying to keep them steady in that jostle of elbows. The projectionist was yelling for everyone to sit down. Saying he'd stop the movie. No one took much notice, they weren't watching anyway.

Johnny was surrounded. He circled slowly, very deliberate. Then he dropped his guns and inched his hands above his head. The kids relaxed a little. They glanced at each other and grinned. Johnny, eyes down, subdued, moved softly along our row and sat down in his seat beside me. He crossed his arms and leaned back, watching the screen. The kids watched us a for a while, I think they felt disappointed, then settled themselves back on the forms. For about a minute there was nothing on screen but the shadows of heads and bodies scrambling to find places to sit.

On the walk back to the cabins the band talked about Saturday night when they'd be playing at the Soundshell. What if it rained, and how many Hollywood talent scouts were liable to be in Napier on a Saturday night in January? Jan was quite friendly to them. She talked as if we'd be there for sure, so I dared to let myself think about it. The singer's girl. *Me*.

ON THE THURSDAY Jan and I were on the way to the dairy for ice blocks when Johnny and the drummer pulled up beside us in their old blue van. They were going into town to buy guitar strings and spotted bow ties. Jan didn't want to go. I said I'd meet up with her down the beach. She didn't object.

First we had a good look at the Soundshell. I stood on the stage and bowed and Johnny and the drummer clapped and shouted and yelled, more, more! The drummer bought me a windmill on a stick from a fairground kind of stall in front of the beach. Then we walked through town looking for a music shop and the kind of place that might stock spotted bow ties. We were buying each other things on the way. The drummer would look in a furniture store window and point to a table and say to Johnny, I just bought you that table. And Johnny would say, That's the very table I always wanted, thank you, you're a real mate. Then Johnny would point to a hernia truss in the chemist's and say to me, Just a token. You're too kind, I'd say. You spoil me.

So we were outside a newsagent's shop and Johnny had picked up the triangular billboard sign and was trying to give it to the drummer, and the drummer was saying, No, no, I've got one of those, and Johnny was saying, Exactly, it needs a friend. I've heard it crying in the night. And I was standing with my windmill, giggling, and suddenly there at my elbow was Aunt Elly in her green and white spotted sunfrock and her white peep-toe sandals, with her long white teardrop earrings crashing against her neck. Uncle Roy was just behind her, clutching a freshly wrapped shoebox and looking nonplussed.

Johnny and the drummer saw them at about the same time. The drummer walked off casually like a passerby. Johnny carefully put the billboard down on the edge of the pavement. With what felt like enormous maturity I said, Aunt Elly and Uncle Roy, this is Johnny of Johnny and the Rockbusters.

Pleased to meet y', said Johnny. He held out a pink hand but they didn't appear to notice. Aunt Elly gave the kind of smile babies give when they're about to throw up and Uncle Roy nodded vaguely as if he was trying to draw attention to the shoebox in his hand.

We're just on our way home, said Aunt Elly, clutching me by the wrist and dragging me towards her. I think it was the first time our skins had ever touched, hers and mine.

No one spoke as we drove back to the beach. I sat in the back seat watching the windmill spin in the breeze from my window. I tried to imagine I was cutting up Aunt Elly's sundress to make four unforgettable bow ties.

The next day we packed up and went home because Uncle Roy had developed a war wound headache.

After Max

NOT YESTERDAY BUT the day before or maybe the day before that Max went. A car drove right in at our drive and they got out. It was a man with a sticky sort of smile and a lady who kept her glasses on a yellow lead. They came to take Max away. The man opened the boot of the car and picked Max up and put him in and shut the lid down tight. Mydad looked at Mymum. I saw him. Max in the boot was crying and scraping but the man said he'll be fine good as gold. Soon as he's settled in the man said. The man he didn't look not once at me or Luke or Bubby. I think in case we saw how he was lying.

Things felt different after. There was no Max and there was no shutting of their door either with me and Luke and Bubby in the hall together and Luke pulling my clothes into a lump in his fist. The three of us waiting for them, Mymum and Mydad, to stop all the meanness and be nice and all of us then maybe go for a walk up the road or sometimes hide and seek. And they would both be so nice and so sort of soft even to me.

There was a day — the first day after Max — and I came home from school and I went inside. It seemed there was no one at home no one at all. And I started first in our room — no one. Then in theirs and I saw him, Mydad, with his knees stuck up next to his head and his face down I couldn't see. Only it was shaking his head and his legs and that. Just a bit and I seen it before — two times or four — and I don't like it, all the wet hair on his chin and his mouth so wobbly. I stand and hold on to my stomach. Bubby she would go up beside him and put her little head against his and make those dove noises she makes to be kind. Even Luke he would do something but me I just stand. That's me, how I am. Mydad crumpled up and crying and me, I just stand then I back away out the door.

MAX IS SCARED of the dark said Luke. And he curled his thumb in my school dress making it crumply. Mymum was listening.

Her eyes were out the window but she was listening with her hands in the sink holding the dishes not putting them up. Sometimes I dry them. I stand on a chair and be careful.

Max's bowl had gone from its place beside the big drawer in the stove. They'll take my clothes just like that. My yellow dress with the white clouds, even my rabbit slippers. Everything will be there then gone.

We had curried eggs for tea the night Max went. Why I said. Mydad said we told you why. Those people want him and they can look after him better than us, he'll be better off. He was too big, Mymum said, the way he ate and ate. We told you that. Would you want to go hungry so Max could eat.

I didn't say yes. I looked down at my plate. All that was left was a few bits of rice stuck up with yellow gug. I pushed them into my mouth and saw Luke staring. We couldn't afford him I said out loud. I knew the words but they didn't quite tell me why.

I say it at school in Talking Time — our dog has gone, we couldn't afford him. Mrs Steel sits down between me and Kelly at morning break and she whispers to me did I bring anything for lunch. Why I say but she doesn't tell. She just pats my hand — I'm so sorry about your dog. He doesn't like bread I tell her. Three peanut butter sandwiches I have. I'm sure he's happy she tells me but I say no he's scared of the dark. And Mrs Steel starts blinking her eyes like Bubby does when she's ready for a big wet bawl. Mydad cries I tell her so she will feel better but the words are wrong and Kelly is hearing them and I see how she thinks that is dumb when I wanted to say it as something really awful, the way he was crumpled up on the floor and now all the time I am scared for all of us but mostly for me.

Bubby will stay because everyone, all of us, say she is cute dead cute and also she hardly eats mostly blowing it out again all bubbled up back in the spoon. Luke is their boy, Mymum and Mydad, and he never does talk all the time driving us crazy. I am the biggest too and always wanting. I can remember when their door never did close with us in the hall and how the snow came down on the road when we were driving — Mymum says to Nana's but I can't remember, only the snow.

Why won't our car work anymore. Kristy shut up says Mydad why why all the bloody time. Kristy says Mymum go outside and take your mouth with you and I see she has not even a teenywee smile. Derek Horner told in Talking Time how his mum has gone run away he said only really she drive. Derek said it's good he stays up till when he likes. Mymum would walk very fast with an angry mouth and if she looked round at me and Luke and Bubby she would never see us the way now she never sees Bubby hold out her arms. I hug Bubby when I'm at home and try and be nice to Luke only he drives me crazy. Kristy he says Kristy Kristy Max gonna come back.

If he did come back it might all turn right is what I think.

I don't eat hardly anymore not even sausages that I used to like best. At night at first I would chew my blanket only now I don't need. Mydad says am I sick and I see he gives Mymum a nuisance look about me. No I say I'm not even a bit sick.

Luke hangs on to my pocket he don't want me to go to school. Why why why why he says. Luke I say shut up why why why all the bloody time.

WHEN I SLEEP the man with the sticky smile chases after me and when I fall over he lifts me up high and I'm screaming and kicking not to be shut up in the dark. And the light comes on and I'm in trouble for waking up Luke and Bubby. What is it says Mymum and I tell her tigers. Luke gets tigers in the night and they want to eat him and I see how scared his eyes have got now he knows the tigers are here for sure. Mymum sits on the floor right next to my bed with the light still on and her hair is all mixed up with mine. She stays there till the tigers must all be gone. I can taste that her cheeks are wet. Why.

When I was still as little as Luke there was just Mymum and me and at night Mydad was home for tea and I stood on the pumpkin lumpy fronts of his boots and he walked us both through to the wash-house.

You love bread with honey Mymum says. I don't I say I don't I hate it. You don't have to shout she says — Mymum — we're not deaf yet. Luke can have it I say but Mydad says no eat it he says. I put it into my mouth just a bit. It's horrible yucky not at all the way I remember bread and honey.

Their door is shut. Me and Luke are in the hall and his nose is running like anything and I feel so lonely for Max I'm starting to cry. In there their voices go zzzzz zzzzzzz like the words are cutting through wood and the wood is bleeding. I can't tell what words except for Kristy. Kristy they say then Kristy some more but I never hear Luke or even Bubby.

WE MAKE A house inside the car, me and Luke, with a blanket roof only Luke keeps pulling it down and I have to hit him. He doesn't tell on me and he stops pulling down the roof. I tell him about the snow and how it was even all over the road. We look out the windows of our car house and pretend the clothesline is moving as we drive past.

There is some grass growing up through the bottom of our car. Why.

Max comes in the dark and licks my face. His tongue feels like dry sand and when I reach out I feel his hair is all knotted. Only he's never there in the morning.

I'm playing tiggy with Kelly and Lee in the playground and I fall down only it's no one's fault. Next thing I'm in the office on the sofa and Mrs Steel is saying they're not on the phone not anymore, I suppose they've just had to cut down. Then next I hear a man his voice through the wall and I think it's Mydad and he's here to take me home. How.

And someone does lift me up but it's not Mydad at all. I can't see who but Mrs Steel is there holding my schoolbag and sort of smiling at me while I'm carried out through the door and it must be a lady because of her lady smell and I turn my head but all I can see is part of her hair and the lead that goes up to stop her glasses getting away. A yellow lead.

I try as hard as I can to get away but she just holds me tighter. I need Mrs Steel to save me but she's not even looking, she's opening up the back of the car. It seems she hasn't been eating she says.

The black comes down slow but even like an old blind shutting out a summer night and I'm fighting not to be taken away and I'm trying not to think about why.

The Married Man

MY PHONE RANG and somehow I knew it was him. He'd be driving down a highway, heading — I hoped — into the city. Trevor removed his hand from the back of my head and grabbed the receiver.

'Don't stop,' he murmured, so I didn't.

'I'm sorry,' Trevor said to my caller, 'but Cameron is unavailable and will be for some time.'

As I reached to snatch the receiver from him I heard it drop back into the cradle. Trevor gave a grunt of laughter and grabbed my outstretched fingers; I felt the wetness of his mouth, then his teeth clamping down — but not quite enough to hurt. He didn't dare; my own mouth was full of him and his agony would have been much the greater.

I wasn't upset, though that was Trevor's intention. I pictured my darling man's state of mind as he considered the nature of my unavailability. Eyes expanding, zipper seam straining. Any moment now, I thought, he will ring back. I rearranged myself so that when he did I could reach the phone before Trevor, and my mind went into my commentary mode. (Sometimes, mothers, it is a social service to speak with one's mouth full.)

The mission at hand was markedly enhanced as I waited for him to call again. Trevor cried out, *Oh yes oh God oh Jesus*, and his eyes rolled out of orbit.

BUT MY DARLING Laurence didn't ring back and I couldn't ring him, didn't have the number. Wasn't allowed to have it. Secrecy bestowed such power — was that the point, or was he simply driven by the terror of being found out?

He disliked me raising such questions. If he wanted that psychological crap, he could get it at home.

'Stick to what you're so good at,' he'd say, repositioning my hand or head or arse. Who was I to protest? Or even point out that, where I was concerned, he had no need to manufacture power. I was more than happy to invest him with as much of it as he wished for. Subjugation brought out my best, most feminine, qualities. Just by stepping inside my door with that iron fist unclenching beneath his trousers, he had me servile and slavering.

HE DID NOT ring back, but the expectation that he would was, for that moment, enough. Trevor all but ceased to exist; my body was entangled with his, but my erogenous zones (and therefore, surely, my heart) were in a late-model white Subaru stationwagon. This, I now understood, was love.

HE LIKED PHONES; they were instant and anonymous. He preferred to listen, but was willing to talk in return. Nothing too creative. He could not be called a sophisticated man. He liked basic descriptions, with much smacking of lips, sighing and moaning. Before we met I never would have placed the telephone high on my list of erotic devices. Having crept, ungracefully, into late middle age, I imagined that my preferences and fancies were pretty much set in concrete. Yet within a few months, at the sound of his voice I would find myself dropping everything, so to speak, and turning into a telecommunications slut. He liked that. And I so very much liked the fact of him liking it.

It never did rival the real thing, but he was a busy man. There was his job as some kind of rural adviser. He travelled around the province talking to farmers and farm managers who fed him scones and leant beside him on lichen-covered gates that left greenish smudges on his cotton shirts. He refused to tell me more — afraid, I presume, that I might turn up at the door of the company he worked for and ruin his image as a regular man.

And perhaps, as things progressed, I would have. Certainly I checked out the Yellow Pages — Farm Management Consultants, and Farm Equipment and Machinery. I considered ringing them one by one and asking for Laurence, then a mumbled surname, hoping the receptionist would take the initiative and reward me. 'Laurence . . . Lovejoy?'

Lovejoy. In my dreams. Even the 'Laurence' could not be relied upon. In his own home he might be Brent, or John, or Andrew. He lived, of course, in the suburbs. Beckenham, he'd said. But even if it was true it told me little, Beckenham being a suburb of leafy streets and solid pre-war houses on the verge of becoming up-market but not quite, so that all kinds of people still live there. He shared the house with his wife (a social worker), a springer spaniel, and a seventeen-year-old schoolgirl daughter. An older daughter worked in Wellington. No names for them, but the springer spaniel was called Skywalker. He wouldn't, surely, have invented that.

Don't worry, I'd thought of it — walking the streets of Beckenham calling 'Skywalker, Skywalker' until the creature ran out to me or barked a response. Not that I have any fondness for dogs, or they for me.

I was appalled at these impulses to *know*. It had never happened to me in the past though, heaven knows, I was accustomed enough to furtive lovers.

Yet his need for secrecy seemed more desperate than theirs. Or was that just a part of the pleasure? The need to so rigidly exclude me from his 'real' life being testimony to the degradation I represented? He was an old-fashioned puritan, my Laurence; disgust and arousal were sides of the same coin and therefore equal in degree — the more disgusting, the more sublime.

This being the case, he must have been excessively disgusted by our mutual activities; for there was a point, I'd regularly observed, where his fabulous Tony Curtis features took on the luminosity of a choirboy who has just caught a glimpse — or a whiff — of the Almighty.

I attended chapel as a schoolboy. It was compulsory, but I would have gone anyway, since the combination of choral voices and the yellow sunlight shafting through the stained glass window was irresistibly euphoric. It's a sensation I've constantly sought to replicate — in my bed, on my sofa and the living-room rug, in public toilets, semi-secluded sand dunes, my cramped and humble Mitsubishi . . . More often than not I succeeded, or seemed to. In those few seconds before my semen blasted into the world I would glimpse paradise.

But not until Laurence came into my life did I *dwell* there. Truly, that's how it felt. A revelation. You think you have explored to the limits and then discover there is more. And beyond that, perhaps more again? The possibility of *limitless* rises like a moon to fill your mind. Obsession? Certainly. Over time his face, in my eyes, grew from merely handsome to beatific; *angelface, my angelface.*

I began studying myself with interest as I shaved, wanting to know what it was he saw there. And it felt as if I was looking with his eyes, for the angles and creases around my eye sockets and jaw looked like the product, not of age but of decadence. I detected a hitherto unremarked on resemblance to Peter O'Toole (pity about the height, but Laurence surely preferred the fact of having to stoop to kiss my lips).

AND YET, UP until that afternoon when Trevor took Laurence's call, I had still not admitted, even within myself, to love.

HE DIDN'T RING back. Not that day, not that week, or the next. Not even the week after that. Three weeks! He'd left it that long before, but this time it felt different. I was in anguish. It was as if we were a married couple who, for the first time ever, had gone to sleep on a quarrel. I felt frantic; this mustn't be allowed to happen. Yet what could I do?

At first I presented myself with the rational options. A — there had been some unreported rural crisis and he was terribly busy. B — he'd been called away to a family funeral. C — he'd caught a bad dose of the 'flu. (Images of him sweating between sheets, his rump and thigh bearing the small, damply engraved lines of creased bed linen, the pungent grassy smell of him. Oh, the waste of it when I could be nursing him, kissing him better in my very own bed. Asparagus soup and fresh linen. Nothing would be too much trouble; I'd take leave from work to tend and pamper.)

Then the perhaps equally rational, but much more disturbing, option. He had been ringing to tell me it was over. He'd met someone tastier, naughtier, better hung. Or the coin had finally settled on self-disgust and he'd given me up.

BUT, JOY. IT was none of those things.

'I was angry,' he said indistinctly though a regrettable cableknit jersey, pulling it over his head.

'Angry, Angelface?'

'Jealous.'

Jealous. A flutter of joy in my chest, running all the way down to my balls. I put on a look of disbelief.

'But you're the one with the wife.'

'Right, I know, it's not rational, but it's how I felt.' He stopped undressing and stood there looking perplexed. Unhappy, perhaps, about this unforeseen erosion of his power?

'So all this time you were sulking?' I couldn't restrain a smile.

Slowly he began to smile back. 'Sulking and wanking.'

He pulled me close and he kissed me. Mouth wide and hungry, lion devouring gazelle. Gazelle offering up her flesh — *let us prey.*

'Did you suffer?' He broke free to ask this. 'Did you miss me?'

He sounded plaintive. Reversing our roles. Was it all just a game?

'No,' I said. 'Hardly at all. Your absence was barely noted.'

A low moan. He liked that; I'd got it right.

'Why is that?' he whispered. 'What have you been doing? Tell me, tell me.'

I raised my hands, palms up, in a shrug. I pouted and arched my eyebrows — *where to start?*

He moaned again, scrabbling at his shirt. A button came away, bounced delicately on the polished floor. I made a note to look for it, sew it back on before he left. That way he couldn't go rushing off in his customary indecent haste, clothes hauled on almost as urgently as they'd been removed. Avoiding my eyes.

'You know me.' I fingered his nipple, the aureole sprouting grey hairs. 'Can't keep my hands to myself.'

'Were they gay?' He read the ironic crook of my eyebrows. 'Well, you know, queers?'

'Let's see.' I feigned deep thought. 'A couple of them.'

Queers didn't count for Laurence.

'And the others?'

'Oh, you know . . .' Folding my jeans, carefully. A thing he never did, just left them on the mat where they dropped. 'Married men.'

I watched his eyes, the flicker of tongue. Yes.

'The one who answered the phone?'

'Trevor? Yes. Married. Five kids.'

The truth, as it happened. I preferred them married. A nice wife who hasn't an inkling gives a husband that emotional edge. Besides, a married man was easily ditched when things got boring.

'What did you do? Tell me. Show me.'

DURING THOSE WEEKS when I was in coventry, our anniversary had come and gone. It was now one year and fifteen days since we met, and never had I felt bored with Laurence.

I'D FOUND HIM at the YMCA gymnasium, several months after my messy but inevitable break-up with Hugo, who is best forgotten. I'd not felt a need to get fit, but for a show of physical effort I was able, at the gym, to browse and exercise my imagination. Laurence wasn't the first I'd found there, but he was by far the best.

I noticed him the moment I entered. He was unfamiliar with the gym equipment, a late starter. I knew the scenario; he'd reached that mid-life stretch where a man looks in the mirror and panics; romance, youth, procreation, anticipation . . . it was all behind him, and ahead stretched a desert of routine and then death. Right now he was ready to snatch at anything that might delay the journey. Get into shape, climb a mountain, sleep around . . .

I caught his eye as he wiped the sweat from his temples. He gave me a rueful grin. *Unfit.*

Tell me about it, my smile commiserated. Bond established, so far so good.

A few moments later he looked across at me, a certain look, sustained. Then he broke the glance and pedalled insanely, head down, beating the devil out of the temple. *Oh yes*, I thought.

I contrived, of course, to follow him to the showers, stepped under the adjoining spray. Only a minor paunch and casually muscular arms. Long legs. Rumpled dick. A stream of hair from belly to groin. He watched me look him over and didn't turn away, but his glance down me was fast and furtive. Insultingly so. Despite myself, I'm still in good shape.

As we dried ourselves off I murmured, offhandedly, 'That earns me a drink.'

'What I was thinking,' he said. Towelling his hair. Loose dark curls just a little too long, grey at the temples.

I folded the towel and reached for my sweatshirt, bending low, taking my time.

'The Dux is handy.'

'Fine,' he said. 'The Dux.'

He held the bar door open for me and bought the first round. We talked like any two strangers in a pub. Our jobs, our living arrangements (I had to ask), the price of joining a gym, the difficulty in finding the time and motivation to go regularly. We chatted, but the desired tension was there. I bought the second round and, as I placed the glasses down, he asked, avoiding my eyes, 'Why me?'

'I liked the look of you.'

'I mean, what made you think that I might . . .'

Does it show? Poor Laurence. I was sorely tempted to make him suffer. *Honey, it's clear as day. Written all over you.*

'Intuition,' I said.

We went back to my place. Afterwards he fled, not looking me in the face. Three weeks later he knocked on my door. My sister was staying with me, only for the weekend. I invited him in, but just for a beer. He declined. I walked with him to his car and gave him my phone number, which he wrote on a parking ticket. I kissed him quickly on the lips.

His visits, every two or three weeks, began to take on undue importance. There were also the calls; mostly from his cell phone, but occasionally — wicked and treacherous — from his home. For him I dug up my salacious past and embellished it with remembered segments of porno movies and a little imagination. His need to hear things said was insatiable, perhaps a trifle pathetic but *endearing* was my translation.

He no longer went to the gym — it had served its purpose. I sometimes did, but the few resulting liaisons felt oddly vicarious. The excitement lay in the retellings, the reenactments.

Once, when I'd stopped at a money machine on my way to work, he walked right past me. He was alone, he saw me, and walked right on. It hurt. He would never agree to us meeting for a drink somewhere, or even walking together. For that first year there was only sex; he'd burst in through my door, shedding clothes like leaves in an autumn storm. Afterwards he'd snatch up his garments and rush to the bathroom to wash and dress. Reappear, mumbling and mortified, to leave almost as urgently as he'd arrived.

That is, until the Trevor incident. After that he allowed himself to be a little kind to me, which pleased us both. He was — and I'd always sensed this — a naturally affectionate man. He began to bring me small gifts — pickles, a mango, a bottle of wine — and would sometimes drop by for coffee and a chat as if we were simply friends. I was pathetically grateful for those visits, and though I learned nothing more about his home and family, my need to know diminished.

ONE MORNING I'M woken by the chalk-on-blackboard screech of my doorbell. Ten twenty, but it's my week on late shift. I'm expecting no one so I decide it's the Mormons or Jehovah's Witness and ignore it. But then there is knocking. I go in my nightshirt by way of rebuke, though I know this has no effect — to be asleep in the daytime, for no matter what reason, proclaims sloth and turpitude

It's Laurence. It is only two days since he was in my bed, and he knows this is my sleeping time.

'Darling, what a surprise! Come in.'

But he just stands there. 'She knows.'

'Oh dear,' I babble. 'Come in. You've spoiled my beauty sleep already. I'll make us a coffee — or does this require something stronger? Coffee, right. Sit down, darling, it's not the end of the world. Now are you sure? How could she know?'

'I told her.' He's staring at me in a kind of disbelief, as if stunned by his own stupidity. I sense he's expecting me to somehow sort this thing out for him. I'm incredulous, until I realise that married men are used to having things sorted out for them. It hasn't occurred to him that this isn't just his crisis — that I might also be concerned. Angry even.

'How very intelligent of you!' I set out two saucers, two cups. I shut the cupboard door too hard.

'Cameron, I had no choice.'

I hear the guilt brimming, about to spill over. I don't want to know. Let's keep this pertinent. 'So it's over, then?'

'Us?' A short laugh, as if that's of no account. *'She and I might be over.'*

Such self-pity. Such terror.

'Perhaps,' I swirl hot water in the plunger, 'you should have kept it to yourself.'

'I couldn't. She sort of found out.'

The wife had been on some social worker mission of mercy, delivering a client home from Accident and Emergency. Saw his Subaru parked in my driveway, the number plate. Asked Laurence some innocent questions about his day and they didn't tally. Accusation and denial. A night awake in separate beds — the first time in their whole revoltingly happy marriage — reduced him to confession.

'You could've been a little inventive?'

'She thought that I was having an affair. Another woman. I saw that the truth would be less hurtful.'

'How thoughtful. And what exactly did you tell her? "It's all right, love, I'm only bonking a queer?"'

Which earned me a don't-be-mean look.

'It was still a hell of a shock to her.'

'So what did she say?'

'Not a lot, actually. AIDS, of course, she was worried . . . Said she needs time to work out how she feels.' His voice crumbling at the edges. 'I don't want to lose her.' His eyes have moistened and are staring at me in accusation. 'I love her. I really do. And there's the kids. Everything. I must've been crazy to risk all that.'

The past tense, I notice.

'If she throws you out there's always a bed for you here.'

I have the decency not to look hopeful, but it's still not what he wants to hear.

And what about me?

'So — no more naughty?' I say it lightly, but my heart is banging about like a shutter in a storm.

He gives me a puppy look of regret and sudden longing. I run a finger down his cheek and along his bottom lip. He sucks my finger into his mouth and bites softly. His eyes slide down to my moving parts.

'One for the road?' I offer.

FOR THE FIRST time he returns from the bathroom to dress in front of me. He gives me a smile and a lover's kiss goodbye.

TWO DAYS LATER he phoned. 'Hi. How are you? What are you doing?'

'None of your business — you've given me up.' Then hope, and flesh, stirring. 'Darling, she's thrown you out!'

'No. Actually, things are great between us. We've talked and talked, it's brought us closer. She doesn't mind me seeing you now and again. Are you busy?'

THE URGENCY WAS gone. He chatted, he smiled, he licked.

'What is this?' I said. 'Foreplay?'

'No hurry,' he soothed.

It wasn't the same. I watched his beloved face as he came. No roar, no bulging eyes, no obliterating moment. A spasm, a whimper. Well, I told myself, he's been under stress.

He lay on my bed, unwashed, shed condom trapped in the palm of his hand.

'She'd seen men looking at me in that way. That's what she said. It's been estimated that one male in three is a practising or potential bisexual.'

'*Really!*'

My leer, if noticed, was ignored. He was frowning. 'I don't know how they worked that out. But anyway. So long as I'm not emotionally involved — that's what she said.'

'Your wife is obviously very broad-minded.'

Nodding happily, proud of her. 'Should've told her from the start.' He smiled. 'She wants to meet you.'

Oh lord. 'I don't know about that.'

He took my hand. 'It's okay, Cameron. She's a good person. You'll like her.'

Well, I owed her, didn't I? Here we were touching, talking. The tenderness I'd so often longed for. 'I guess we could all go for a drink some time?'

He kissed my cheek.

At the door he said, 'I'll give you a ring.'

'Right.'

Why didn't I ask, then, for his phone number? His full name?

Three weeks passed. In the meantime Tim had walked into my life on a work transfer. We looked at each other over the registry counter; simultaneous eye contact. I gave him room 224 overlooking the river.

Laurence rang.

'It's me. How's things?'

Ooh. I hadn't got over him. Tim was nothing, no one.

'Great,' I said. 'Just great. And you? Feeling a little bit naughty, are we?'

'*Naughty?*' As if he was weighing the word in his palm, finding it . . . absurd. 'About that drink we were all going to have. Can we make it a meal?'

'A meal! Good gracious. Who will eat who?'

'You'll have to behave yourself,' he said.

HEATHER (YES HEATHER) had chosen the restaurant. A wine bar with an intimate little eatery in the back. She was anxious for my approval.

'Lovely,' I murmured.

Any hunger I'd felt had vanished the moment I saw them there cosily knee to knee. Jealousy a splash of acid in my gut, spilling out into my veins, promoting another appetite.

Heather was charming, really she was. Wanting to know about my life, my job, my star sign. Laurence was quiet. We threw each other the occasional longing looks, but his felt less than convincing. More for her benefit that mine? Or perhaps he was feeling threatened by the chumminess of us two girls chatting away.

I refilled Heather's wine glass. Her third. We'd got on to

snow — should we expect it that coming winter? She thought yes, Laurence thought no; I felt the clammy breath of boredom.

'Frankly,' I said, 'I don't give a shit one way or the other.'

Heather gave a cracking laugh that turned the heads of the well-dressed couple at the other table. Then she knocked back two-thirds of her wine, and leant towards me to confess she was 'a little bit jealous' of my 'relationship' with Larry.

'I call him Laurence,' I said. 'It's *that* kind of relationship.'

She wasn't reassured. Laurence reached for her hand, the one with the cluster of ownership rings.

'There's no reason.' He looked into her eyes. 'Truly.'

'No reason at all,' I said. 'To Laurence I've never been more than an optional extra.'

I saw Heather only just stifle her instinct to deny, to comfort, to reassure — *Oh but I'm sure that's not true!* — and I felt the need to intensify her discomfort.

'He's ashamed of me and what we do. So ashamed he's never even given me his phone number.'

'Oh! Oh, that's no good.' Heather gave me a motherly look. *There, there!* 'Don't worry, from now on it's going to be different.'

She reached down for her bag — a scruffy suede number long past its use-by date — and fumbled in its depths for a pen. She wrote the phone number on a paper napkin. Laurence became suddenly interested in the framed poster above us — Charles Laughton, no less. I watched the small pulse in his throat throbbing in agitation and stifled a smirk of triumph.

'There.' Heather gave me the napkin. 'Out in the open. Consenting adults and all that.' A shy sort of smile, just for me. 'Friends, Cameron?'

'Friends,' I reaching to squeeze the hand that Laurence had recently held.

'Let's drink to that.' I topped up our glasses with dry white and we clinked them together — mine and hers, hers and his, his and mine. Eyes meeting, merging, in that same order.

'Friends,' we murmured.

I was happy, disarmed by their eager, artless affection. I

smiled at Laurence. 'I can see why you love her. I think I do too.'

Heather laughed in a pleased but embarrassed way, and Laurence smiled back at me — an unguarded adolescent kind of smile that was new to me, and agonisingly attractive. I held his eyes and I puckered my mouth. Heather watched. Laurence checked her out with a sidelong glance, then blew me a kiss. Heather's mouth smiled at us beneath glazed grey eyes.

They offered to drive me home but I make it a point to walk as much as I can. It was, at most, fifteen minutes to my apartment. I walked with them to the car and gave each of them a hug. Laurence kissed me. On the lips. Not a lingering kiss, but a kiss none the less.

'See you soon,' we told each other. I waltzed home on footpaths golden with fallen leaves, euphoric.

TWENTY-FOUR DAYS went by. Winter had arrived. My apartment, though well heated, felt cluttered and dark. I'd copied his phone number into my tartan-covered address book, but I should not be the one to call.

Tim had left the hotel to share a flat with a morose and recently separated colleague. We still saw each other, in a casually regular kind of way. Touching, kissing, entering Tim I would think of Laurence.

ON THE TWENTY-FIFTH day I abandoned all pride. Heather answered the phone, seemed happy enough to hear my voice. We chatted for a few minutes about how busy we'd been and the increasing likelihood of snow.

'I guess you want to speak to Larry? Just a minute. Darling.' Not quite a shout, so he must have been nearby. Then a muzzling of the mouthpiece, but not sufficient to obliterate the sound of her voice coaxing, his refusing. And, far in the background, a dog barking. Skywalker. Then Heather was back with me.

'Cameron, I'm sorry. He's . . . ah . . . kind of busy at the . . . Hang on.' A door was closed, her voice became intimate. 'Look, are you still there? Cameron, I think it's best to be honest. The thing is Larry says he's kind of gone off . . . I think it was a phase he went through, if you know what I mean, some kind of mid-life crisis. I'm sorry, Cameron, and he should be telling you this himself. I enjoyed meeting you, it was a nice evening we had. I really am sorry.'

I was seeing her face; the way she'd leant across the table, those forthright grey eyes. My hand was trembling. I was trembling.

'*Are* you, Heather? *Are you really?*'

She was shocked. 'What do you mean?'

I hung up. *Figure it out for yourself, bitch.* Twenty-two years together — she knew how his mind worked. *No secrets*, she'd cooed. *Everything out in the open. Friends.*

How calculated. How cunning she was! You almost had to admire . . .

I was sorely tempted to ring straight back. Let her answer. Hiss down the line in her husband's voice, *Suck my dick.*

IT'S WINTER AGAIN. My new lover wears forest green tights beneath his shredded jeans, and unlaced boots. He calls it fashion. He's unemployed, but obliged, through the courts, to spend his mornings at an anger management course. On the advice of the anger management counsellor he began working out at the YM. Just as promised, it changed his life direction.

I've introduced him to opera, olives and feta cheese. Despite his choice of clothes he's open to new experiences. In some ways he reminds me of myself when I was his age, although it's difficult for me to convey, and for him to grasp, how different things were back then.

Last night I took him on a tour of my old haunts, some of them places I'd all but forgotten. A number of the pubs and clubs have been torn down, others remodelled beyond recognition.

We drove to a certain park, the public toilets. I hadn't been there in thirty-five years but the park and the building looked unchanged. My young man said he was familiar with the place from his schooldays, when he and his friends would stand on each other's shoulders to look in through the gap between roof and concrete wall.

'It's the pits,' he said. 'You'd'a had to be bloody desperate.'

'It was different then. The risk was only of being arrested. And losing your job, your friends . . .'

He wasn't listening. '*Gladiators* will be nearly started.'

As we drove off I saw a white Subaru stationwagon pulling up. I went a few metres, did a U-turn, drove back. Perspiration beaded the edge of my hairline.

'Gladiators, Cam-moron!' He leant to look at my watch. 'We got two minutes to get there.'

Laurence had got out of the car and was walking away from the streetlights towards the toilets. Over a year had gone by but just seeing him again my stomach knotted.

'You're fucking me off, Cam.'

'Okay, okay.'

He was no longer in sight. Concrete underfoot, black water trapped in the hollow beneath the handbasin. The dank, distinctive smell of rotting pine needles and ammonia. Two cubicles and the rough hole gouged between them. No reason to suppose anything had changed.

I drove my young man home and watched him watching rippling bodies performing decent and criminally meaning-less acts with knotted ropes and disabled escalators. I thought of ringing the wife to wise her up and gloat, but what good would it do?

An Alternative Life

IT WAS AS if the grime began to grow like moss from the moment Diane got her mother's letter.

Before that the cottage had looked cosy and bright, and somehow honest. Definitely clean. But after she'd read the letter she began to see grime everywhere and the sight of it brought a dry and bitter taste to her mouth.

She went around all the shelves and windowsills with a damp cloth and a bottle of Jif but it was only partly effective. The cracks and corners were full of scunge, like dirty finger-nails. If she examined it closely and identified the different ingredients — dead ants and a few larger insects of unknown species, the stickiness of spilt sugared coffee, green wood mould, hair — it seemed less repulsive. But for the most part she just saw it as grime and it brought a ripple of nausea to her stomach. She took her scissors and scraped the corners and cracks with the narrowest blade. The stuff came out like plasticine.

All that week she made these special cleaning efforts on shelves she hadn't noticed for months, but it only seemed to encourage the spread of the dirt, the way trimming is supposed to make hair grow faster and stronger. The cottage had begun to seem less and less cosy and bright and honest; more and more dilapidated and grubby.

She knew it was all in her mind. She kept trying to take her vision back to seeing the place the way it used to be. Not when they had first moved in, when it had been sullen with disuse — littered with broken fishing rods and rusty biscuit tins and funny little chipped enamel candleholders. Two smashed windows and a sea of old newspapers, yellow and rat-shredded. Not that way, but the way they had made it. For Mike had put new glass in the windows and repaired the broken fireplace and tacked hessian around the walls of the main room. And he had brought home a chair from the dump, which Diane had covered with a crocheted wool rug in bright reds and oranges.

Someone had given them an old wooden table and Mike had sawed off the legs so they could eat sitting on the floor. A spare mattress, folded in three, made an easy chair. Like their bed, it was covered with Indian printed cotton that looked at the same time bright yet faded. They had pulled up the filthy tattered carpet and scrubbed the boards underneath.

The warm, clean look of the wood had always pleased her, though the cracks between were large and ominously dark. They had got the old wood stove in working order and a friend had lent them the tilly lamp that hung from the rafters, giving Mike just enough light to work by when he's in the mood.

She had felt so fond of their cottage; it was bothersome to have it change so suddenly, slide into another perspective. Diane wanted to hope that, by wiping and scraping at the dirt, she could transform it back to the homely little nest it had seemed.

Her mother's letter said that the train got in at 5.30 p.m. on Friday the 16th. *I do hope I'm not being a nuisance, but it seems so long since I've seen you.*

On that Friday Diane got up unreasonably early, considering that Wednesday and Thursday she went into the township to work in the fruit shop and Fridays she usually slept in a bit. Fridays she had nothing to do but tidy the cottage and cook the evening meal and maybe put in some time on the vegetable garden if it was a fine day. She never slept in for long. If she stayed in bed until late morning, as Mike almost always did, her day would seem to consist of nothing but making a meal and tidying up. A wasted day. With the extra time she gave herself by getting up earlier she would go for a walk, or do the garden, or write letters to people she used to know. It wasn't so very much but somehow it made a big difference.

Still in her nightdress and warm from bed, she lit the stove and filled the kettle. While it was heating — the stove took forever to get hotted up in the mornings — she tidied the kitchen and the main room, though there was little to tidy, and found some terrifying new areas of dirt. The back of the taps; how was it she'd never noticed that there it was thick with rubbery dirt? She had to scrape it first with a knife or she would have been rubbing away for hours.

The night before, after they'd finished tea — and she was tired, too, from a day standing in the shop and the bus ride to and from work — she had removed the books from their bookcase, all of them, and dusted their tops and wiped down the shelves. Mike had sat watching her with a slight, mocking smile he seemed to be trying to suppress. (He's pretending to be trying to suppress it, she thought.) The night before they'd talked about her sudden obsession with dirt. Insecurity, Mike said. And she had thought, Well, he's probably right — she couldn't remember ever having felt what she'd describe as secure — but knowing you felt insecure did nothing to help your insecurity.

Don't you see, he'd demanded, that you're being hypocritical? The dirt doesn't really bother you. It hasn't before. So why are you pretending to be something you're not?

Maybe, she'd said — though she didn't believe it — maybe I just want to please my mother because I'm fond of her. Mike had raised his eyebrows in an exaggerated way. Comical despair over her silly hang-ups.

It was a favourite reaction of his. She sometimes wondered if she oughtn't to find it offensive, but the truth was she didn't. In fact it made her feel loved and protectively enclosed. It made her laugh at herself and relax a bit. And he hardly ever did it when they had company.

Later she'd tried to tell him some of the things she felt about her mother's visit, though it was just a jumble of thoughts, none of them clear in her head. You have to consider, she said, how *she* will see things; the cottage itself, the loo way out there in the bush, the being so far from everything and no transport except the bus and that a fair walk away.

I mean, said Diane, she's been very good so far about you and me and the moving here and everything. I just think we should . . . well, you know, try and meet her halfway sort of thing.

What she wanted to say was, I think you should get up earlier while she's here and do a few hours on your leather-work — four, or even five, a day — so it looks like you're actually making some kind of living at it, the way I've said you are in my letters. And maybe you could even dig the garden a bit and cut back the jasmine so we can walk out to the letter-box without getting scratched in the face. Or just do *something* so that you look just a little bit energetic because that kind of thing's important to my mother.

But she couldn't possibly say such things to Mike. He would lecture her about her uptightness and the importance of personal freedom and her tendency to be rigid and judgemental. Yet at the same time it was Mike who always insisted that you should say exactly what was on your mind. The trouble was that the things on Diane's mind were almost always things which Mike considered totally trivial.

When she did mention them he always seemed slightly surprised that anyone could harbour such mundane thoughts, let alone muster the energy to express them.

Still, he'd been quite willing to discuss her mother's visit, which he considered to be of some academic interest — the filial struggle for independence. You'll have to stand up for yourself, he said. Make it clear to your mother that she has no right to interfere in your life. Explain to her that this is the kind of life you have freely chosen, that you have your own values and priorities.

It's not that simple, she thought, but there didn't seem any point in saying so.

As she scrubbed at the back of the bench (though she'd already done it only three days before) she wondered why it was that Mike seemed to be —and to always have been — immune to the niggling complexities of human relationships. She had met his father only once. In fact he had taken them both out to dinner at an expensive restaurant that had one wall entirely covered in deep red velvet. He had been polite but distant, as though his mind was elsewhere. She had thought he was like an adult taking a couple of kids on a picnic, prepared to share their conversations but preferring not to.

Diane had never met Mike's mother. She visualised her as a kind of extension of his father. Elegant, remote and rich (which they were — they wrote to their son in turn; brief letters containing brisk sentences about the activities of people he'd gone to school with, and always a couple of crisp twenty-dollar notes inside). Diane didn't think about Mike's parents often. She had never really known any rich people and she rather believed they were a different species.

It was the explanation she gave herself for the things about Mike that annoyed or bewildered her (and sometimes that seemed to cover everything about him). Most of all she attributed his amazing confidence to his parents' wealth. She could imagine the family sitting down to dinner when Mike and his sister were younger; the very air around them had a crystal clarity, the conversation was positively crisp and the silences were positively silent.

Her own family, when she put them in that same situation, were surrounded by a haze of hesitations, self-doubts; the air was heavy with second thoughts censoring first thoughts that had never been voiced. Even the silences were fuzzy with discomfort.

Mike's confidence impressed and frightened Diane. It lay across her mind in precisely the way his body lay across their bed at nights — diagonal and spreadeagled, leaving her to apologetically occupy one corner. When she pointed this out in the mornings he would be sorry and a bit amused. And of course it wasn't deliberate. Perhaps it was, if anything, her fault for not being more *substantial* as person. Everybody else's ideas seemed to intrude on her own. Her head contained so many ways of looking at things, how could she settle on any one perspective and say, This is mine?

Did she like the way they lived? Sometimes she knew she did.

She liked the garden she had built. She liked the silence, she liked walking on earth instead of asphalt, she liked the smell of things infinitely growing, and the country moon. She used to like the cottage. And she preferred their friends here to the people she'd known in Wellington during her four years at the insurance office.

Lonely years; when she looked back on them she saw them that way. Yet there had been a kind of security in the normality of her life then. Her job, the flat she shared with quiet, creeping Ellen, the boyfriends she'd gone around with . . . there had been a rightness about it all. She'd never had to balance up the pros and cons of the way she lived, or worry whether the advantages her mind kept discovering weren't, in fact, merely justifications.

THE KITCHEN WAS clean. She was satisfied of that. It still looked somehow scungy, but this couldn't be helped. Kitchens with wood stoves and rough board shelves could never compete with the gleaming formica palaces of suburbia. Her mother would surely realise that.

In the main room she had piled Mike's jeans and sandals on the table while she swept the floor. She gathered them up and took them into the bedroom. Mike was asleep with the blankets gathered round his head, his mouth open and joined by a thread of spittle to the pillowcase. It always made her angry, the way he slept so peacefully while she tidied the house. She took a drawer and slammed it as loudly as she could. He opened his eyes, looked at her without expression and closed them again.

If she shook him awake he would be in a mood for the rest of the morning, and yet he ought to be working. There were three orders for handbags and the shop in town was happy to take all the belts and small purses he could turn out. And, God knows, the money would help. We're getting by okay, Mike would say if she nagged him. Which they were sort of, but only because of her job in the fruit shop, which she didn't enjoy at all. Or he would say they should spend less, eat more pipis and cockles. Or maybe he'd say, yes, he really was going to get on to the bags tomorrow but today he wasn't in that kind of mood but tomorrow he was really going to get into it and work like a demon for a couple of weeks.

Or he might say, disarmingly, Oh I'm a lazy bugger, such a lazy bugger. I'm lucky you don't go off and just leave me to rot in bed forever.

And, much as his laziness exasperated her, she was also, in a way, grateful for it because sometimes it seemed his only human flaw. He was so clever and good-looking and witty, and he could do anything — mend the electrical wiring, get motors going, write poetry, bake bread, play the guitar . . . anything he set his mind to when the mood was right.

She didn't question whether she'd done the right thing in leaving her job and coming away with him. There had seemed no alternative once she knew him. He'd said they'd fix up this little old neglected house he'd come across. She'd agreed because it was inevitable, she knew that in her bones. Even if it turned out badly for her, she had to go with him.

And it hadn't turned out badly. Except that now she had the feeling that her mother's visit was going to make it seem that it had.

She could, perhaps, have faced the prospect of her mother with some degree of confidence if it hadn't been for the baby. She suspected her mother was coming only because Diane had written that she was pregnant. The baby made Diane feel both vulnerable and defensive. She might be able to justify her own life in this cottage, but was it right for a baby?

SHE COULD PICTURE her mother waving the foetus about like a weapon, wanting to know how her daughter could dream of bringing a child into such a primitive set-up.

She knew the right answers. Love was the important thing. A child didn't need electricity, didn't need possessions. A child needed love, and that they would give it. (Or would they? She would love it, surely, but Mike might do so only when he was in the mood. Which could be once a month. She supposed she and Mike would be better parents than some, but what kind of basis was that for child-raising?)

Perhaps, if she worked out a strategy of defence, she could give an impression of confidence? Her mother, after all, was no dragon. Just an ordinary woman, not unduly opinionated or overbearing. She was, in fact, somewhat diffident. It ran in the family. Even if she was seething with disapproval she would have difficulty putting it into words.

She'll wait, thought Diane, until we're doing the dishes tomorrow night. Mike will be huddled in a corner plinking on his guitar. She'll be standing there with the grey-white teatowel and she'll be wearing a beige skirt and a blue blouse. She'll say, Darling, I don't want you to feel I'm interfering or anything but I can't help wondering if you've got any idea at all of how hard it will be when you're trying to cope with a new baby in this . . .

Or perhaps she'll just get that tight look and drop the occasional ambiguous phrase. Then when she's leaving she'll crush some money into my hand and say, conspiratorially, Do come home for a visit soon, Di. Perhaps you could come down when it's due and stay for a while (forever) and have a rest?

She might be terse with Mike or too obviously polite. Her concern might drift between the three of them like an uneasy cloud, causing Diane to weep in bed at night and hold unsatisfactory whispered conversations with Mike, who would find her tears intriguing.

If her mother did raise the matter in a way that demanded some reply, how should Diane respond? I'll be defensive, she thought. And that's the very thing I shouldn't be. I'll start chattering wildly about all the orders Mike's getting and the plans we have for setting up a workshop and putting a sign out on the road. I won't be able to stop myself.

Perhaps she could bring the subject up herself? In a light way, to show she was aware of her situation but in control. Mike, she could say in a warm voice, is incredibly lazy but . . .

But what? But it's only a phase and he plans to change? But that's a comparatively minor fault? But I love him?

The last was by far the best, but she couldn't make a bald statement like that to her mother, who never uttered words that weren't suitably dressed.

Maybe, as Mike had advised, attack would be the best strategy. I don't know, she would say to her mother (they would be doing the dishes again), I don't know how you can bear to live in the city among all those meaningless and soulless possessions of yours. When I look back on my childhood, you know, I'm amazed that I came out of it remotely sane. I'd never bring a child of mine up in that kind of environment.

The thought of saying those things out loud made Diane grin. She reran the words as she poured herself a cup of tea. She tried to give her mother a convincing reaction. Was it possible that she, also, would laugh? That they'd laugh together?

And she saw herself and her mother sitting, giggling together, on one side of the table and Mike on the other side. And Mike, on his side of the table, looked so very alone that she had to shake the picture out of her mind and pour a second cup of tea. Then she took them both into the bedroom.

THIS TIME SHE looked at his sleeping face and felt only happiness. She put the cups beside the bed, pulled back the bedclothes and slid herself in beside him. His arms went round her. You're dressed, he said with disappointment.

Here's a cup of tea beside the bed, she whispered.

Never mind, he said, unbuttoning her skirt, if we're brave and we ignore it it might go away. Why did you get dressed?

I've been up for ages. She was smiling because of his joke, repeating it to herself as she struggled to slide her skirt off. I thought, she said, that I had a lot of things to do but I must have been wrong.

She lay still, looking at the pink glass beading they had hung from the ceiling, the smile still with her, the warmth of Mike's hand sliding up under her shirt.

Of course you were wrong, he murmured and she stiffened a little, noticing at the same time the huge cobweb that stretched from the glass beads right to the far corner of the room.

The National School of Beauty Therapy

YOU RING WORK and tell them you have a temperature, you think it's a bug. Your son — the one who is doing a small business course and therefore still living at home — overhears on his way back from the bathroom, and tells you he also feels crook; he almost barfed in the handbasin. The way he says it you know he holds you responsible for wanton contagion.

You don't tell him you're just taking a sickie; you've always tried to lead by example. Besides he would want to know why.

There are brown marks in the toilet bowl, no bigger than fly spots but harder to shift. You wonder why you are the only person in the household who is capable of lifting a brush to slosh the bowl clean at the time. And you wonder if it was the pork pieces, since you couldn't remember how long they had been in the fridge. Your own bowels are fine — but now you remember that all you ate that particular night was a couple of cheese-flavoured crackers. You've had no appetite since *that* Friday.

Odd how, in one brief moment, a life can be tossed into the air and then land in a barely recognisable form. Whisky and cask wine are now your primary caregivers; you can't imagine how you might get through the day without them. Food is an addiction you once had but certainly don't miss. You haven't yet tried, but it's very likely that already you would fit into the last pair of jeans you ever bought. From a factory shop in Marshlands Road — a pair for you and a pair for the youngest son, who still had a plaster cast on his leg, so he would have been eleven. Nine years ago.

There is always, you think as you run a wet cloth around the plastic seat, a plus, a silver lining.

YOU STRAIGHTEN THE duvet on your bed and marvel at how

smooth the sheets have remained, at how little impression is made when you sleep alone. Then you remember that you were only in bed for, at most, four hours. Unable to sleep, or read, or watch television, you got up and cleaned the pantry shelves. An exceptionally clean house is, surely, another plus. Not a large one.

You sit for a time on the bedroom chair that normally never gets used. Your mind drifts into a kind of sluggish backwater where nothing is going on, but outside time is passing at speed. This is a state your former self was unfamiliar with. From time to time you glance across at the mirror, hoping to catch your reflection unawares and see yourself as he sees you. You're waiting for your at-home son to leave for his course, so you can go out and humiliate yourself in a public street.

Of course you may not actually go, you may just intend to and leave it at that. But now you have a whole day for yourself and your home, like the food in your pantry, has lost all its attractions. Being there fills you with impatience.

Your son's door is closed. You knock and go in. The smell of unaired sheets and unwashed socks seems, suddenly, more stimulating, more *real*, than your own rituals with picked jasmine and old-fashioned roses. Your son is in bed with a comic book at the end of his nose. He is, surely, too old to be reading comic books. You tell him he'll ruin his eyesight. You're only aware that you've said this when you see him sigh and roll his eyes. Critical observations, you have to suppose, dribble constantly from your mouth without you knowing. You resemble a tap with a faulty washer.

'Your course,' you remind him.

'I told you. I've caught your bug.'

'I could give you a lift in.'

'I thought you were sick?'

'I am,' you say, 'but I've got things to do.'

You notice the way his shoulderblades jut and the creamy skin of his inner arm. You notice how even his freckles look brand new.

He is almost the same age as her. Crumpled sheet over pliant, peach-ripe flesh. That thought ignites inside you and explodes like a Double Happy.

Quickly — but not indifferently — you get yourself dressed. Leggings and the lemon shirt that covers your thighs. You decided on these last night before you gave up on trying to sleep and began on the pantry. You're aiming for a look that doesn't shout middle-aged yet is nonchalant. She must not have the satisfaction of thinking that you have been driven to a tragic attempt to compete with her at this level.

You're standing in front of a Christian bookshop. Directly across the road is the National School of Beauty Therapy. You look at the titles in the bookshop window — *Go the Distance, Timeless Treasures, Soul Management* — and wonder if she is a reader of books and, if so, what kind. You've never met a beauty therapist, let alone a beauty therapy student. When Greer heard what she did and sniggered it made you feel much better, but Greer, as your friend, is obliged to be totally unobjective.

The school opens at 10 a.m., but students are required to be there ten minutes before. You know all this because you rang the School of Beauty Therapy for details of their course, claiming a daughter with an interest in the field. Their brochure, when it arrived, made you glad that you had not, in your own youth, desired to be a beauty therapist. Students were required to wear uniforms, and the school rules took up two whole pages.

The brochure contained grievous grammatical errors, a fact that gave you unreasonable satisfaction.

You cross the road to stand just outside the entrance to the building that houses the beauty school. You are looking out for a young woman with blonde hair, neither short nor long. Shoulder length, you imagine. She is tall — exactly his height, which is five eleven — and slender and (naturally) beautiful. She may or may not be called Emily; your husband is protective of her. The less you know, the safer she is. Just what is it he imagines you might do to her?

You're not even certain about the National School of Beauty Therapy, except that Greer remembered seeing him one afternoon around four, standing almost where you are standing now. Driving past, she'd tooted, but he'd failed to look her way. In retrospect, she found that significant.

You put this together with the one piece of information you felt certain of — the beautician training — and consulted the Yellow Pages. Bingo.

Twenty is the age you were when you got married. Twenty-two years and three sons ago. You weren't sure, at the time, if it was love or just fantastic sex. Only time, you thought, could tell.

Time said love. Emphatically. You only had to look at the relationships that other people put up with. At social events you would still gaze around with available eyes and choose him over everyone present. After twenty-two years and three sons the sex was perhaps less consuming than the need to have the lawn mowed, but there were compensations suited to your stage in life. Children, companionship, stability, affection.

You were lucky; you felt it in your bones, and other people told you so. Lucky, but not complacent. How could you be, when every year it got harder to think of anyone who hadn't split up and found someone new (not necessarily in that order). And then maybe split up again. In the midst of so much wreckage and turmoil how could anyone not know they were sailing in dangerous times, treacherous waters?

Perhaps that was why you'd got to feeling a little benumbed. Sometimes things in the books you read and the movies you saw (and you had more time to pursue these independent pleasures now that you and he were past the obsessional inter-dependency of earlier years) made you tremble, yearn or weep. Other people's passion would blow a draught of air on the charcoal embers of your own, causing a glow and a flicker, but never a great leaping explosion of flame. Yet you would remember, would *seem* to remember, holocaust, incandescence.

Sometimes you found yourself wanting to know how it would feel to split up.

TWO YOUNG WOMEN cross the street, heading towards you. They wear tailored dark blue skirts and jackets. Air hostess uniforms, you think disparagingly; out-of-date, conservative, dreary. You wonder why and by whom they were chosen.

Both young women have dark hair. They enter the building, and wait in the foyer for the lift. You also enter the foyer and study the list of occupants on the marbled wall. The National School of Beauty Therapy is on the seventh floor, between a solicitor and the Alzheimers Society.

Four young women come in together, just in time to catch the lift. You barely get to look them over. Two are Asian, one is Maori or at least Polynesian, but the other is blonde — you try not to stare. She is no taller than you, and plump. They're holding the lift, waiting for you. Flustered, you smile and gesture them on their way.

You will watch the numbers for where the lift stops, just to be sure. Seven.

Classes at the National School of Beauty Therapy are, they told you, small, with twelve students at most.

A MAN IN a suit enters; cell phone, briefcase, the works. You look towards the street as if you're expecting someone — which of course you are. You don't want a repeat of the lift-holding business.

Three more trainee beauty therapists scamper in giggling and rolling their eyes. For an irrational second you think that somehow they know who you are and why you are there, but as they jiggle and groan over the lift's slow arrival you realise that their laughter is the nervous kind, and concerns the repercussions of being late. A strawberry blonde, her hair in a ponytail. But she can't, surely, be twenty? And you couldn't say, even in kindness, that she was beautiful.

You walk back out the glass door and onto the street. The clock above the watch shop shows three minutes to ten. Either she arrives at class very early or she's running late. If she is late, why is she late? What has kept her?

Your husband has moved into Minka and Tom's sleepout in order to think things through. In other words, *to choose*. For the last eight days and nights, you conjecture, he has been writing out lists of pros and cons, comparing the demands of conscience and libido, and unsettling Tom with the irrepressible note of prize-winner pride that sneaks into his voice whenever he talks of her. So young. So lovely. So eager to please.

Is she, too, appalled by his indecision? He knows what he wants — he wants you both. An option she's grown accustomed to and is content to accept. You are the problem. Your refusal to be as accommodating.

You, too, have decisions to make and feel incapable of making them. You surely must understand, he pleads, that he is not in a state capable of thinking things through in a rational way. You concede that point — he looks exhausted. But when you consider what it is that has exhausted him you want to smash him around the head with something jagged and heavy. He was wise to move in with Minka and Tom. These rather exciting waves of insanity keep crashing upon you. You could be compelled to smother or strangle during the night.

You can't sleep, at most an hour here or there, yet you have an extraordinary supply of energy. He remarked, the day he moved out, on the amount of energy you had. He said that was his principal reason for going: he had a backlog of sleep to catch up on and you wouldn't leave him alone.

He told the resident son that he was taking a fishing trip up the Rakaia with Tom. You insisted the lie should come from his lips but, since you have to sustain the pretence, the lie is also yours. Yet you don't want to burden your son with something he may never need to know.

It feels necessary to keep this disaster contained, as if it's blood from a severed artery. The smaller the spread, the easier, quicker it is to mop up. At the same time you need to talk about it, because right now there is nothing else — absolutely nothing — that is of interest to you.

So Greer knows and has no doubt told Mick. And Tom and Minka, of course, know — have known, it seems, for quite some time. Which could mean that half your friends know, but are still pretending they don't. Minka has told you she felt terrible about it, but he was Tom's oldest friend and, well, these things happened. Had you noticed that she just couldn't look you in the face?

No, you hadn't. But you will never again see Minka's face without wanting to pummel it out of shape.

Fishing with Tom was what he'd claimed to have been doing on some of those nights. Then on Thursdays it was the

Continuing Education class, Introduction to Western Philosophy. Turned out he'd only attended the first night and on the way home stopped off for a drink. That's when he met her, she was there with a friend. Outgoing, he's told you, and friendly the way that young women are nowadays.

That being so, you wish those young women would lavish some of their friendliness on your resident son, who seems in real need of it.

She said he had nice eyes. Or maybe that came later when she told him she liked married men: they were more together and didn't make too many demands. Also they had money. (He didn't tell you that bit; it's your own deduction made on a careful perusal of his credit card statement.)

'Don't blame her,' he said. 'She didn't *ask* me to spend money on her.'

That left you speechless. You could just see him sitting at that bar, a stupid ripe plum waiting to be picked.

She had a lifestyle to maintain. Her own flat and a late model car with eyelids. The beauty course was costing her twelve thousand dollars, and her wardrobe was full of fantastic clothes. She liked to have nice things, he said. You were trying to keep communications open, so you just bit down on your tongue.

SHE RUNS PAST you, late and breathless. The hair is pinned up with combs with a few strands trickled over her face so it's hard to gauge the length. You look at her face which has a wide-eyed Goldie Hawn prettiness, and you wait for some internal signal because after so many years you must surely know exactly what would attract him.

You can't be absolutely certain but she's probably the one. You follow her into the foyer and stand beside her, waiting for the lift. Your heart is crashing away in your chest. Is it possible that she knows what you look like? Who you are?

The lift doors open and you both step in. She presses button seven then looks at you questioningly, meets your eyes. The breath goes out of you and it takes several seconds before you realise she's waiting to know what floor.

'Eight,' you tell her. 'Thank you.' You recall that eight is the Alzheimers Society. Unusual encounters may be common-place in this elevator. *Talk to her,* you order yourself. *If it's not her you can gallop off in unrelated sentences.* But if it is?

Ask her anyway. *Are you Emily?* Go on, ask.

'You have nothing to say to her,' he's told you. 'I'm the one who betrayed you. It's me you should hate.'

But you don't hate him, how can you? You don't even hate this young woman standing beside you, not even when you consider what may have made her late for class and a six hundred-volt sensation, which three weeks ago you couldn't even have imagined, throws your heart into a higher gear.

At least, you tell yourself, she has good taste.

It's Minka you hate. Never, ever, will you forgive Minka.

You remind yourself about the credit statement — enough to have had the house repainted. This toughens you up.

You know exactly what you want to say to her, but there are only three floors to go.

What goes around comes around, you want to say. *Think about that. There's a kind of power in being young. All of us sense it at the time, though it's only in retrospect that we recognise it as power, and by then, of course, it has gone.*

Power has its responsibilities.

Let me paint you a picture. There's a man; he's attractive and flattered by your interest. You fancy each other. You discover he's also a great lover, kind to children and animals, and generous (you may wish to rearrange the order of importance). Despite your intentions you fall in love with him. He finds this irresistible and falls in love with you.

Everything is wonderful, except for his guilt. As I said before, this is a nice man. He felt bad enough when it was just an affair, but now that it's love he decides his wife must be told. Clearly there are decisions that need to be made. You discuss the options. He's besotted with you, ready to leave his home and family and move in with you. But that isn't quite what you had in mind. True, you'd like to spend more time with him, but not all your time. The advantage of married men is that they don't want to move in. You want the good times to continue and — you have eyes, you have parents, and you know there are lots of other women out there just like you — you know that co-habitation is a bad move.

You tell him to get a place of his own. It's a reasonable suggestion, but this is a man who likes to have a home and a garden and someone to feel his brow if he has a temperature. He hates the thought of living alone, or living with anyone other than you, or his wife and resident son, both of whom he is very fond of.

So, after much inner struggle in the sleepout, and drunken discussions with his best friend Tom, he decides he might stay with his wife, who these days has a rather exciting intensity.

So you and he have one last tragic, passionate night together, and he moves back home. And for a while it's like it was all those years ago, when they first got together. But as the wife's adrenalin level subsides and her husband sinks back, with a measure of relief, into normal life, they realise that things will never really be as they were all those years ago. Sour, unfamiliar emotions slide like bilgewater in her gut. Distrust, resentment, even dislike.

It takes maybe a couple of years. Possibly she meets someone else who has also been betrayed and they find they have much in common. The husband then goes looking for you, but you haven't even thought of him in months. You have someone else who may or may not be married.

Everything has fallen apart, you see. And maybe that's just life — or maybe it's a tragedy that could quite easily have been averted back on the day he first told you he was married.

YOU REACH THE seventh floor. The lift goes *ting* and the doors glide open. She walks out. You haven't said a word but it doesn't matter, at least now you have a face to hold in your mind.

You get out at the eighth floor, step straight into the reception area of the Alzheimers Society.

'Oops, wrong floor,' you mutter, embarrassed.

The lift is already on its way down. You can't wait here in the presence of this pleasant-faced woman who obviously has her life in order. You take the stairs — all the way down as penance for cowardliness. You almost run down those steps, suddenly light-headed, and part way down it comes to you that your life has reached a pinnacle. You are *up there* where the air is thin, and it's a heady, dizzy feeling. You're looking around and wondering which route will get you back down, and you suddenly realise you can't lose.

One route has you and him together and it's okay, it's better than okay and will stay that way despite her, or maybe even because of her. And the other route has you on your own, *starting again*. Which seems, all of a sudden, to be not so unthinkable. Even exciting. For you know now, having looked in her face — you can't explain it but you know — that he is the one who will be left with regrets.

IT MAY NOT, of course, have been her at all. This thought returns just as you walk out of the building. At four o'clock you may have to come back and look again.

All Things are Possible

'WITH LOVE ALL things are possible,' the letter began. Caitlin takes it, now, from the pocket of her smock, and slides it across the cafeteria table to Audrey. 'Came in the mail.'

Audrey is fighting the Gladwrap on her sandwiches, so it's Michelle who shakes the letter from the envelope and unfolds it.

'With love all things are possible,' she reads in a put-on voice. 'This letter has been sent to bring you luck. Provided that you do not break the chain you will have good luck within four days. THIS IS NOT A JOKE!'

Her cackle peppers the room like rusty gunshot. Silence. Stares.

Caitlin hates this.

'I dunno whose writing,' she whispers to Audrey.

'It's typed.' Audrey whips the letter from Michelle's hand.

'The envelope.' Caitlin turns it right way up. A local post-mark. 'You know anyone that writes like that?' Caitlin's name and address in tight uneven printing, such as you might expect, let's say — just for argument's sake — of Duane Kemp from stores. *With love all things are possible!*

But Audrey is skimming her way through the letter. 'Send no money,' she reads out, 'as fate has no price.' She pauses to blink and scrape her teeth over her lower lip. *Fate has no price,* she repeats to herself. Caitlin, watching, reads Audrey's lips correctly. She mouths the words out herself, without even meaning to, but luckily nobody sees.

Audrey continues. 'Send this letter and twenty copies to people you think deserve good luck. You must do this within fifty-six hours.'

'It came yesterday,' says Caitlin, unasked. 'Someone must think I deserve good luck.' She adds a small laugh to show it's no big deal, and waits for one of them to say maybe it's Cute-lips Kemp. They must have seen the way his eyes slide past her and then return and freeze a moment, just as if she'd pressed the pause button — time, sound, everything stopped.

Michelle can't stand the way the other two are pissing about. She snatches back the letter and reads.

'The chain was started by Angus Archibald de Groot, a dentist in Argentina. Elizabeth Nolan received the letter in 1956 and a few days after she sent her copies away she won £300 in a Sweepstake. ALL THIS IS TRUE.' Michelle's voice is rising. 'Ignatius Rothschild, an office worker from New Hampshire, put the letter aside and forgot it. Soon after he was fired from his job. When he found the letter and renewed the chain he got a much better job with another firm.'

Michelle's voice disappears into a squeaky void. Caitlin wants to snatch the letter back. It just doesn't seem right, like making fun of a dumb animal.

Audrey wouldn't laugh if she was Michelle. It's not, she says, that she's superstitious but she doesn't make a habit of walking on cracks or under ladders. She got a chain letter once. It only cost her a couple of dollars for photocopies and a little bit more for stamps and, well, who knows? As they said once on *Star Trek*, there are more things in heaven and earth.

Caitlin thinks she probably agrees. If they didn't work, why would anyone write them in the first place?

Michelle, recovered, says they're probably written by the managing director of New Zealand Post, and Caitlin must stand up to such ludicrous psychological blackmail.

Right in front them, she tears the letter into shreds.

'There,' she says, 'I've done it for you.'

But Caitlin is looking over Michelle's shoulder at Duane Kemp striding in at the doorway with a smile to die for. He catches her eye. He's heading her way. She remembers the envelope, still intact, in time to snatch it up and hide it away in her pocket.

'Hey,' he says, 'you ladies heard my news? Off to Sydney. For good. Won me thirty grand on a scratchie.'

Diary of the Victim

TODAY BEING SATURDAY and Sam away at work I pull on my Garbo raincoat and tell Daniel that I'm going out for a walk. Knowing how it will be.

'I'll come with you,' he says very quickly.

'It's so wet out there. I won't be long. You know how fast I walk.'

He is anguished. 'You don't want me to come.'

Exactly. But there are no classes for emotional self-defence and I have no natural skills in that direction. His pain is mine, making me victim and assailant.

I say, but ungraciously, 'Okay then, if you really want to come.'

As we head up the hill Daniel describes to me the various shooting capacities of a rifle, a shotgun, a pistol. His words are little bullets deflected by my armour of repugnance. My inability to assimilate facts is a constant challenge to him. When he was about three years old his favourite bedtime stories detailed the hydraulic systems and cubic capacities of articulated vehicles. Our spheres of reality have only ever touched in passing.

He takes my hand. I know I'm being softened up; he has a reason. 'I wish, I wish we could move back home.'

'Home?'

He gives me a narrow, sidelong look which I probably deserve. 'Auckland,' he hisses.

I walk four steps then ask, with a foolish flicker of hope, 'The three of us?'

He looks down at the street and doesn't reply.

TONIGHT SALLY AND Justin stayed to dinner. Sam, in the kitchen carving the chicken, called, 'Who wants the wishbone?'

Justin was nearest and quickest. Daniel stood at the doorway drowning in his anger. 'You mean pig, you did that on purpose,' and he fled to the refuge of his bedroom.

Sam gave me the look he keeps for these occasions. He thinks Daniel should be noble and polite. Sam was a noble and polite child.

After an indecisive wait I went to Daniel's room. His desolate pose, body flung on bed, face to the wall. 'He hates me. I hate him. He did that on purpose.' Not looking at me.

I sat on the bed in my counselling pose. Justin, I said, was a guest. And besides, he got there first. (Not a counsellor so much as a handy mechanic; patching up our faltering domestic machine with sticky tape and chewing gum to keep it grinding along for a few more days. Waiting for its total collapse or perhaps a miracle.)

When I returned to the table it was draped in reproachful silence.

'I'll put Dan's in the oven,' I said.

Sam snorted. Sally began to talk too cheerfully about the time when she was driving buses. Sam was ostentatiously silent. I kept being especially polite to him, hoping we could leave it at that. (When you've seen the movie many times before, you get to want to leave before the end.) But Sam was determined to stay with it; when Sally began her usual lament about how bored she is with this little town Sam pushed aside his plate and headed for the bedroom. I followed him, of course, after the required interval. Sam, flung across our bed in his infuriated pose.

'I've just about had enough.' Talking straight up at the ceiling.

I sat down on the edge of the bed. After a suitable time of silence and sorrow I reached out my hand and took it in his.

O, the monotony of our regurgitating melodrama. The audience in me hoots and hisses. Then I remember it's me centre stage and I seem to have written most of the plot.

SUNDAY, AND SALLY has taken Justin and Daniel to visit her uncle's farm. Why have I never taken him to a farm? I feel sad to miss out on the spillage from his delight.

Sam and I talked of spending the day in bed but the sky is so blue and the prospect of a whole day on our own is so amazing and exciting that we're dressed and breakfasted by ten o'clock and eager to go somewhere.

We walk all the way to the beach, arm in arm like skaters. I want to breathe on the day and polish it up, it seems so glowing and flawless. I'm feeling completely lucky and optimistic, daring to believe in happy-ever-after.

'Every day of our life could be like this,' says Sam, if . . .'

My gut curls up like a hedgehog.

DANIEL IS IN his room, transporting three-legged cows around his farm, but watching us all the time through the open door.

Sam says, 'He makes damn sure I never get to feel I'm alone with you. It's not natural even.'

After tea Sam tells Daniel, 'Your mother and I are going next door to Mick's for a while. You can stay here and play, okay? We won't be far away but we want you to stay here.'

Daniel looks at me, betrayed. 'You'll be all right,' I say.

But at Mick's I'm on edge. I sip the sweet sherry and sort out my cards and make bids but I'm really next door with Daniel, who's alone.

When I make an excuse to leave Sam sighs. I find Daniel crouched in the dark peering next door at Mick's lights and crying.

Sam comes home, much later, drunk on sherry. 'Why didn't you come back? I missed you.' When he's been drinking, he sounds like Daniel.

'I DON'T WANT to interfere or anything,' says my sister. 'It's just that . . . well, you must admit he's disturbed. And it's only since . . .'

While she was inside nibbling at the lunch I'd made for us Daniel climbed into her shining car in his muddy gumboots and stood all over her sales charts, then turned on the motor. When I rushed out and attempted to remove him he shrieked and fought and swore, making the most of a new audience.

As she is about to drive off my sister says, 'Mum would love you both to go up and stay for a while.'

'Both?' I ask. 'Which both?'

She smiles and waves.

'I DON'T EVEN like you,' he screams. 'You're a bitch. You stink. Why can't we go back to Auckland? I was happy there.'

'I wasn't,' I yell. He looks at me then turns away. I'm appalled at my own cruelty. In Auckland there were just the two of us and I didn't know then that I wasn't happy.

Yesterday he threw a mug across the table and it smashed the glass in the sideboard. He was screaming and flailing. I looked to Sam for help — it's his sideboard — but he just sat there shielding his face with a book. 'Perhaps,' I told him later, 'if you could try to be more of a father figure . . .' He laughed.

I daydream about solitary train journeys and a little house where I live alone. It has a rack full of spices in the kitchen and the rooms echo when I walk.

HIS TEACHER SAID, 'He's not at all a happy child. I wondered if perhaps there are difficulties at home?'

'No,' I said, feeling my eyes go blank as cats' eyes.

NEARLY A WEEK passed without a scene and my hopes springing up like radishes, but tonight Sam accidentally stood on Daniel's combine harvester and it was all on again.

Later Sam said, 'It's no good, is it? I want to say you have to choose, but I know there isn't a choice to make. He's your son. But I've had all I can take.'

But when I began to pack he stopped me. 'Maybe it's just a matter of time.'

A FINE SPRING morning in the city. This morning Daniel brought me breakfast in bed. Boiled eggs, weak tea and his grateful heart served up on a rose-patterned tray. I ate my breakfast in a single bed with yellow floral sheets in a room that used to be mine. I ached all over in a vaguely pleasurable way, as if recovering from an illness. My mother beamed at me from the doorway.

'Didn't our boy do well? He's so chirpy this morning. You can see that you've done the right thing.'

I lay there thinking about all the things that had to be done. Find a flat, get Daniel enrolled at school, look for a job.

I stared at the clock and tried to imagine precisely what Sam would be doing. At work. Sawing? Measuring? Saying to his offsider, my missus has shot through?

If I think of Sam very hard my thoughts of him and his thoughts of me might touch, might intertwine.

My mother packed us a picnic lunch and we took it to the park. Daniel held my hand all the way, without design. He skipped, he sang. 'We're happy now,' he ordered me.

We ate the sandwiches and he went off to play on the swings. He no longer bothers to keep me constantly within sight.

I begin to realise that I may never forgive him.

Distance in Kilometres

SHE WAS STANDING on the roadside south of Papakura. Two small bundles of clothes in plastic shopping bags — the kind you get in Woolworths — and a large dog. The clothes showed through the gaps in the bag, bright pinks and purples. The dog was a brindled boxer.

They had just left the service station. Cigarettes for Kate, half a tank of fuel and a litre of oil. A whole litre. Rings, or possibly worse. Probably worse. And the gearbox newly reconditioned. Money thrown after money . . .

Thought Paul as he pulled up beside the hitchhiker.

Kate looked at the plastic bags flashing bright cotton colours and at the woman who was, probably, mid-thirties.

'Where'a you heading?' Kate asked through the open window. She imagined this woman grabbing clothes blindly from a drawer and shoving them into the bags, slipping silently out the back, down the yard where cabbages are running to seed and the fork lies beside browning potato plants and through the gap in the fence; hoping, hoping the neighbours will not see and that *he* won't come round from the front. Trying to frighten the dog into staying, yet pleased, in a way, that he is determined to come, *someone loves me*.

The woman with the dog said, 'Wherever,' and smiled brightly, her hand already opening the back door of the blue Torana with suspect rings.

That 'wherever' had somehow removed a stepping stone to the settling-in conversation. But Kate made an attempt, 'You come from Papakura?'

'Not exactly.' The woman was moving things from the back seat — the latest *Listener*, a box of tissues, the camera — and putting them up the back out of the dog's way. Paul pulled out onto the highway. The woman rustled her plastic bags onto the floor.

So okay, thought Kate, you don't want to talk about it. But she felt mildly irritated — no need to be so bloody mysterious. What's it to us?

And she groped back into her thoughts, which Paul had interrupted by stopping the car. Fumbling for the severed end, — like finding a lost page, but that would imply some kind of prior existence of thoughts yet to come. Or would it? And why had Paul stopped for this one, who had looked so . . . *unconvincing*. As if she was just waiting there, perhaps for a friend.. Because of the service station, probably. Once he picked up speed he hated stopping. As if the physical effort involved — eyes to mirror, hand to gear stick, foot to brake — was almost impossibly arduous.

The baby, that's where her thoughts had left off. Simon's baby, Kate's grandchild, not yet an individual presence, but *real* now that she had seen it turn over, relocate its tiny body in the dark barrel of Trish's flesh. Now that she'd laid her hand against an absurd protrusion and felt the *solidity* there. Their first grandchild and with it a flutter of memories . . . belly button popped out like a balloon not quite fully blown, the inexpressible certainty and inadmissible uncertainty, and then the stretch — not, as you had imagined, just of flesh but of some outer boundaries of emotion and with it a sense of . . . *infinite comprehension*. Thirty days and thirty nights in the desert: men needing to dream up extreme adventures, tests of inner strength. Then having to repeat them in case they'd missed the point. And Freud, the fool, had talked of penis envy.

'So where are you heading?' Paul asked, moving his head so he could see the woman's face in the mirror. He'd heard Kate ask this already but the reply had been drowned out by the highway's erratic roar.

'Anywhere's fine,' she said, looking into the mirror. The corners of her mouth twitched up in a smile that was all for him, and Paul was left with an urge to shift the mirror and take a look at his own reflection; what was there about it to earn such sudden intimacy? Surely his eyes, beneath the dark sunglasses, weren't even visible. So how come she seemed, for a time, to have held them? *Squeezed* them, in fact.

'Where are you going?' She made the question sound dutiful, a matter of indifference.

'Wellington,' Paul said. 'Well, north of. Plimmerton.'

'Sounds fine,' she said.

Kate looked at Paul. He saw the very deliberate way her head turned and he knew without lifting his eyes from the road, that her eyebrows would be arched and her mouth open. He pretended not to know; it helped keep reality at bay. Here was this woman, like something his imagination might have conjured up — enigmatic, anonymous, and perhaps available.

Kate peeled the cellophane strip from the cigarette packet. Paul disliked her smoking, especially in the car. She was doing her best, down to ten a day. The money she saved she kept in a tin. Her bedroom rug fund, an incentive to quit once and for all. She decided against offering one to the hitchhiker. But even before she'd got the packet open the woman said, 'Do you mind if I have one?'

Kate took out a cigarette and lit it, then passed the packet and the red lighter over her shoulder. The dog was panting heavily, his head was close to Paul's ear.

Paul said, his voice raised to reach the back seat, 'A bit hot out there for walking.'

The woman passed back the cigarettes and lighter.

'I just wait,' she said.

'So where are you from?' he asked, encouraged.

'Nowhere in particular.' She sounded amused, pleased with her inscrutability.

Kate had an urge to turn her head and stare. She tried to reassemble the face she had seen through the window. (Fair, straight hair hanging to just below the shoulders, a rounded baby face — pink from the sun or the heat — which had looked curiously worn-out.) She waited to see if Paul felt the remark was worth following up on. It seemed he didn't.

THEY TOOK THE bypass out of Hamilton. The silence felt somehow deliberate. Kate looked at her husband. He was watching the road ahead, his eyes staring steadily out through the dark lenses. Kate continued to look at him for several seconds — almost always, if she did this, he would turn to her and say, a little defensively, 'What?' — but this time his eyes never moved from the road. What was he thinking? Her eyes slid cautiously down to his groin. No communication there either. Or was it muzzled by heavy denim?

The dog stood up and rearranged himself so that his head poked between the front seats. His saliva dripped cool on Kate's arm. She reached up and scratched his chin. She wondered if Cleo had behaved herself for the Garlicks and whether they'd relented and let her sleep indoors.

'Can I have another cigarette?'

The third already. The only three sentences spoken over seventy kilometres. A chain smoker. And chain smokers ought to buy their own. Kate passed the packet and the matches over her shoulder. The cigarettes were supposed to last her till Monday. It was her rule. She listened to the lighter hissing and felt deprived. *You don't really need one.* She inhaled a wisp of floating smoke. The dog licked his own saliva off Kate's arm. The woman must have seen this for he was suddenly jerked backwards. 'Sit down,' she hissed.

'He's all right,' said Kate, but was ignored. The woman and the dog seemed to be wrestling in the back seat then the woman was back behind Kate and the dog was just a steady shunting sound somewhere over Paul's side.

The woman said, 'I don't suppose by any chance you'd have a joint on you?'

'No,' said Kate. She heard her own voice, sharp with indignation. Which would be taken as disapproval. So what? Let her think what she liked. In her head Kate resorted to sarcasm — *But there's half a bottle of gin in the boot, could we offer you that? Or our clothes? A whole suitcase full?*

But Paul was saying in a pleasant, rueful way, 'Alas and if only.'

They were coming into Cambridge — affluence and tree-lined streets. Kate had a second cousin living in Cambridge. She'd met him only once. It was the year she started high school. He was grown up. He asked her to show him the back garden, then down by the hen house he took her hand and pushed it into his trouser pocket and across. He held her hand there for quite a long time. His body was moving of its own accord, like a restless baby in a blanket. Then he let go and she took her hand away, but that night at dinner they watched each other. That was all. He and his sister and brother-in-law left soon after that. But for the next few days Kate had felt tight and urgent, like a breath being held.

'Isn't this is where your cousin lives?' said Paul.

'My second cousin.'

He smirked. 'We should stop off and visit him.'

She said, 'Perhaps I made it up.' But she felt pleased because the woman would be listening and somehow this established them. We are partners, it said. We embody twenty-five years of confessions and confidences, concessions and conspiracies. Our lives are interwoven tight as a carpet, the colours have melted together, no wedge or blade can divide us. Anything that might happen on this journey will happen only by mutual consent.

For Kate acknowledged, now, that she was waiting; all three of them were waiting. The air that circled between them was curled up tight and urgent. Like — yes — a breath being held.

The woman said, 'I just happen to have the makings of a joint here if you'd like one.'

Kate left it to Paul. He said, 'Why not!'

The Woolworths bag crackled as the woman dragged it up on to her knees. The dog moved forward again and shoved his head on Kate's shoulder. She scratched him behind the ear. He turned his eyes towards her, grinning and drooling.

Paul asked the rear-vision mirror, 'What's the dog's name?'

'Pedro.'

All Paul could see in the mirror was the crown of her bent head. He adjusted the mirror and she looked up and gave him a little smile. She was licking the edge of a cigarette paper and her tongue seemed like part of the smile. Paul tried to think of another innocuous question. Kate usually handled all that social stuff, filling silences, putting out biscuits. But now she was just sitting there fiddling with the dog. Was she sulking? Hard to tell anything for sure — sunglasses had always made her look remote. Arrogant, even.

Almost grandparents. No getting away from something like that, it was so final.

'You wouldn't have another bag? Mine's got a hole.'

Kate fumbled vaguely in the dashboard. 'No,' she said, 'sorry.'

Paul overtook a stationwagon. Its back window was filled with bedding and a deflated floral plastic thing that might have been a paddling pool. His palms were sticky against the steering wheel. Everyone's going home, he thought, now the hot weather has begun. Well, not *all* of us going home. Or was she intending to come home with them?

'Could I have the lighter, please?'

Kate passed it over her shoulder.

The smell of the stuff was instantaneous, nostalgic. Pedro was pushed aside and the woman's hand came over, the joint held delicately between finger and thumb. Kate took it and passed it straight to Paul. Paul kept it a while, feeling the fluidity seep into his head and his bones. He passed it back to Kate and this time she took a drag. One. Then passed it over her shoulder.

They went through the same routine three or four times over and the silence began to seem less explosive. Kate returned the final dog-end. Paul said, 'That was nice,' and Kate said, 'Yes. Thanks.' Though her tone was somehow begrudging.

'Can I have another cigarette?'

Before handing them over Kate lit one for herself. Alcohol or dope, she thought, it was always the same, your willpower shut down. This time she put the packet and the lighter on the floor between the front seats. 'I'll leave them there so you can help yourself.' She wondered if that had sounded sarcastic. She hadn't meant to but, despite the ritual sharing, she sensed the woman's dislike of her. Had sensed it from the moment the woman and dog climbed into the car. But had mistrusted her own instincts; such instant aversion seemed nonsensical.

Yet now Kate's sense of the woman's hostility was so strong that she had a sudden dreadful image of those slim pink hands sliding round from behind and choking her. She edged down in her seat, protecting her neck, pretending tiredness.

She stayed like that all the way to Tokoroa. At one point Paul said, 'We'll have to get that thing fixed. I miss having music.' He was talking about the cassette player. And Pedro must have gone to sleep for his panting had given way to a faint irregular snore. Apart from that there was silence. And even the silence, thought Kate, was somehow being manipulated from the back seat.

The woman smoked two more of Kate's cigarettes.

Just south of Tokoroa she laughed out loud. At least it sounded like laughter but it could have been a bout of shrill sobbing. It went for several seconds then stopped as suddenly as it had started. Kate looked across at Paul, who glanced back at her without perceptibly turning his head. His glance was the equivalent of a shrug. Kate felt with certainty that the laughter — or sobbing — had been directed at her. She was expected to turn and confront the woman. She would, therefore, ignore it. After all she was pretending to be asleep.

Laughter, Paul supposed, though he couldn't be sure. He considered adjusting the mirror back so he could see her face, but the sounds she had made had seemed so false, so . . . *confrontational* that he wasn't eager to meet her eye. Besides, he had been enjoying the mirror where it was. Once she'd straightened up after rolling the joint he'd been left with a vision of two large breasts pressing against a blue cotton-knit shirt with just a hint of rolling flesh beneath them. Then, between one stolen glance and the next, her left hand had come up to cradle her right tit, with the thumb making small encouraging circles over an ever-extending nipple.

All the way from Putaruru to Tokoroa that hand had pleasured that breast; at first through the fabric and then — just past the second bridge — it had snaked down the neck of her shirt and moved in sly ripples over the heavy swell of flesh. Knew he was watching. Surely she must? Then what had the crazy laughter meant?

Furtive now, Paul looked in the mirror. The big blue tits pouted towards him, untouched by human hand. Their angle had changed slightly and behind them a forearm moved in regular soothing rhythm. Fondling the dog. Paul set his eyes back on the road ahead. Pine forests coming up.

Shade at last. If she did know, had she grown bored with the game?

Lucky Pedro.

Suddenly Paul was back at the mirror, moving it now, like a searchlight. And there was the crown of her head with its curtain of fair hair and her right arm still moving in a hypnotic motion. But, twisting the mirror further, he could see only his own pale green shirt and his arms looking unexpectedly brown. So he turned his head. The need to see was a fever. He turned his head. They were just coming up to a bend. The Torana went straight on, heading for the edge of the seal, long dry grass, taut new fence with glittering wires . . .

'*Paul!*' shrieked Kate and grabbed the steering wheel. He was back in control in an instant. Bumping on an uneven surface, the swish of grass beneath them and then they were back on the highway just as if nothing had happened.

'How's that for reflexes?' he said. Kate was still clutching hold of the seat belt. Her knuckles were white with anger. 'I must have nodded off for a minute,' he said.

'Shall I drive?'

'No,' he said, 'No. I'm fine now.' And for all that what had he seen? A flash of brindle-coloured flank, a pink arm leisurely moving. 'You all right?' he asked of the back seat.

'Nothing a cigarette won't fix.'

Paul waited a few seconds, then adjusted the mirror back to where it had begun. There was a campervan coming up behind.

'I need a cuppa,' said Kate. 'I'm starving. If you see a place.'

'There's probably nothing till Taupo.'

'Taupo then.'

Why didn't she pack sandwiches and thermos flasks like other wives did? Every time they travelled they would see families picnicking at rest areas and Kate would say, 'That's what we should do. That looks so nice. Next time I'll pack us something.' But she never had, not even when the kids were young. Takeaways, and foul coffee in polystyrene cups, up and down the country.

If, today, she had packed a picnic lunch they could pull off somewhere in the shade of the forest and lie on pine needles looking up at the fragments of blue sky. Pedro could bound off on opossum trails the way that Cleo always did. *She* might feel inclined to roll another joint (and anyway there was half a bottle of gin in the boot), and they could stay there all afternoon if they felt inclined. He didn't start work till Monday and Kate had another whole week. And lying on pine needles in the summer shade, the sharp questions drug-cushioned, who knows what might happen . . .

Thought Paul.

And, if, today, she had packed a picnic lunch they could pull off somewhere in the shade of the forest and lie on pine needles looking up at the fragments of blue sky. Pedro could bound off on opossum trails the way that Cleo always did. She might feel inclined to roll another joint, (and anyway there was that gin), and they could stay there all afternoon if they felt inclined. Paul didn't start work till Monday and she had another whole week. And lying on pine needles in the summer shade, the sharp questions drug-cushioned, who knows what could happen.

Thought Kate. Except did it have to be someone so weird?

Just as the forest was thinning out, the woman made the same hysterical laughing sound. Louder this time, and and it went on a little longer. Paul and Kate looked at each other without even pretending not to. And this time Kate turned around in her seat and looked at the woman. It seemed very odd that after nearly three hours of travelling together she still didn't really know what this person looked like. Almost from the start she had felt . . . well, superstitious about looking round. Like Lot's wife. Or was it Lot?

The woman was leaning forward and so when Kate turned round they were almost nose to nose. (And even that close it was hard to tell if the sound which was snuffling to an end was humour or grief.) The immediate, disconcerting impression was of a new-born baby — the face was so pink and damp and scrunched up and the mouth so wide open. The teeth seemed out of place, and then just ugly, full of dark grey fillings and a front one broken to a sharp point.

'What's so funny?' Kate made herself smile because somehow this face substantiated her vague sense of being at risk.

'Nothing,' said the woman, still grinning. 'It's personal. Just something I thought of.'

Paul knew without even looking, just by the way that his wife settled back in her seat, that she was wearing her good-grief expression. But he stifled a sharing grin; he'd seen that emboldened nipple, that gently coaxing thumb. He drove steadily now, with care; he wanted to prolong this part of the journey with the three of them trapped together in this abrasive state of infinite risk and possibilities.

The woman lit another cigarette. When she dropped the packet back between the front seats Kate snatched it up and examined the contents. Then she lit one for herself. She put the packet and the lighter on the dashboard.

There was a large Coca-Cola sign coming up. Above it, a sign: WAYSIDE TEAROOMS. Paul eased his foot back. 'This do?'

'Do me,' said Kate, 'what about you?'

He shrugged indifference.

'I'm starving,' said the woman suddenly, 'and I could really go a cup of tea. But I happen to be broke so I hope you don't mind shouting me.'

Kate had bent to gather her bag from the floor. For a second or two she froze, head down. Paul pulled in beside a dusty Ford Escort van and turned off the ignition. The silence between them was sliding down into his lungs, causing his throat to tickle. And now Kate was staring at him in an angry, impatient way. Leaving it up to him. His wife, who was so parsimonious with herself but such an easy touch for others. His wife, who now sat in silence.

Paul switched off the motor. The three of them sat there. Kate gathered her cigarettes and lighter from the dashboard. Eventually the woman said, 'I take it that's a no?'

Kate took a deep breath. 'I don't like feeling pressured into something,' she said. 'I think people should take some responsibility for themselves.'

None of them moved. 'Oh, all right,' said Kate, angrily. 'What the hell. It's no big deal. Come on, then.'

'No thanks,' said the woman. She opened the car door. 'I think it would choke me.'

Kate and Paul sat staring stiffly through the windscreen as the woman and the dog began walking up the road.

'That was a bit mean,' he said finally.

'*You* could have said yes.'

'I got the message,' he said.

'I didn't like her. There was something about her.'

'Yes,' he said wistfully. 'There certainly was.'

She looked at him with exasperation. 'Then why didn't you. . .?'

'Don't be ridiculous.' Paul opened his door, 'Are we going in or aren't we?' His voice was full of rage.

'Of course we're going in.'

But she wasn't very hungry, after all. One tomato sandwich, one cheese and onion. Paul had a pie. They ordered a pot of tea but Paul didn't drink his. He was thinking about the picnic lunch they might have had back there in the forest.

Kate felt misjudged. She wanted to explain. 'That laughing,' she said. 'Now that was pretty weird.'

'So what's wrong with weird?' he demanded. Kate sighed and finished her tea.

'You realise,' he said, 'we'll have to pass her. She won't have got a lift so soon.'

'So we just drive past.' She watched his face and felt sorry. Now that the woman wasn't with them the sense of infinite and undefined possibilities returned to her. 'Whatever,' she said. 'You decide.'

'Perhaps she'll have got a lift,' he said. Mostly that thought was a relief.

Two hundred metres up the road, round the bend, and there they were; Pedro, the woman and the plastic bags. 'Oh Jesus,' said Paul. He pulled over and stopped. The woman was right outside Kate's window. This time Kate had a good look at her — big bust and solid thighs, a loose cotton-knit top and pants to match. The fabric stretched where it met with flesh. White sandals.

'This feels pretty silly,' said Kate out the window, 'but do you want a ride?'

'No thanks.' said the woman, baring her fillings, the broken tooth. Paul drove off. He watched them in the rear-vision mirror for a time. The woman looking back along the road for approaching traffic. The dog sitting patiently on his haunches.

THE SILENCE WITHIN the car was no longer agitated and brittle, but nor was it the soothing unconsidered lack of speech they had shared from Auckland to Papakura. This was a bruised silence, heavy with regret and inevitability. Yet comfortable, too, in that it was familiar. From time to time Paul's eyes jumped to the mirror and he remembered the hand beneath the blue shirt, nuzzling and sinuous as a new-born puppy. That began to seem enough in itself.

Kate reinvented a woman she could talk to. A confident, cheerful woman who would appreciate the difference between an adventure and a competition. A woman . . . okay, with a brindled dog and her clothes in plastic bags, but friendly and with good teeth. Kate — comfortingly — supposed no such woman existed, but *if,* just *if* she did, and *if* Kate had packed a picnic lunch . . .

She left the story hanging there. Already her body was intervening, her breasts rubbed themselves against loose cotton fabric, her groin sighed and yearned for attention.

The sign said: REST AREA 200 METRES. Kate saw it and thought, 'It's bound to be one of those exposed places with gravel and picnic tables.' Besides, Paul was still being remote and aggrieved. So she pushed the thought away until Paul put on the indicator light. Then she saw it was a gravel road that ran among trees and she turned and smiled at him.

'It seems familiar,' she said, following him down a track that led to a creek. She wished he would just stand still so she could unzip him and nuzzle at the burgeoning flesh beneath the yellow briefs. An inclination as urgent as this could be hard to sustain. But outdoors it was always like this — he would stomp around looking the right private patch, just like a cow about to give birth.

'We've been here before,' he said. 'Years ago, when Vicki still got carsick and I turned in here, remember, and it was just in the nick of time. She put one foot out the door and spewed all over a gorse bush.'

Kate remembered. Sixteen years ago, at least. 'Please,' she said. 'Here'll do.' She pulled the straps of her sundress down over her shoulders and cupped her naked breasts in her two hands. And he turned and came back, with his greedy mouth and his heavy-duty zipper to offer in exchange.

His teeth teased gently at her nipples and the liquid sound of the creek flowed into her mind. Her fingers adjusted metal and fondled flesh through cotton.

'She was playing with herself,' Paul whispered. 'For me.'

His tongue curled in her belly button. Her hands forced his jeans over curving haunches. 'Tell me,' she begged.

He made her wait. His mouth moved soft and damp against her inner thighs.

'She was touching her nipples. Caressing them, round and round. Watching me in the mirror.'

'Oooh,' moaned Kate, seeing it. Her fingers were slippery with fluid and the creek ran through her head like a silver thirst.

'We could've brought her here,' she sighed. 'Just here. And she would've taken off all her clothes, and yours, and pushed your head between those big pale thighs.'

Paul groaned softly, easing them both to the ground. She could feel twigs and dry leaves etching her flesh. And maybe pine needles. 'And you,' he said softly, nuzzling her breast, 'would've offered her these to feast on.'

Kate could feel a broken tooth on the edge of her nipple and yellow hair brushing her neck.

'And then,' she said, 'and then I would have taken her nipple in my lips and circled it with my tongue. Like this.'

Paul's tight, hair-tufted nipple expanded beneath her tongue into a fulsome teat and the creek in Kate's head was gathering speed, bouncing off boulders, tumbling through rapids. She was ahead of Paul and trying to hold back, but unable, now, to speak, for her breath must be saved for the impending rapids.

'I think,' Paul said, 'she's got a thing going with that dog.' His voice was a hoarse croak now and his body a force beyond him — earthquake, thunder, tidal wave.

And Kate closed her eyes and went gasping, spinning, screaming over the edge of the waterfall and down, down finally into that vast, calm pool beneath.

As SHE SLID back into the car Kate reached for a cigarette. The packet was empty. She sighed. Beside her Paul was slumped in his seat wearing a vacant smile. She reached for his hand. His fingers curled around hers. They smiled at each other.

'I guess I was mean about the tearooms, wasn't I?' said Kate. 'It's just that I really hate to be *used*.'

D_o

'HOBBIES?'

The man looks at his wife before answering. 'I do the garden. Vegetable garden. And . . .' He tries to imagine a day, any day. The things that fill it in. The others are waiting. He moves on to the weekend. 'Rugby,' he says. 'I mean I watch it. Our boy plays. And on TV I watch it.' The interviewer notes this down in careful lettering. Soon she will look up and wait. The man tries, desperately now, to think of what else he does.

'And cricket,' says his wife.

'You play cricket?'

'No,' he says,' I watch that too.' He smiles wanly, ashamed.

'Clubs?' prompts the interviewer helpfully. 'Do you belong to any . . .?'

The man shakes his head slowly. He is a dull person, and his life is humdrum — he sees that now, and it makes his movements heavy.

WHEN THE WORKS closed they set up a resource centre in the canteen to help people adjust to redundancy. We went there a couple of times to see what was on offer. We sat around drinking the free coffee and chatting to the others who were in the same boat. The mood was almost jovial, as if we were all starting out on an adventure. But that was early on.

At the resource centre they had all the appropriate officials — Employment Service, Social Welfare, Iwi Authority, Inland Revenue. They also had leaflets on how to handle redundancy, and a Job Vacancy screen with cards for experienced computer operators, book-keepers and door-to-door salesmen. The resource centre committee was applying for money from the government so that in the new year they could start up work schemes for all the people who hadn't managed to find jobs by then. Because of that — the safety net — we told each other things weren't so bad. **It was the Job that was made Redundant, Not You.**

LET'S HANG ON in, we said. For the sake of the kids as much as anything. It wasn't even three years since we'd moved here, and they'd hate being dragged away from school again.

'I FISH SOMETIMES,' the man says. 'Go fishing.'

But the interviewer, daunted by the silence, has turned to his wife and speaks at the same time as he does. 'What about you?'

'That's right,' his wife says. 'He goes fishing. And we do a lot of things together: family stuff — picnics, visiting. Most of our friends live in other places. We haven't been here all that long.'

'Of course,' says the interviewer. She grimaces. 'We've been here eight years and we barely know our neighbours. Unless you join things . . .' She bites her lip and looks at her questions. 'Are you in any clubs? Committees? Groups?'

The wife shakes her head, smiling at the very thought. 'I'm not that type,' she says. 'I sew a bit but I don't enjoy it all that much. I like gardening. And dancing. I used to like dancing.' She gives her husband a small glance of rebuke. 'Music. We both like music. And reading. Watching telly when there's something halfway decent on, though with kids you tend to end up with what they want. Anyway I don't suppose those are *hobbies* exactly?'

'If you enjoy doing them, they are.' The interviewer is hunched over her papers, getting it down. The husband stares at his wife, impressed by her ability to make dullness sound so energetic.

HE WAS A permanent seasonal worker. That means he'd been laid off six months before, at the beginning of winter. **Work out a weekly budget by looking at how much you spend.** Even then there were rumours that the place would close but no one really believed it; there had been such rumours every off-season for as far back as the old hands could remember. Most likely we'll lose one chain, they told each other. Even though factories and freezing works had been steadily closing throughout the country they were certain it couldn't happen to *theirs*.

I WAS A bit surprised that my husband would go along with such unreality. He had reason to know better. It was less than four years since he left his forestry job because of the rumours that they were all about to be laid off. He'd been offered a job with a trucking firm. We talked it over for a week. It seemed too good to turn down.

When the forestry men got their redundancy pay most of them headed for the city. **Managing Your Redundancy Pay: hope for the best — but plan for the worst.** The trucking company lost business and had to put off drivers. Last on, first off. No redundancy agreement. You live and learn, we told each other. DO — **think in terms of how you can make the most of it. No 'chips on the shoulder'.**

I did a horticultural course at polytech. I couldn't get into the computer course or media studies, so I took horticulture. At the end of the year I got a certificate. This would give me a better chance of getting into horticultural college if we could afford it. At least it's something to put on your CV, they said. I thought, at least it got me out of the house. I've never wanted to get away from him before.

While I was out he put in an asparagus bed and tended his cabbages and broad beans. DO — **keep yourself busy.** Then he began going down to the pub and playing the machines though he'd never been a gambler. It fills in the day, he said. And it's only till the works open.

Some weeks our neighbour, Veronica, gives me a few hours' work in her gift shop. She pays me cash so it won't affect our dole payments. We tell people I just help out because she's a friend. But now she's offered me a regular job four days a week and late night Thursday. The shop barely makes a profit but Veronica's husband is working and I think she feels sorry for us.

I'm not sure whether to accept. Not because it feels like charity, but because it might seem a betrayal. In making dole payments Social Welfare divides the money equally between us, but *he* is the one who is registered as unemployed; *he* must report in, fill in the forms, sign the declarations. If I earn the money even that token sense of contribution will be gone. He might feel he had no substance.

'IT DOESN'T EVEN need to be things you *do*,' says the interviewer as if she's just remembered her briefing. 'It can be things you'd *like* to do if the opportunity was there.'

'Anything?' says the wife. She looks at the interviewer with suspicion. 'Regardless of cost?'

'As long as you'd like to do it. Some people have said "travel", things like that.'

I KEEP REMEMBERING school. That's how it feels. The playground and the teachers shoving you into teams — c'mon, you, over there and get rid of that long lip. You've got an attitude problem, know that? Better start shaping up, make something of yourself.

Then I escaped to the real world and it was so good, like landing on cotton wool. No attitude problem, not out there. Fell in love and she wanted me. We had a boy, stillborn. But then a girl and a boy and another girl. And despite the kids, or because of them, I kept falling in love with her every six months at least. Making comparisons and feeling fortunate: happily married, family man, content.

Lately her movements have got sharper. Her head jolts when it turns. Her voice has a thin black outline. The children have noticed; when she's in the room I see them think before they speak.

At first I only took five dollars a time. Twenty-five chances. The first time I went down the woman before me won a hundred and fifty dollars.

Last week I won a hundred and twenty. Now I allow myself ten dollars a time. When I wake up in the morning I look forward to pushing the button, watching the numbers spin. At least it gets me out of the house. The day I win two hundred I'll take it home to her and I won't ever play the machines again.

I keep remembering school. The teachers always had to be right, to have the last say. It's as if they've been lying in wait for me all these years.

Personally, I can't see much wrong with Australia, but she's against it. We're New Zealanders, she said, and our kids should be New Zealanders. Why should we have to crawl away from this country like refugees?

I thought, every refugee must have asked that question. What makes us think we're so different? But I didn't say this. Instead I peeled back the petalled layers of her words to find the accusation within and slipped it into my pocket with all the rest.

'WELL, TRAVEL, OF course,' says the wife. 'Everyone wants to travel. All the same, I don't see the point of information like that.'

'They must have a reason,' says the interviewer, 'though I'm not sure what it is. Perhaps if a lot of people want the same thing they'll try and organise something along those lines.'

The wife laughs sourly. 'What? Take us all to Europe for a couple of weeks?'

This upsets the interviewer. She squares her shoulders and looks primly at the sugar bowl. The wife sees and tries to make amends. 'It might be to do with personality,' she offers. 'To give some sort of guide on what kind of potential . . .' Her voice falters. The three of them sit there in silence, stifled by a gust of futility.

THE RESOURCE CENTRE organised a house-to-house survey of all the redundant workers. DON'T — **harp on about it to everyone around you.** Then they went to the Minister of Employment to ask for funds to set up work schemes which could utilise the skills of those people. At least that's what we were told.

And the Minister of Employment has — REMEMBER **first impressions count** — announced in the paper that the government does not believe in creating jobs. However she has promised the resource centre enough to pay for a full-time co-ordinator and two social workers.

DON'T — **worry about it to the point of losing sleep.**

'BUNGY JUMPING,' SAYS the wife suddenly. 'I think that would be amazing. And hot air ballooning. Imagine that.' She smiles across at her husband.

The interviewer snatches up the ballpoint and bends over her papers with relief.

'Water skiing?' The wife tries to tempt the husband into this game. 'Gliding. On a perfect summer day with just a few feathery clouds . . .'

The interviewer finishes the list and looks, hopefully, at the husband. His wife is also watching him, her smile collapsing slowly as she waits. He tries to think of something, if only to restore the smile, which had been for an instant so . . . *unlimited*. But all his imagination offers him is flashing fluorescent lights and that little mechanical tune of success that plays while the coins spill out into the tray.

The Assassin Bug

CRIPPLED. IT'S STILL the word I use in the privacy of my own head. Strangers use it too, forgetting the rules have changed. 'Have you always been cripp—?' Then they remember, try to suck it back in, redden around the neck. I refuse to offer them comfort, watch stone-faced as they frantically search their mental files. Find it lying there, just where they left it. Oh, the relief. 'Handicapped.'

'Have you always been . . .?'

And they glance at my still-immobile face and realise that handicapped is also past its use-by date. Some scurry back to their files. Disabled. Whew. Third time lucky! Others give up, pretend they haven't said a word. Quick thinkers improvise.

'Have you always been . . . in a wheelchair?'

'No.' I tell them. 'This is quite recent.'

I don't say how it happened. It's always what they want to know, but I make them ask; it cuts down the numbers. And then I give them only the basic details. 'Car crash,' I tell them. 'Broke my neck.' Which isn't entirely accurate, but a broken neck has a timeless, almost mythical, ring to it that satisfies. Even me. I get an image of dolls with their heads wrenched off and remember the horror of the dismemberment, and the joy of discovering that a smear of Uhu could restore them miraculously to almost as good as new.

I believe people feel the same way when I tell them I broke my neck. They see my head tumbling to the ground or dangling from some umbilical artery and marvel that here I am. Alive, if not exactly almost as good as new.

Crippled, in fact.

I like the word. For me it conjures up Quasimodo . . . Porgy . . . tragic but deeply appealing figures. A big improvement on *handicapped* (the third leg at Trentham) and even the bland *disabled*. A sterile sort of word, reminding me of hospital wards and the metal parts of a wheelchair. I choose *crippled* but, on principle, won't condone its use.

Hamish, my partner, is one of those people who sniggers over vocabulary refurbished in the interests of social change. Even *partner* makes him twitchy. He argues that language should evolve naturally, like a patch of bush. Death, regrowth, adaptation, mutation, with no outside interference. I've told him that, in that case, he better start blowing up the advertising agencies, TV networks, politicians — all those big-time manipulators of language. Either we destroy them or we join them. He said, 'You're right. My crippled missus has an incisive mind.'

Whenever he's in the wrong, which is often, Hamish comes out with that sort of thing. Disarming. For years I found it so. Then one day at work a customer insisted on telling me about the 'assassin bug' that sneakily injects its predators with a poison which causes them to dissolve inside, though outside they remain intact. And I had this flash of Hamish smirking.

That night I pointed out to him that resorting to flippancy or whimsy was just a technique he used to ward off any truth he found unpalatable. I explained about the assassin bug and the obvious parallel. This was unwise of me, leading, as it did to a childish discussion about whether, in the case of the Hamish bug, I was predator or prey.

So, he would still make me laugh, but from that day on a little sign would flash in my brain. 'Manipulation,' it said. I began noting how often this happened and under what circumstances, and this made me aware of other things I had noticed but not really thought about. Habits he certainly didn't have, or had kept under wraps, during the first years we were together.

Mañana sort of habits. The unwashed dish pushed beneath the sofa because the sink was so far away, the abandoned sock, the underpants and shirts that clung to the sides of the laundry basket staring down at their peers which had slid to the floor (necks all broken). The lawnmower not returned to the shed. The bathroom mirror flecked with toothpaste spittle . . .

Things that took only a moment to set right, so I would. And sometimes I remembered to mention to him, reproachfully, that I had done that which I ought not to have had to do. Yet in a way that made it worse. I didn't want to be the kind of person for whom hanging up the bathmat was an activity that warranted conscious thought, let alone discussion.

All this, of course, was before the accident. In retrospect it seems ironic that I was upset over a few minutes spent doing chores that I would now be delighted to be able to do. I have to remind myself that there was a principle at stake. Also, that I suspected that, unchecked, this would prove to be just the thin end of a vast wedge of dereliction.

Besides, I had an obligation to my past as a leading feminist.

I have newspaper clippings that show me in overalls clutching a loud-hailer . . . being forcibly arrested outside Parliament Buildings . . . leaving a Wellington courtroom. I am quoted — even, once, in the headlines.

All of which causes my daughter, Cassandra, much mirth and incredulity. I should be proud of Cass, she's the woman of the future we'd all envisaged back in the early seventies when we were fighting for change.

Ellen Fuller, my business partner, has a daughter just like Cass. There are, we notice, a lot of these young women around. Ellen and I talk about our daughters the way Linus Peach, our only regular skinhead customer, talks about Adolf Hitler. We're full of admiration but at the same time find them kind of scary.

This particular year Cass had come down for Easter and I had watched her only just holding her tongue over some of the little things I'd got into the habit of doing. Nothing arduous: a button on a shirt, a get well card to his mother, cutting lunches.

When he left the dinner table and his emptied plate to check on the cricket, and didn't return to the kitchen for the doing of dishes (despite my exaggerated clattering and clashing as I stacked them), my daughter lost patience. She clomped into the TV room and said a few words. Hamish said a few words back. Well, only two, apparently. Historic German words. And he saluted.

It wasn't calculated to disarm; it was a declaration of war. When Hamish and I decided to pool resources and live together, Cassandra was still a schoolgirl, and living with me. He used to complain to me in private that my daughter watched him the way a hawk might watch a calf with a tubercular cough.

Cass stormed back in the kitchen where I had my hands in the sink. She appeared to have entered a dimension beyond words and just stood staring at me, shaking her head. I looked for the teatowel she had been using — the rack was jammed full of plates and cups and knives and forks — but her hands were clenched together, white-knuckled and teatowel free. After a time she huffed out a lungful of breath (technically it was a sigh but the word didn't suit at all) and marched outside to kick the chrysanthemums.

I went in search of the teatowel — there was no point in dirtying another — and found it draped over Hamish's head.

'Is that,' I ventured, 'some kind of joke?'

'I think not,' he said. 'Ask your daughter.'

He tugged the teatowel off, screwed it into a ball and bowled it to me, as near to overarm as is possible while lying on a sofa. I fielded it and stood for a moment copying Cass's technique, the too-disgusted-to-speak headshake. Hamish's back shot up from the cushions. 'Yeah!' he said, slapping his thigh, 'Yeah. *Fan-tastic*. You see that?' Even then he didn't look at me, eyes glued to the screen. 'Look. Here's the replay.'

I finished the dishes on my own. If I minded doing dishes I'd have bought a dishwasher long ago.

I left it until Cass had returned to Wellington — to her flatmates, her partner Michael and the in-the-meantime job she loathed — then I turned off the early evening news and made a speech. Things, I told him, had to change, I was no longer prepared to be jollied into habitual servitude.

He said I was right, he'd been sliding back into the slothful habits. His mother had been shockingly overindulgent to both her sons. He was glad that I had the guts to take a stand. That was what he liked about me, I was a strong woman. With good legs. And a grippable arse.

Then we made love very nicely on the polyurethaned floorboards. He begged me to go and put on the black garments, flimsy with lace and inventive apertures, that he had bought several Christmases back. I couldn't. As I'd told Hamish many times, that kind of stuff just wasn't *me*. I could put it on but I wouldn't be able to carry it off. I'd get the giggles, and feel ridiculous, if not humiliated. Even the fact that he wanted me to wear it was, I had to say, a bit of a worry. *Totally retro,* as Cass would say.

When we dragged some clothes back on and switched on the TV the mid-evening news was just starting. Hamish was pleased by that. He had this conceit that the sex he and I had was better and more prolonged than other people's. All the time he was assembling evidence as if some day there would be a judicial inquiry into our sex lives. After reading one of those magazine surveys on the sexual activities of the average couple he would get a smug look that could last for days.

For possibly a week after our little talk Hamish displayed an awesome amount of domestic energy. Everything, it seemed, that I went to do had already been done. So that when I saw that energy dropping away it seemed, at first, that he was still *in credit* and for a time I wasn't concerned.

But decline was rapid. Within three weeks the sofa, when shifted, revealed an empty Ice Beer bottle, three unsuccessful scratch tickets, a plate with several grains of rice glued in congealed sweet and sour sauce, and four screw-on beer caps.

And when I brought it to his attention Hamish overdid contrition. Then, two days running, when he was last out of bed, the duvet was merely dragged up to hide sheets clumped like seaweed. He claimed, in mitigation, that he couldn't bear to dismantle the evidence of my unbridled passion. But by the time his towel was found mouldering on the bedroom floor I had become — and I quote — *obsessive* and *irrational*. It was at that point that I began to keep a record. HILPA, I would jot down in my work diary with disturbing frequency.

'What does that mean?' Ellen asked, thumbing back through June. I had to think fast. Hamish Is Lazy Prick Again, it stood for, and, from what I knew of Charles Fuller, Ellen would have understood only too well. But I was scared she'd tell her bolshie daughter, Annie, and Annie would write me off as truly pathetic.

'It's code,' I said desperately. 'To . . . help keep track of my menopausal symptoms. Hot Flushes In Lower Parts Again.' I felt rotten lying to Ellen, especially about a bonding sort of subject like menopause, but she started to laugh. She thought it was hysterically funny. For three whole days HILPA kept flashing into Ellen's mind and making her fall about, wiping her eyes and telling me she was sorry, really she was.

On the fourth day she'd settled down enough to tell me that at least she now understood why I'd been so dithery of late. I wasn't aware that it showed but of course I had been dithery — back and forth like an adolescent on a high diving board: *Shall I? Shan't I? Get it over with . . . don't have to if I don't want to . . .* I'd been that way for weeks now. Waiting to be shoved.

Friday night. Thursday is our late night but Ellen and I were stocktaking. When I'd rung Hamish, at four thirty, to say we'd be knocking off about eight, I could hear the rugby commentator in the background. 'I'll make Chinese,' he said.

At ten to nine I walked into the kitchen. The bench was clear, the oven was empty, so was the microwave. There was no wok in sight, not even a saucepan, and the fridge had nothing to offer.

From the passage I could hear him in the bedroom singing 'Volare'. His grandmother was Italian. I pictured him lying naked on the bed singing in a Pavarotti voice, just for me, and it made me furious. My stomach was rumbling and I was desperately tired. If I'd wanted to see a naked man lying on a bed singing I could have gone to the movies.

The worst part was that I knew that if it was the other way round — him the one who had just got home from a hard day's work and me the one who was singing and naked — his hunger, his exhaustion would count for nothing from the moment he saw me there.

In fact he was getting dressed, zipping up his newest trousers with the front pleats. His hair was tousled and damp and a towel lay on the floor beside his naked feet, but he could still be intending to return it to the bathroom.

He saw me at the door. 'Thought we'd eat out.'

'Did you,' I said sourly. I was grubby and hungry and tired. I didn't want to shower and dress. I hadn't the energy to make decisions on what to wear, where to go, what to order. I wanted to eat right then and in my home. Since we had, both of us, put so much thought, effort and money into making this house the kind of place we wanted to spend time in, it seemed stupid to go out and sit around in some less appealing room with fake wood walls and relentless music. Especially when it was his night to cook.

'I've booked,' he said. 'For nine thirty.'

'Who's paying?' I heard myself with some regret. I could at least have asked him, first, where we were eating. He gave a loud what-I-have-to-put-up-with sigh and it came to me that we'd both been giving rather a lot of those kind of sighs in recent months.

'I thought it could come out of the kitty. It's only Thai.' He sighed again. 'I'll pay then.'

I told him money wasn't really the point. He should have consulted me, I was tired and smelly and ravenous. If it was too much effort to cook, why not just get takeaways? He acted misjudged, said he'd just wanted us to have a nice night out together. Talk to each other. Romantic.

Of course that won me over. He said he'd pour us a drink while I had a quick shower, and he handed me his damp towel to take back to the bathroom since I was going that way.

The bathroom was clammy with condensation. I opened the window before I saw the bath with the facecloth slumped at the plug hole and a scummy grey tide mark a hand's width from the top. I decided to give him time.

I had my shower, got dressed, put on make-up, drank my gin and tonic and, just as we were ready to leave, I checked out the bath. Tide mark still there. *Right*, I thought, *that's it*. I felt very calm and definite.

We went in Hamish's car. I resolved not to say anything until I had food in my stomach. I looked out the window and thought of ways I could possibly raise the money to buy his share of the house. Taking in Asian students was the best I could come up with. Unless my parents should both suddenly die and turn out to have a drawer full of Brierley shares and no will bequeathing the lot to the Masonic Lodge or the Rugby Union.

In Manchester Street a young woman in a black mini-skirt and strappy high heels was leaning into the window of a dark green Mercedes. As we approached she stepped back from the car with the pouting bottom lip of a disappointed child.

'Nice,' murmured Hamish.

I knew he meant the long legs and the flesh above and below her skimpy top. It was maybe five degrees Celsius out there. Even in the car I was wearing my coat and was only moderately warm. 'Poor thing,' I said, 'she must be freezing.'

Hamish gave one of his weighty and deliberate sighs.

I no longer cared about food by the time I looked at the menu. Hamish had told the young man who allotted us a table that we wanted to order as quickly as possible, but food had lost priority so I just picked a number and, as soon as the waitress had gone, I told Hamish that I wished to live on my own and why.

At first he had trouble taking it in. 'You want us to separate because I forgot to clean the bath?' He'd raised his voice. The couple at the next table looked our way.

'You can put it like that if you want to.'

'That's insane.'

'Not to me, it isn't.'

I saw the woman at the next table nod her agreement and felt strengthened. In my activist days I had great faith in the sisterhood.

'You could've asked me,' he said. 'You could've said would I please wipe down the bath before we left.'

'The point is, I shouldn't *have* to ask. Having to ask means a clean bath is my responsibility.'

'Jesus!' growled the woman's partner, loudly. Her reply was sharp but unclear.

'Why shouldn't it be? You're one who wants it cleaned after it's used. By rights you should clean it. I'm quite happy to clean it *before* I use it.'

'It's not the bath,' I hissed. 'It's everything. It's pulling your weight.'

I heard the woman give an approving grunt.

'Ah,' he said. 'Fair enough, let's discuss it.'

I counted to eight under my breath. 'We have. Many times. And you've promised to get it together.'

'That was just rehearsals. For this time. This time is the one that counts.'

The man at the next table was leaning towards us with a floppy grin of approval. The woman jabbed him in the arm. 'You make me sick.' His grin shrivelled up.

'Forget it,' I told Hamish. 'It's over. Finito. End of the line.'

Hamish glanced at the couple, as if they had become an integral part of the proceedings. He may have been hoping for male support, but the pair were now embroiled in a fight of their own, hissing at each other across the table. Her face was splotched red and white with sudden anger. When I looked back at Hamish he seemed very pale. His voice was calm.

'So when are you moving out then?'

'I'm not. You are.'

He shook his head. I realised I hadn't thought this through very carefully. I said, 'I'm not the one who's caused the problem.'

He smiled at me, 'But you're the one who wants us to split up.'

I suspected he might, legally, have a better case than I had. Certainly I'd never heard of the courts ordering someone to leave a house because he'd failed to wield a wet mop or clean beneath the grill. Yet I could think of a couple of cases where women I knew had called a halt to long-standing relationships and their partners had obligingly moved out and rented a flat. That was rather what I'd expected of Hamish.

'So,' he taunted, 'when are you shifting?'

The waitress brought the bottle of red we'd left at the counter for uncorking. We both smiled at her with the desperate friendliness of people who feel unlovable. The waitress had the anxious face and limited English of a recent immigrant, and may have thought our manic smiles were normal New Zealand behaviour, for after that she kept glancing at us and flashing a rather insane smile of her own.

'When?' Hamish harped.

'I'll need to see a lawyer,' I tried to sound casual yet digni-
fied. I saw Hamish's mouth twitch and I knew he was thinking, already, about the making up. About how we could best
make use of all that adrenalin. Just reading his mind, my
crotch went twittery.

Our meals came and we ate without speaking, but not in
silence and not even in a state of enmity. Along with everyone else in the room we had become the stunned audience of
the couple alongside us who, by then, were having an argument so loud, so full of invective and astonishing accusations
that our dispute seemed piffling and half-hearted.

On the way home Hamish hummed 'With A Little Help
From My Friends' and I fought to rekindle my resolve.

'I'll sleep in the spare room,' I announced as we entered
the house. Hamish said nothing. The answerphone light was
flashing so he pressed the button. My mother's voice came on,
hesitant and anxious the way she always sounded.

'Oh dear, these things . . . Merran, are you there? It's me,
your mother. Can you ring me back? As soon as you can, dear?
Or Hamish? Bye bye.'

It had to be trouble. My mother didn't ring her daughters
for a chat. As Cass had got older I'd begun to see the sadness of
this, but there seemed to be nothing I could do about it. Mum
had made her choice and my sister and I had made ours. It was
a long time ago but not much had changed in the years since.

Sheila, my sister, still drove down to visit Wyn from time to
time, though not at the house. They would rendezvous at the
park or a coffee shop for an hour or so then Mum would scurry
off home to put on the dinner and Sheila would call into a pub
for a drink or two before driving back over the ranges to
Palmerston North. At the pub she would run into neighbours
or people we went to school with and (she said) the message
she got, either straight up or reading between the lines, was that
Angus (our father, though we never called him Dad, hadn't
beyond the age of ten, it was either *him* or Angus) was still the
same bullying sexist loudmouth that she and I remembered.

When I was ten and we lived in the house that neither of us
will visit, I abandoned my sister, who was two years younger
than me, in favour of a girl my age called Emma Tonks. We

were best friends, Emma and I, and I spent much of my time at the Tonks' house. Up until then Angus was the only adult male I had real knowledge of and I imagined all men were like him. Emma's kindly, jovial father was a revelation.

Not that Angus directed his violence at us girls — we just got the spillage of what was meant for Wyn. In fact, when we were small, I suspect he saw us only as an extension of his contemptible wife. Angus had expected sons — that was his most frequently and loudly expressed reason for knocking our mother about. Not only had she botched the order, but she had managed, in the course of expelling Sheila, to damage her womb beyond use or repair.

It was not until, as adults, Sheila and I threw ourselves in the women's movement and became, almost unwittingly, what is now called *high profile*, that Angus appeared to realise his daughters were individuals — and therefore worthy of contempt on their own behalf. Wyn got a bit of a rest while his rage was redirected at us.

When I took my small daughter and exchanged my philandering husband for the DPB, Angus wrote letters to the *Herald* and the *Dominion* disowning me. I was less than devastated, but the Fight For Family Society made him their honorary president.

For years we tried, Sheila and I, to get Wyn to leave him. We reasoned, we bullied, we bribed, we got drunk and banged our heads together over the extent of the woman's denial and the transparency of her excuses for staying. Finally we gave up in disgust. She'd chosen him over us — it was hard to believe and even harder to forgive. We went through the motions of keeping in touch with her, Sheila more conscientiously than I, but she lived much closer and didn't work full time.

That Saturday night I had to look up my mother's number. As she would have had to look up mine. I took the phone into the bedroom so as not to get bad news alone. Wyn answered far too quickly.

'Mum,' I said, 'it's Merran. Is something wrong?'

'I can't get hold of Sheila,' she said. 'No one's answering.'

'They'll be out.' I rolled my eyes for Hamish, who was waiting to hear. 'Are you all right, Mum?'

'Not bad,' she said. 'I had the 'flu for six weeks but I finally threw it off. Your father seems to have passed away.'

I couldn't believe she'd said this, and in that order.

'Angus is dead?'

'Seems to be,' she said. 'There's no breathing. I tried with a mirror the way you see on TV.'

'Angus,' I mouthed to Hamish whipping a finger past my throat.

There were a couple of clunking noises, then Wyn was whispering with great clarity as if she'd climbed inside the mouthpiece. 'His eyes are open. I haven't been able to get hold of Sheila and Roy.'

'What about the doctor?' I said. 'When did this happen? You have rung the doctor, Mum?'

'I should've,' she said. 'Of course I should've. I just couldn't think and you girls weren't home, either of you.'

'So what have you done?'

'What do you mean? I haven't done anything. I've been sitting on this chair waiting for one of you to ring.'

'Mum,' I said. 'Wyn, listen to me. Hang up now and ring the doctor. Have you got his number? I'll ring you back in ten minutes.'

I waited for her to hang up first. 'My father's dead,' I said. It felt like I was trying the words on as I might a hat, to see if they suited me. 'Probably dead,' I amended, and saw Hamish's jaw drop open.

'I'll find out for sure when I ring her back.'

Hamish came around to my side of the bed and sat beside me. He took my hand which was, unaccountably, shaking. The business about one of us leaving had been swept right out of my head.

When I rang back the doctor was on his way and so was Sheila. Wyn sounded more confident. Angus was definitely dead, she said. She'd pushed his eyelids down the way they did on TV and it had made her feel much better.

WE TOOK AN early flight to Wellington and hired a rental car at the airport. I'd arranged with Cass that we'd pick her up at her flat and so had a Wellington street map spread over my knees. Cass had moved twice since I last came north.

'I hope she's got coffee on,' I said as we turned into Cass's street.

'What number?'

But as soon as he asked we saw Cass on the footpath, half a block down, with a backpack and a couple of bags.

'So much for coffee,' said Hamish.

I told him we could stop in the Hutt, we weren't in a hurry, and I got out to give Cass a hug. She was all ribs and elbows.

'You didn't need to be this ready,' I told her.

'I did,' she said. 'Believe me.'

A young man in a tattered bathrobe was sitting on the fire escape. When I glanced at him he gave me the nicest smile.

'I'm Michael,' he advised me.

'D'you mind?' Cass said and slammed the boot of the rental.

'Hello, Michael.' I said. He was only sitting there. Two months ago she'd told me he was 'totally cool'. Unless this was another Michael.

'For God's sake, Mum, ignore him. 'She threw herself into the back seat and slammed that door. Hamish was looking agitated and tapping the steering wheel. It was only a rental but it was almost brand new and (he'd told me) an absolute pleasure to drive.

As we sped off I couldn't help but look back at the young man. He was standing, by then, leaning on the fire escape railing. Beneath it was a slash of white thigh, above it his arm stabbed the air with two upturned fingers.

After advising Hamish on the quickest route to the motorway, Cass explained that she had moved out of the flat the night before, not long after my call. She had dossed at a friend's place, and wouldn't be returning to flat with Michael, who was basically a wanker and had neglected to clean the congealed blood from the bottom of the fridge.

'*His* congealed blood,' she said, in a voice of vegetarian disgust.

Hamish's rolling eye caught mine and maybe saw ambivalence there, for he quickly turned back to watching the road.

In all the excitement of finding myself bereaved I had forgotten that he and I were all but separated. Michael was both a reminder, and a reproach to my vacillating resolve.

Cass wanted to know about Angus's death. It seemed that she had gone up on the train to visit her grandparents a couple of times, but not mentioned it to me. And once, the year before, when they were visiting Wellington, Wyn and Angus had taken Cass to lunch in an almost empty hotel dining room with white damask tablecloths and dire food. Her grandfather, Cass now told us, had on each occasion seemed a rather sad old dinosaur who bore no resemblance to the sniping and snarling drunk that Sheila and I 'obsessed over' whenever we got together. He was still a big man, she said, and fit. He and Wyn had travelled down by train, to save driving in city traffic, and they had walked from the station to Courtenay Place and back again as if it was just an evening stroll.

I wasn't in a mood to debate Angus's nature. If he had developed a good side then I was glad that Cass had got to see it. She was his only granddaughter and no doubt less of a disappointment than his grandson, Tim, who walked with his thighs pressed together and whose self-published book of poems, *Time Honoured*, had sat in our bookshop — mine and Ellen Fuller's — for two years, all eight copies, not even on sale or return because he was my sister's child.

I told Cass that Angus had died in his bed. In his sleep, I supposed, though Wyn hadn't said so. When Wyn couldn't get through to Sheila or me she had made herself a cup of tea and sat by the phone waiting for it to ring.

We stopped in Upper Hutt for the coffee we were in need of. As Cass and I sat down at a table she asked me who was paying for the rental. I knew by rote where this was leading and my resistance was automatic.

'Why?' Smiling nicely. 'You want to chip in?'

She gave a small, unamused laugh. 'If I did would I get to drive?'

'Probably not,' I admitted. Then had to add, 'I don't mind being a passenger.'

'Don't you?' said Cass. 'I hate it.'

I was awed by her vehemence. It seemed so unconstrained, especially for someone who didn't own a car.

ROY'S MIDDLE-AGED BMW was parked in the driveway. Beside its haughty substance the rental felt suddenly cheap and tinny.

'Academics,' grunted Hamish. 'Always whining they're underpaid.'

I was taking stock of the house after so many years and feeling a kind of mindless anxiety. I focused on the shrubs which felt both familiar and safe. These days I even knew the names — pittosporum, pyracantha, coprosma . . . They had not grown larger; Angus believed plants should be kept in their place. The house looked smaller and excessively tidy. Roy, then Sheila, came out to greet us. We kept our voices low but I could hear in Sheila's voice, and in my own, a kind of jumpy glee.

'Is he . . .?'

'No. They've taken him away. To do that business . . .'

Was I relieved or disappointed? I'd been imagining how I might feel, looking down at him. Steeling myself against pity or unbidden memories of moments of casual kindness or charm.

'Embalming,' said Hamish helpfully.

'No. Well, I suppose, but also the coroner has to make a report.'

'What for?'

'Apparently,' said Roy, 'it's routine. If someone's not under current medical treatment.'

'It was a heart attack?'

'Probably. But of course he'd been dead for nearly three hours by the time the doctor saw him.'

As Cass handed me the box of groceries we'd bought in Carterton, Sheila pinched me on the hip. Leant for my ear, breathing wine fumes.

'Pssst. How are you feeling?'

'I'm not sure,' I said. 'How's she taking it?'

'Dazed. Doctor gave her some pills. I feel bloody ecstatic. I thought the bastard would live forever. I'm gonna dance on his grave, Mer.'

I smiled at her. She was halfway drunk and it wasn't even lunch time. But then, it was a special occasion.

Our voices had woken Wyn, who was taking a nap. She threw herself into boiling the jug and the logistics of who would sleep where. She wouldn't hear mention of motels — there was room aplenty. She dispatched Roy and Hamish to the garage to drag out and dust off the old double mattress stored above the rafters while she and Cass cleared the sunporch of its two wicker chairs, plant stand and little glass table. They crammed all these into the lounge, which began to resemble an auction room. I took over the tea-making, and Sheila poured herself another glass of sauvignon blanc from the cask on the bench.

Wyn looked glazed but happy. This was the first time all of us had been together in this house. The whole family except, of course, for Angus, and Sheila's son Tim, who was in Chicago at a summer school for performance poets. Wyn allotted herself and Cass the spare bedroom that once was mine and Sheila's. Sheila and Roy would have the dusted-off mattress on the sunporch floor, while Hamish and I were given my parents' bedroom.

We protested. Wyn should have her own bed, we could manage in a single. Wyn was adamant. It dawned on us that she didn't want to sleep in the bed where her dead husband had lain.

Neither did we, but we couldn't say so.

'Don't worry, guys,' smirked Sheila. 'We changed the sheets.'

Already Wyn was worrying about our lunch. We told her not to. There was plenty of food, I said, and Sheila and I would deal with lunch. Cass gave me a look of deep pity.

'I wish I'd had a son,' I told Sheila as I washed the lettuce.

'So do I,' said Sheila and laughed in a slightly manic way. There was something bitter and angry in the laughter that reminded me of Angus. I searched for something to say in defence of Tim, but the truth was I hardly knew him. The images that came were of Sheila, sixteen, pregnant and terrified. At the time I'd believed she was determined to have the baby only because Angus had ordered her not to.

Other images belonged a few years later, when Sheila and I were caught up with campaigning and Tim was coming up school age. He was one of three children and maybe a dozen women (for a time I was one of them) in that rambling Aro Street house. The children's care was organised week by week, up there on the blackboard along with all the other chores. *Veg co-op sort — Sheila, childcare — Angela.* We made it into a virtue, telling each other about the advantages of multiple parenting and communal toys and kelp granules and uncovered floorboards, when the truth was simply that the alternatives — for families like Sheila and Tim — were even worse.

Though I did my share of childcare duty I did not come to know any of the children as individuals. Perhaps none of us did, not even Sheila. Was that what was wrong between her and Tim?

But then, Sheila says things just for effect, always has. Which is why she was such a good speaker for the movement. I was the literal one, who provided facts and figures. The media liked the idea of us being sisters, found that colourful and so pushed us both to the forefront.

We played a part in changing things, Sheila and I. I'm proud of that. But to Cass it's history and of no account. 'Look at you now,' she would say. (These days my *condition* obliges her to be more tactful.)

As we prepared lunch Wyn was kept busy answering the phone. In some circles Angus was a popular man, and Wyn reminded us this was so each time the phone rang. He was a former coach and ex-president of the local rugby club, he'd served on the town council . . . Already word had got around.

'Yes,' Wyn kept having to say, 'it was very sudden . . . he was fighting fit . . . totally unexpected . . . barely a day's illness in his whole life.'

I thought Roy or Hamish could be handling the calls but Wyn insisted on doing it herself.

'So many people admired him.'

We took it that she was making a point for us, his daughters, who didn't. I gritted my teeth. Sheila crashed open an egg and dropped it into a bowl.

'Wonders never cease,' she said in a loud voice.

I glared at her. It seemed important to keep things friendly, the man was dead. I considered the way Cass was with Hamish and, for the first time, wondered whether Sheila and I hadn't exaggerated Angus's abominability. Surely there must have been something besides her own lack of courage that had kept Wyn at his side for forty-eight years?.

Cass came to help or hurry us with lunch. It was one of the times when Wyn was on the phone and Sheila and I were discussing her future. What would she do? What could she do? Which of us was best placed to have her?

'But I barely know her,' I heard myself protesting, 'after all these years.'

Sheila's eyebrows shot up. 'Well, here's your chance,' she said.

'Gran might have her own plans. Have you asked her?' Cass poured herself a glass from the cask. It seemed like a good idea, being almost lunch time. I rinsed myself a glass from the sink.

'Well,' my daughter said. 'Have you?'

Sheila and I looked at each other. 'Cassandra,' said Sheila imperiously, 'surely you're old enough to know that once one is grown up it becomes impossible to talk to one's mother!'

Cass and I laughed, as we were intended to, but I was thinking, Many a true word . . .

The warm-up to the relayed test match had started, so the men took their lunch plates through to the living room. Wyn helped herself, quite heartily for a brand-new widow, and set off after them.

'Mum,' I said, 'they're just going to watch the rugby. You don't like rugby. Do you?'

She paused at the door. 'I've got used to it, Merran. He liked me to watch. It gave us something to talk about.'

'But —,' I said, to no one for she had gone to join the men.

She had effectively silenced and united the three of us who remained in kitchen.

'Did she mean,' Cass wondered, eventually, in a small, winded voice, 'something to talk about to each other? Or to the neighbours?'

'Both,' Sheila and I said in unison. Our accord confirmed our right to feel depressed. I was awash with that old recurring feeling that any woman in her right mind would vacate this country and never return. Maybe Sheila was having the same thought for she suddenly began questioning Cass about her life, in a market researcher voice.

Cass's life, as elicited by Sheila, turned out to be slightly worse than I'd thought. The lack of a partner I was ready to envy, but when it was accompanied by the lack of a job (she'd walked out of her last two workplaces) and nowhere to live, it lost all its glamour.

'There must be some decent jobs out there,' I said. To comfort myself. I registered the look of disgust Cass threw me, but couldn't stop my mouth. 'Three years in design school. A twenty thousand dollar student loan she owes the state.' I was talking to Sheila, but for the benefit of Cass, who didn't seem able to see the dreadfulness of her situation.

Sure there were jobs, Cass snapped. If she wore pastel mini-skirts, and shirts you could see her tits through and nice little pearl earrings people'd be falling over themselves to employ her.

To which Sheila said 'typical' in a heavy Germanic voice that meant she was drunk. But — because I was the mother and didn't want my daughter's life to be hard and miserable, I said that sometimes the end justified the means, and it didn't hurt to compromise your principles. Cass nodded and sighed in a world-weary fashion and said, quite kindly, that she could see what I was saying but she'd prefer not to end up like me.

Sheila was bewildered. What did Cass mean?

'She means Hamish,' I said. 'Me and him.' I turned to Cass — perhaps it was because my father was dead, but suddenly I felt old enough to be a dispenser of wisdom. Nobody was perfect, I told her. Every human being had failings.

'What are yours?' Cass asked.

I searched my mind; it really did seem that I was faultless. Sheila and Cass had begun to giggle at my silence. Perhaps this jogged my memory.

'I'm too ready to compromise.'

This made them cackle out loud and brought Roy to the door, frowning, with a finger pressed to his lips on Wyn's behalf.

'I'll bet you started it,' he said to Sheila. She poked her tongue at him.

Cass said, pulling herself together. 'When I die people are allowed to laugh but not allowed to watch rugby.'

'It's a test match!' objected Roy and disappeared.

'Who are they playing?'

'Poms,' said Sheila. 'Isn't it?'

Through the wall the crowd roared, Hamish screamed 'yes, yes' and Roy gave the sort of yodel an electric cattle-prod might be expected to induce. Sheila leaned towards Cass. 'Did your boyfriend-that-was follow rugby?'

Cass shook her head. I could see she was sick of us. As she escaped the table she said sourly, 'No. *He* had a brain.'

I wanted Sheila to come up with a smart response but she just pulled a face. Left on our own, we got back to the problem of Wyn. Sheila said, with a sigh, that they were expecting Tim back home in August when the course ended, and the spare bedroom had been taken over by Roy as his office.

Hamish and I had two spare bedrooms, but now I remembered.

'We're going to sell up.'

'Oh, come on,' said Sheila. 'That is pathetic. She's not that bad!'

'But we *are!* Probably.'

'Your lovely house?'

'We're splitting up.'

'You're not! Merran? My God, I can't believe . . . There's someone else?'

'No. It's just . . .'

Put into words it would sound so foolish. If Wyn came to stay I would have to forget or postpone the whole business. Hamish would win by default.

'. . . we're going through a rocky patch.'

Even as I said it I could hear Sheila and Roy discussing this news in bed. With concern, but also the relief of discovering that a couple who seemed to get on so well were in fact on the brink of separation.

The All Blacks lost. This meant that Sheila and I felt rewarded for having been left in the kitchen to clean up and do the dishes, but Roy and Hamish were suddenly disconsolate and bored. They flung themselves into chairs, nagged at us about the lack of funeral arrangements and paced the kitchen until we sent them off to the undertakers to get some answers.

Wyn, meanwhile, had been thumping about in the master bedroom with the door firmly closed. When she eventually emerged it was to distribute chosen possessions among us 'girls'. She insisted on doing this, even though Cass, who had returned a few minutes earlier, argued that it should be Angus's possessions she gave away. (How could she, I thought, knowing how fiercely we had hated him. And for a moment the sadness of what we had done to our mother in our single-minded contempt of Angus — deserved or not — hit me with such force that I had to reach out and steady myself.)

To Sheila, Wyn gave her paua shell and silver necklace with matching bracelet. To Cass she gave her wedding dress, a voluminous satin affair that would have looked at home in a gay pride parade or a production of *The White Horse Inn*. To me she gave her fox-fur coat. As we made, in turn, suitably gratified noises, we carefully avoided each other's eyes. I asked myself if each generation was inevitably blind to the person-alities of their children, seeing only an image of their own invention. But, in part at least, Wyn's selection of gifts had been based on practicality. I lived in the chilly south; Cass might yet get married. What logic connected Sheila with the paua shell jewellery I could not imagine, and didn't dare try, because it would surely trigger my laughter.

I stroked the fur and remembered doing just that as a child. If I put aside fashion and ecological objections, the coat was a quality garment, a symbol of luxury belied by Wyn's life where all the extravagances — the whisky, the gambling — were Angus's while she 'made do'.

'It's beautiful,' I said and all the laughter down in my gut died away.

Sheila was still protesting. Why now? she wanted to know.

'Just in case,' Wyn told her.

'In case of what, Mum?'

'In case there's some kind of trouble.'

'What kind of trouble?'

'Complications,' she said.

Because Friday night — who could believe only Friday, it seemed so long ago already? — Angus had come home under the weather. Had stumbled and hit his head on the wood-burner, a nasty gash, but Wyn had cleaned it up and got him to bed. The policeman who came when the doctor was here had looked at the woodburner. But of course there was nothing to see, Wyn had wiped it clean.

'I don't think I should've,' she said. 'It was evidence.'

We patted and smiled and clucked indulgently. 'Oh Mum,' we said. 'Oh Gran. You think he suspected you!'

'They're keeping his body a long time,' she fretted.

'It's only Sunday now.'

'The men have gone to talk to the undertaker.'

'It's the weekend, Mum. And the coroner must have to come up from Wellington.'

'Of course. Of course.' Wyn cheered up. 'I just want it over with. You people don't want to be hanging around — there's your jobs to think of. Have we put it in the paper?'

'In the morning we will, Mum.'

'The undertaker's wife works at Countdown. She's a friendly sort of person.'

'Caterers,' said Sheila. 'Have we thought about caterers?'

'No,' said Wyn. 'They cost a fortune and all you get is a bit of this and a bit of that.'

'Maa-um,' Sheila objected.

But I agreed with Wyn — why pay someone to make sandwiches if you can do it yourself?

'So much to do,' said Wyn happily. 'Cassie and I'd better make a list.'

Wyn was more fond of Cass than of me or Sheila. And why not? Cass had caused her no anguish.

I lay the fox-fur coat on my parents bed and joined Sheila in the kitchen. She said she was going out for supplies and rattled Roy's car keys. I took them from her and said I would drive.

'So the old bastard was drunk!' said Sheila, as I backed out the drive. 'What a surprise!'

'It's genetic, Sheila.' I said.

'What is?'

'Alcoholism. You inherit it.'

Sheila rolled her head towards me. 'Got a drinking problem, have you?'

'No. But you have.'

'Christ. You sound just like Roy.'

'Sorry about that,' I said lightly.

There, I was thinking. I've said it. It's off my conscience.

'I was waiting for that little lecture,' Sheila said. 'You're so bloody predictable.'

'Now you sound just like Hamish,' I said.

Then I thought about it. *Was* predictability a fault? Did I perhaps have faults I imagined were virtues?

When we got back with wine and beer and grapes, from shops that had changed surprisingly little in thirty years, Cass was waiting, all twitchy and pink-faced.

'Oh shit,' she jabbered. 'Oh bloody hell. Hurry up, hurry up, there's something I've gotta show you guys.'

She beckoned us through the side door into the garage.

'I sent Gran for a nap,' she whispered, pushing past Angus's baby blue Triumph and raising the lid of the chest freezer. 'Look, look at this for fucksake!'

I squeezed in beside her. Looked down at sausage rolls, biscuits, cake. Wyn belonged to generation that baked. Cass's excitement began to seem a little weird.

'She always had full tins,' I said. 'We were porky little girls, thanks to Wyn.'

'You don't get it!' Cass was still whispering. 'Look. I asked her, "What's all the food in the freezer for, Gran?" And she said it was for the funeral. She said there were bound to be lots of people coming so she's been doing a bit every day.'

'She hasn't baked since we've been here,' said Sheila.

We stood there in silence staring at each other, taking this in. Angus had been dead less than forty-eight hours.

'He didn't pong or anything.' Sheila was reading our minds. 'I didn't look closely, but if he'd been dead for days the doctor would've said so, to me and Roy.'

I closed the lid on the freezer. The window of the garage was half covered by a spider web. Sheila suddenly let out an odd, high-pitched sound which I didn't recognise as laughter until her face collapsed. I couldn't, right away, see the funny side. Sheila was clutching my arm in an urgent way trying to get out the words.

'The worm . . . finally . . . turned!' Sheila raised her fist in a clenched salute the way she used to at protests. Cass and I just stood there. I was trying to work out what I felt. Hollow. Or maybe solid but numb.

'Well, he deserved it. He bloody deserved it, didn't he, Mer?'

I opened my mouth but my voice was unavailable.

'To die?' squeaked Cass. 'If he was that bad, why didn't you lay charges?'

'It wasn't us,' I said. 'It was her he laid into. And back then nothing would've been done.' (Sheila and I crouching, holding each other, behind the wash-house door. Doing nothing to stop him or get help. Saving our own hides at her expense — that's how I felt it to be, and me the oldest and therefore most to blame. But the shame not ever as strong as the fear. His drunken face — I saw it, still, in horror movies. Freddy Kruger/my father — the features are fluid and interchanging, the terror is once-removed yet exactly the same.)

'Why didn't she just leave him?' Even as I said it I remembered Hamish's sneering, 'So when are you moving out?'

'For Godsake,' hissed Sheila, 'what we have here was the ultimate feminist act. We're on her side.'

I nodded a feeble agreement. The truth was I no longer knew where I stood.

'Hamish and Roy must not be told.'

I wanted to object. In most matters I have great respect for Hamish's judgement.

'You don't think,' Cass ventured, 'that when they see Gran defrosting half a tonne of finger food . . .' She couldn't finish. Suddenly we all had the giggles. We were reduced to third-form schoolgirls, our knees collapsed and we draped ourselves over Angus's Triumph (Wyn had never learnt to drive) or slid to the concrete floor. We laughed until our bellies ached and our eyes ran. When we had almost regained control Sheila lifted the freezer lid, we all looked in and the laughter hit us again.

We had pulled ourselves together and were flopped about the kitchen, limp and depleted, by the time the men got back to report that the funeral was booked for Tuesday. They made it sound like a dental appointment. Angus would be transported straight from the hospital mortuary to the funeral parlour — would that be okay with Wyn? We said it would. Our mother was still sleeping and we had no wish to wake her.

'You ladies look exhausted,' said Roy.

Then Hamish put his arm around me. 'We'll get takeaways for dinner,' he said.

That night, in the double bed, I told him. He had insisted on having Wyn's side of the bed, was squeamish about resting his flesh where a corpse had lain. I'd felt some unease about this myself but was able to push it aside. Suddenly not telling Hamish seemed ridiculous.

When I finally convinced him I wasn't making the story up, Hamish wanted to go out to the garage and look for himself. I talked him out of it. If Wyn caught her son-in-law (possibly both of her sons-in-law because Sheila may also have blabbed) sneaking out to look in her freezer in the middle of the night, she might become agitated.

Hamish slid his legs into bed again and lay back.

'If we don't report it we're withholding evidence,' he said.

'We don't *know* anything.'

'Withholding evidence makes you an accessory to murder.'

'Manslaughter. He was the aggressor.'

'She'd planned it. That's murder. And you heard her mention wiping down the woodburner.'

We speculated, then, on how she had carried it out. Pushed him? Hit him with something heavy? Such as? Was he in fact drunk or had she drugged him?

Bit by bit we transformed Wyn from our pathetic mouse of a mother into a pathological killer. I began to feel anxious about Cass sharing the bedroom. Into my mind came a picture of Wyn slipping out of bed, silent and wild-eyed in sprigged winceyette, clutching a stretch of piano wire.

At daybreak Sheila and Roy came into our room to confer. ('He guessed,' said Sheila defensively. I told her so had

Hamish.) There was nothing new to be said, but the situation was certainly thrilling enough to merit revision.

'Someone you'd lived with for forty-eight years!'

That was the part that shocked Hamish most. The *disloyalty* of it, I supposed.

'All the more reason.' I told him grimly.

'She's right,' said Sheila. 'Forty-eight years of just some pesky little habit would drive me to the edge.'

'Like mother, like daughters,' said Roy, and we all laughed except Hamish.

Even two days before I would have been appalled at being likened to Wyn. Now I felt flattered. I saw Hamish watching me in a wary way and that, too, pleased me.

It rained all that day. We milled around impatiently in Wyn's cramped house, lifting the net curtains to peer out, making coffee, switching the TV on, then off again. Sheila opened a new cask of white. None of us could settle to anything, though Wyn's only cause for anxiety seemed to be the realisation that her house was too small to serve as a reception venue. I said never mind, it wasn't too late to hire a place, and notices of the altered venue could be passed out at the service. I fetched the Yellow Pages to look for halls, but Wyn said no, I should let the men do it, they were better at that kind of thing. I looked at Sheila with my jaw hanging. She winked back. I closed the Yellow Pages.

'Of course they are,' I said.

I was thinking, *We've got this all quite wrong — this woman hasn't taken fate into her own hands and never, never will.* I felt cheated.

Delegated to arrange for the hire of a hall, the men pushed aside the Yellow Pages and went off in the rain. Wyn had by then persuaded Cass that more baking was required. I hadn't been a baking kind of mother so Cass had a lot of finger-and bowl-licking deprivation to make up for. The men returned with a pack of cards and an okay to use the rugby club hall for free, and I had to admit that was better than I would have done.

Sheila, Roy, Hamish and I were playing five hundred in a jumpy, light-headed way, when we heard the car pull up.

Sheila went to look through the curtain.

'Here we go!' she said in a sing-song voice. 'It's the cops.'

She stepped back from the window, still watching. 'He's not flashing his lights,' she reported. 'And there's just the one. I thought they had to work in pairs.'

He hammered on the front door, which opened into the living room where we were. We stared at the door, we stared at each other. I was incapable of moving. It was Hamish who threaded his way through the excess furniture to the door and let the cop in. A freckle-faced man about our own age. He wanted a word with Wyn. We kept our eyes and lips free of give-away signals. Hamish led him through to the kitchen, and a moment later returned, accompanied by Cass.

He wanted, they whispered, to have a word with our mother in private.

We dealt the cards and played another self-conscious hand in case, through the wall, the officer was listening for a suspicious silence. I was imagining Wyn in jail, at the mercy of tough, sharp-faced women, and perhaps in a cell with a potty instead of a toilet. We dealt another hand. Cass slipped out into the rain to spy for us through the window and came back to report that they were drinking tea.

After another twenty minutes the policeman left by the back door and ran to his car. Wyn came in to call Cass, her baking assistant, back on duty. She looked quite calm. 'What did he want, Mum?' asked Sheila, as Wyn was about to retreat.

'Nothing much, dear,' said Wyn, then added. 'Your father was well thought of in this town, and no one wants that to change.'

After tea, at Wyn's request, we took the baked food out of the freezer and spread it on the bench to defrost overnight. Gingerbread, shortbread, afghans, cinnamon fingers, ginger crunch, melting moments . . . Enough, as Wyn herself observed, to feed an army.

We saw the policeman again at the service. The church was almost full, and when I looked over my shoulder as the congregation was being asked to stand, I saw faces I recognised from my childhood, yet could not place. Almost all the mourners were male.

The cask was pale pine. I hadn't looked in before it was closed, but Hamish had. He'd looked for bruising, he whispered, but had seen none. Perhaps it had been the back of the head? That cheerful song from *The Wizard of Oz*, the one about the witch being dead, was stuck in my brain.

I reached for Hamish's hand. Thoughts of Angus always reduced Hamish's failings to charming foibles. Hamish's hand lay in mine, unnaturally lifeless. I've lost him, I thought, with a stab of panic. My predictability, my indifference to black garter belts and peekaboo bras had stifled his affection. Not once since we'd arrived at Wyn's had he tried to discuss my demand for a separation. He was willing to let it happen! Hamish would find someone generous enough to gather his clothes off the floor without minding, and air-headed enough to relish romping in a g-string.

Soon he would be saying to our friends, 'In fact, for me it was the best thing that could've happened.'

'Sweetheart,' I whispered and he turned his head. I gave him a smile. He looked at me for a few seconds as if I was someone he didn't know very well and then smiled politely back.

At the reception I ferried round enormous plates of biscuits and the sandwiches we'd all put together that morning. Hamish was pouring the tea. Wyn's baking proved very popular; strapping men in sports jackets who I guessed were rugby players, accepted two or three biscuits at a time. They were unimpressed with the offer of tea so we sent Roy out to get cans of beer.

The policeman stuck to sandwiches and told me he'd been in the same class as Sheila at primary school. 'But she wouldn't remember me,' he said. 'I expect everyone claims to know you once you're famous.' It took me a moment to work out that he meant Sheila, or maybe both of us.

'That was ages ago,' I said. 'And I thought everyone in this town would have disowned us.'

'At least people remember your face,' he said. It sounded wistful. I wanted to tell him that a uniform made a face harder to recall, but it would hardly have cheered him up. I saw Sheila slipping out the door and, when my plates were empty,

I went to find her. She was round the side, sheltering under the eaves and tucked out of view from the windows. I stood beside her. 'It's almost over.'

She nodded.

'What's going to happen to her?'

'Nothing,' said Sheila. 'She's pulled it off.' She laughed.

'I mean, where's she going to live and all that?'

'Didn't they tell you? Your daughter's staying on for a while. They've sorted it all out between the two of them.'

I felt a flash of bitterness — kill a man and win Cass's heart!

'Good,' I said. 'So it's not our problem. Are you okay?'

'No,' said Sheila. 'That useless twerp only came back with beer. I can't drink beer all afternoon!'

We left first thing the next morning. The rain had stopped but it was still overcast, almost muggy.

'I'm so glad you like it,' said Wyn, stroking the fur coat as we hugged goodbye. 'But where are your slacks, dear? Won't you be cold?'

'D'you want to drive?' asked Hamish, ready to toss me the key.

'No,' I said. 'No thanks.' And I glanced at Cass, pleased that she'd heard. (After the reception Hamish had done more cleaning up than any of us. Cass couldn't fail to have seen that. Sheila had jabbed Roy in the ribs — 'Look and learn.' I felt proud, but in a way that disgusted me. I felt like one of those mothers who push their daughters on stage and bask in the reflected glory.)

We made our farewells quickly, eager to get going. I was longing to be at home. I sat hugging myself with furry arms, watching my beloved from the corner of my eye. He was driving carefully through the morning traffic of the township.

We hit the highway. Hamish stretched and sighed with relief. 'There's something I want to tell you,' he said, his eyes still on the road. I felt a queasy surge of fear.

'It taught me something,' he began. 'Wyn and your father, and all that . . . It showed me something. I'm going to be different, Mer. I swear it. The more I was getting fed up with work, the more I was dumping on you at home. I see that now. It's not just laziness, what I've been doing is a kind of low-key manipulation.'

I wanted background music. I wanted to hang on to those words and press them in an album or light them up with neon. It was better, a hundred times better, than hearing *I love you.*

'You just don't want me to do you in,' I said.

Hamish laughed. 'There's that too.'

I waited a few moments. 'I've got something for you,' I told him. I pulled open Wyn's coat. It felt like diving into freezing water — though in fact the air in the car was less cold than I'd expected — just cool enough to be exhilarating. Hamish looked at my exposed and tingling flesh and his face took on a look of . . . not lust, as I expected, but a combination of delight and immense gratitude. I saw his face, the lovely expression it wore, and at the same time I saw the truck coming towards us.